ABOUT THE TRANSLATOR

KARLA GRUODIS is a translator, editor and artist based in Vilnius, where she founded and edited Lithuania's first English-language newspaper, *The Lithuanian Review*, in 1990. She is the editor and author of *Feminist Excursus: The Concept of Woman from Antiquity to Postmodernism* (Pradai, 1995) and was active in the post-Soviet Lithuanian women's movement. Her translations include Leonidas Donskis's *A Small Map of Experience: Aphorisms and Reflections* (Guernica, 2013), Antanas Škėma's *White Shroud* (Vagabond Voices, 2018) and regular contributions to the online literary journal *Vilnius Review*.

OTHER TITLES IN
THE WORLD SERIES
BALTIC SEASON

Kai Aareleid, *Burning Cities* (translated by Adam Cullen)

Kristīne Ulberga, *The Green Crow* (translated by Žanete Vēvere Pasqualini)

PETER OWEN WORLD SERIES

'*The world is a book, and those who do not travel read only one page,*' wrote St Augustine. Journey with us to explore outstanding contemporary literature translated into English for the first time. Read a single book in each season – which will focus on a different country or region every time – or try all three and experience the range and diversity to be found in contemporary literature from across the globe.

Read the world – three books at a time

3 works of literature in

2 seasons each year from

1 country or region each season

For information on forthcoming seasons go to peterowen.com

DARKNESS AND COMPANY

Sigitas Parulskis

DARKNESS
AND
COMPANY

Translated from the Lithuanian by
Karla Gruodis

PETER OWEN
WORLD SERIES

WORLD SERIES SEASON 4 : BALTICS

Peter Owen Publishers
Conway Hall, 25 Red Lion Square, London WC1R 4RL, UK

Peter Owen books are distributed in the USA and Canada by
Independent Publishers Group/Trafalgar Square
814 North Franklin Street, Chicago, IL 60610, USA

Translated from the Lithuanian *Tamsa ir partneriai*
Copyright © Sigitas Parulskis 2012
Copyright © Alma Littera 2012
English translation copyright © Karla Gruodis 2018

Preface copyright © Sigitas Parulskis 2015
English translation copyright © Romas Kinka 2015
Originally commissioned by Writers' Centre Norwich 2015

Afterword © Tomas Vaiseta 2018
English translation copyright © Karla Gruodis 2018

Paperback ISBN   978-0-7206-2033-7
Epub ISBN   978-0-7206-2034-4
Mobipocket ISBN   978-0-7206-2035-1
PDF ISBN   978-0-7206-2036-8

A catalogue record for this book is available from the British Library.

Cover design: Davor Pukljak, frontispis.hr
Typeset by Octavo Smith Publishing Services

Printed by Printfinder, Riga, Latvia

The translation of this book was supported by the Lithuanian Culture Institute.

CONTENTS

PREFACE

The Street with No Name

The very first word that comes to my mind when thinking about the subject of my novel *Tamsa ir partneriai* (*Darkness and Company*) is 'obscenity'.

In J.M. Coetzee's novel *Elizabeth Costello* there is an episode in which the eponymous writer is reading Paul West's novel *The Very Rich Hours of Count von Stauffenberg*. Described in it is the execution of the officers who had wanted to kill Adolf Hitler. Coetzee's protagonist is so disgusted by the naturalistic descriptions that she pronounces the book 'obscene'. Obscene because such things, generally speaking, cannot happen, and if they do they cannot be made public, they must be kept hidden, as has happened in all the slaughterhouses of the world.

To write about the massacres of Jews in Lithuania is also obscene. When *Tamsa ir partneriai* was published, I found out that it was even considered *vulgar*. And, alas, not for the same reasons that J.M. Coetzee was talking about through the words of Elizabeth Costello. Why did I need to write such a book?

I was born in northern Lithuania, on the outskirts of the small town of Obeliai – to be more precise, on the lands of a former manorial estate in one of the old estate-workers' cottages, which still today retain their old-fashioned shingle roofs. Perhaps ten families of peasants, workers and servants had lived there. To the south there was a lake; to the north, on a hill, there stood a windmill; to the east, through the tops of the trees, one could see the twin-towered old neo-Gothic church; and to the west the distillery, built in 1907 by Jan Pszedecki, the former lord of the manor.

Even further to the north, beyond the windmill, which had long ago ceased to catch any wind, among the bushes and the grass, there was an old cemetery. Headstones decorated with large, incomprehensible, angular marks stood there, crooked, frozen in a variety of poses. We, the children living on the manorial estate, would often play war games there. The adults called it 'the Jewish cemetery', and these words sounded most mysterious to us children, almost like the words 'pirates' or 'treasure', because there had been no Jews in our small town for a long time. The Jews of our town were never mentioned, not at school, not at home. It was as if that cemetery dated from the days of the Egyptian pyramids or the Acropolis.

In 2010 I was visiting relatives in London. My second cousin Ernestas and his wife Daiva, who was working at that time as cultural attaché at the Lithuanian embassy in the UK, kindly suggested I come to stay with them and take a look around the city, which I had never before visited. One day we visited the Imperial War Museum, and I came across something there that shocked, distressed and shamed me. In the section on the Holocaust there is a diagram showing where and how many Jews had been killed in Europe during the Second World War, and on that diagram I also found my own unfortunate small town in the north of Lithuania, marked with only the numbers and the bare facts: 1,160 Jews were killed there by the Nazis and local collaborators. I don't know how to explain it, but I suddenly felt unmasked. For forty-five years I had taken no interest in this subject, I had avoided it, evaded it, because, most probably, I had been afraid of the truth. And now this truth was formulated and presented in the form of dry facts. I myself now find it strange how that could have happened in the way it did. After 1990, when Lithuania regained its independence, I had already read about the participation of Lithuanians in the mass murder of the country's Jews, had discussed it, had argued about it, but, all the same, I spoke about it as if it were just my own private, personal matter. As if it were only up to me to confirm or otherwise the participation of Lithuanians in that slaughter. But what I had been thinking about had already been formulated and put on a wall in a museum a long time ago.

It could not have been clearer; it was public knowledge, and it was shameful. It came as a shock to me. Something clicked in my head. And the worst thing was the shame. The shame that I, like most Lithuanians, had in all manner of ways tried to avoid the simple truth. At that moment, in the Imperial War Museum in London, I very clearly understood what the conversion of St Paul on the road to Damascus meant in Christian mythology.

In the autumn of 2010 I spent a couple of months as a writer in residence in Salzburg. During a conversation a local writer asked me if anything had been written in Lithuania on the Holocaust. I could call to mind a couple of writers who had, but their books had been written a long time before. In present-day independent Lithuania, however, I could not think of any such works. Historians had already been working on this subject for some time, but novelists, for whatever reason, had avoided it. That same evening

I found a piece on the internet by the Lithuanian historian Arūnas Bubnys in which he writes about the mass killings of Jews in the Lithuanian countryside. In discussing the Holocaust in Lithuania, the massacres of Vilnius and Kaunas were always mentioned, and it had been the Nazis who had murdered the Jews. I, like most Lithuanians, knew very little about the slaughter that had taken place in the countryside and the fact that, while there were a few Germans in the special squads that perpetrated these crimes, mostly they were Lithuanians. And only because we did not want to know. I did not want to know. And during the Soviet occupation the conditions for us not to know were conveniently created. The vast majority of Lithuanians are still reluctant to speak about this subject, and, if they do, more often than not they fall back on the same arguments: the Jews were shot by the German Nazis and a few Lithuanian degenerates, who perhaps were not even really Lithuanians; the majority of Jews were communists and NKVD agents, and so their destruction under the prevailing conditions of war could be justified; when, in 1940, Lithuania was occupied by the Soviet army, it was the Jews who met the Soviet tanks with flowers and then took a very active part in the government structures of the occupying authorities; they were Soviet agitators and political leaders, and they were the ones who also played a part in the deportations of Lithuanians to Siberia; and so on.

Another very strange, but perhaps no less relevant argument, which I would sometimes hear from my mother, was that the Jews crucified Jesus Christ and that is why such a terrible punishment was visited upon them. In reading the documents and memoirs about the torture, humiliation and murder of Jews in Lithuania, I came across this argument several times. In some paradoxical way, in the thinking of a Lithuanian, Jesus Christ was not even a

Jew. Perhaps it was this idea that prompted me in the novel to give the members of the killing squad the names of Christ's disciples and why they refer to themselves as 'the apostles'. Of course, this is literature, but I needed a form, a certain religious context, because in Lithuania in the mid-twentieth century Christianity was a very powerful force. Even during the Soviet period, religion for Lithuanians was one of the principal ways of expressing identity, national consciousness and resisting the occupation. Even more important in this regard was the Lithuanian language and literature. With the founding of Sąjūdis, the Lithuanian independence movement, in its attempt to liberate Lithuania from the Soviet empire, poetry and folk songs were more important than weapons. At the Sąjūdis rallies talks were given by poets and writers, that is to say, by those who knew the Lithuanian language best and who wrote in it. Of course, the reputation of literature and those who create it is not the same today as it once was, but it seemed to me to be an important act of consciousness to write a book in Lithuanian about Lithuanians who took part in the massacres of Jews. And not just for me but for all our people.

So this was the genesis of *Tamsa ir partneriai*. Why did I decide to write such a novel? In the West it would seem the subject has been covered comprehensively in books, in many films and in countless memoirs. The victims and their executioners are now lying under the ground. The first thing that made my head spin was the opportunity to talk about something that in Lithuania was almost taboo. To write on a subject that carries risk, which is unpleasant, and with which one has to grapple like Jacob wrestling with the angel. And even before beginning to write, one already knows that one will at the very least be left bruised and certainly without any blessing.

What should one do about mass murder, about which both the executioners and the victims have something to say? How should one deal with the obscenity referred to by J.M. Coetzee? Do we really learn anything from the mistakes of the past, and, if we do, do we become better human beings as a result, or do the scum become even smarter and harder to bring to justice? Unfortunately, I was rebuked not for describing the executions but because I had taken on the subject of the murderers in the first place.

I received all manner of criticism – that the Jews had paid me, that I was defaming my motherland – but I called to mind a line from Julian Barnes's *Flaubert's Parrot*, in which he states that the most patriotic act is to tell your country when it is behaving dishonourably, foolishly or viciously. My book caused great controversy. On the one hand I was awarded the title of Person of Tolerance 2012, but on the other I was called a traitor. It was suggested that in my next book I should write about homosexuals – meaning that the subject I had chosen was sensationalist, and I was just courting cheap publicity. I was admonished for not writing about the members of the Lithuanian resistance who had been murdered by the Soviets, for not writing about the Jewish members of the NKVD and so on. The biggest complaint, which I received from a serious literary critic, was that there was no repentance in my novel and for that reason it was not written sincerely and I was little more than a representative of the Holocaust industry. To tell the truth, I find unacceptable the point of view that literature has to *do* something, to repent, condemn, judge, that it has to be ideologically committed. At any rate, I became convinced that there exists in Lithuania the premise that if one writes about the mass murder of the Jews, one is after something shameful: money, attention, undeserved popularity. (Just for the record, in my view, for a writer to seek popularity and to be recompensed for his or her work is not a sin.) It is a simple fact that in Lithuania there is a very strong tendency to believe that it is better not to take on the subject of the Jews, and if one does, one is guilty, no matter what.

Repentance is a complicated matter. A person who repents publically, strenuously, will always be regarded with suspicion, because repentance is a very internal, subtle feeling. Like shame. From the time that I saw that diagram in that museum in London, when I saw the numbers, I was accompanied by a feeling of shame. My favourite Polish writer is Witold Gombrowicz, who spent part of his life in exile. He said that it doesn't matter what complexes a writer has, what's important is whether he is able to transform them into a fact of culture. I do not know if I was successful in turning my guilt into a fact of culture of any quality. Some people turn guilt and shame into aggression; others, spurred on by such experiences, take the path of awareness. I really cannot say if my book is just one more statistical achievement or rather a sign of awareness, of a more real relationship with existence. I don't know.

As regards repentance, I read a lot of documentary material, interviews with Lithuanians who had directly participated in the mass killings, and I was surprised that I found no repentance there. By way of example, here is an extract from the interview of one such:

In the first group of Jews that had been brought here there were about thirty persons. We shot at them from a distance of twenty metres. Our group at that time shot about 300 people, mainly men. We took the things belonging to the shot Jews. I took two suitcases, in which there were two men's suits and a man's overcoat. Chrome-tanned boots, women's dresses, men's over- and underclothes, some strips of material for women's overcoats, two watches – a wristwatch and a pocket-watch – and other things, which I took home with me.

The language used was that of a statement, the facts set out with indifference. Indifference, that is the most terrible thing. Complete indifference. That is how I wanted to portray the killers.

The director Peter Brook conducted an interesting experiment in the 1960s. He gave a student an extract from Peter Weiss's play *Die Ermittlung* (*The Investigation*) about Auschwitz. In the extract there is a section about the bodies of people who had just been killed. The student read the piece with feeling, and his distress was felt and understood by the audience. He asked another student to read an extract on the Battle of Agincourt from *Henry V*, in which the English and the French who died are named. The student made the mistakes typical of an amateur. He read the piece in an elevated tone, with pathos, putting the emphasis in all the wrong places. The audience did not know what to make of it. Then the director asked that the impressions raised by the Auschwitz victims be used to imagine the dead at the Battle of Agincourt, to realize that they were not just figures from literature but living human beings, as alive as the victims of Auschwitz, like ourselves. When the student read Shakespeare's text again, the audience became attentive, because the reader, now feeling an emotional connection with the characters in the play, read the piece in a simple and appropriate manner. Following this experiment Peter Brook formulated some important questions. How much time has to pass before a corpse becomes a historical corpse? After how many years does mass killing become romantic?

What, in truth, can literature do to remind us, to resurrect memories, to connect those memories with the feelings of human beings today, to revive the relationship with the past, with suffering, with repentance? So that those memories are not obscene and a writer does not fall under the suspicion of wishing to profit from a tragedy? In truth, are our lives not a continual profiting from the dead? We are parasites living off the bones of our ancestors, and there is nothing we can do to change that. Human beings today, in all manner of ways, try to avoid suffering.

I do not know if suffering has a cleansing, healing power. Let us take Russia as an example, where people suffered so much during the Second World War. But it does not seem that they understand what a misfortune it is to suffer continually – today they rattle their sabres and threaten anyone who dares not go along with their policies of aggression. You would imagine that the person who has suffered greatly would be more understanding, more aware, better able to comprehend the suffering of his neighbour, but the opposite can be true. A person who has suffered a lot can become even more terrible, more cruel; he can become vengeful and resentful.

During the presentation of my novel at the Centre for Tolerance in Vilnius I was asked if I had any Jewish friends. I wasn't able to answer the question. I don't have any Jewish friends, but I couldn't come up with an answer. Why? It was only later that I understood. They had all died. On 25 August 1941 all my potential Jewish friends had been shot and buried in pits not far from a small town in the north of Lithuania. On the other side of the small town there are only the dilapidated headstones of the graves of their ancestors.

Frances A. Yates, in her book *The Art of Memory*, writes about a mnemonic device. It's quite simple. A person wishing to remember information puts images into places he knows well, and then, walking through those places in his thoughts, he can quite easily reproduce large amounts of information. Where a person is born and grows up is often the place he or she knows best. Let's agree that the small town of Obeliai is just such a place in my memory, a place I know well, but, alas, images are missing, over a thousand Jews are missing, Jews who were erased from the life of that small town, but they have not disappeared from my memory nor, as a consequence, from the map of existence.

To tell the truth, after everything I've written here I have a bad taste in my mouth. As if I've turned myself inside out trying to appear sincere, but I don't believe in the sincerity of writers. A writer is very rarely sincere, he can't really be sincere, particularly if he wants to be a good writer. He only exploits that sincerity, he doesn't give in to it. He uses sincerity as a stylistic device. But there is one unpleasant and strange thing I can grasp – perhaps it's just a feeling – that the impetus behind this text of mine coming into being – and, I repeat, it's only a feeling – is an ember of anti-Semitism deep inside me and the fear and the shame of admitting it.

My mother still lives on the edge of that small town, on the former manorial estate. She is in her eighties, she attends church diligently, likes to watch soap operas on television, sympathizes with all the poor souls and unfortunates of the world. I recently visited her, and the subject of streets came up – she doesn't like the name of a street close by her house. I said to her, what if we changed the name to Jewish Street? After all, the Jewish cemetery isn't far away, and, besides that, so many of them lived here before the war. My mother looked at me as if I'd said the most foolish thing imaginable. What are you talking about? she asked with a dismissive gesture. And, in truth, what *am* I talking about?

Sigitas Parulskis
Vilnius, May 2015

Translated from the Lithuanian by Romas Kinka

DARKNESS AND COMPANY

PIGS

My life is like a cigarette butt, thought Vincentas as he gathered the crushed, soggy ends from the ground. As though not he but someone else had lived his life, had smoked it – Vincentas's life – then tossed it away and walked off. Leaving Vincentas smouldering. It wasn't completely over, but the best part was destroyed, lost, gone for ever. In any case it wasn't easy to find cigarette butts in the British zone. You could go for a few kilometres before coming across a single decent one. In the past he had smoked rarely and not much. After taking a good photograph or making love. He had always smoked after making love. It was a way of extending the pleasure, crowning the achievement. But that was another time, before the war. It might have been a thousand years ago, before Christ even.

It was a day like any other, he was walking along the lake, the sun was shining, he would have liked to take off his clothes and bathe. And he might have done so if he hadn't been startled by a strange noise. His first thought was to turn and leave, but then he changed his mind. He heard female voices. Bathing women – he was sorry that he hadn't brought his camera.

A small group of people had settled by the lake. Through the bushes he could see the women's blonde, shimmering hair; their ringing laughter rolled over the smooth surface of the lake; they were completely naked, swimming and splashing and constantly looking back over their shoulders at the shore where three men in army uniforms sprawled on the grass. He couldn't tell if they were Brits or Americans. With their air of victory they definitely weren't Germans. The girls were German, hungry and yearning, their vigorous young bodies undamaged by the war; he stared through the branches trying not to move, but neither could he withdraw; a painful longing flooded his chest; he thought about Judita, about her white body glowing in his embrace, that he might never again smell her wonderfully fragrant skin or see her moist, slightly parted lips, inviting, unpredictable, intoxicating; the soldiers had brought food, canned meat and bread and chocolate, and there were a few bottles of something – from a distance he couldn't make out the labels, but it looked like wine, red, lip-bloodying, inviting, sensual, unpredictable – the girls ran out of the water, bare and shameless, and lay down by the men and drank from army flasks and laughed with their heads thrown back to the sky, and their lips were bloody like the sunset over the lake, over Europe, he was hungry, but even more he craved a cigarette, they were smoking and tossing long cigarette butts as though they were Americans, maybe they were Americans, it was only in their zone that he would find cigarettes barely a third smoked, the Brits were a bit more frugal, but women can turn your head and upset habits, they could have been Brits, but they definitely weren't Russians. One pair split away from the others and moved in Vincentas's direction, dangerously close to his hiding place, she didn't know a word of English, he understood no German, but it looked like they understood each other perfectly without words, the language of the body is very simple, instinct doesn't need words or explanations, everything that stands in the way of desire is insignificant, unless, of course, it is the Church or the law or the girl's father with a gun in his hands, he had already unbuttoned his shirt, she was gently slipping it off his shoulders, and then the two of them lay down in the tall grass, the young man was smiling, the girl looked focused, as though she was planning to undertake a task that required concentration, she unbuckled his belt, slowly pulled off his trousers and froze for a moment, as though in shock, as though what she discovered was not what she had hoped for or that it exceeded her expectations, Vincentas's hiding place was uncomfortable, he couldn't move or he would be found, and the branches in front of him prevented him from seeing clearly, the girl began to caress the man, he arched his neck, threw his head back and closed his eyes. The remaining couples followed their example and went off to lie in the tall grass a little further away, he heard the women's sighs, the men's moans and saw the rhythmic rise and fall of white buttocks shining in the sun, he felt very weak and for a second thought he had lost consciousness, his eyes went dark, or perhaps a dark cloud had cloaked the sky, a strong wind swept the lakeside, he closed his eyes and held his head in his hands so that it wouldn't explode, he knew that if he let go, his skull would shatter like an eggshell crushed by a heavy soldier's boot, then everything stopped, the wind calmed down, the clouds dispersed, his eyes were still closed, but he now felt that everything around him had changed, that he could move, and although his eyes were still closed it got brighter, he carefully released his palms from his head, a sound reached his ears and forced him to open his eyes – he clearly heard a grunting, as though pigs were grazing near by, and, sure enough, he could no longer see the lovebirds playing their games, strange creatures had strayed near his hiding place, neither pigs nor humans, a girl with a pig's snout, a man with pig's legs, her large plump breasts sprouting thick, whitish bristles, he had cloven hooves instead of hands, and their throats released an awful grunting that sounded like a death rattle, and, unable to bear this ghastly spectacle, he leaped out from the bushes waving above his head a stick he had just grabbed, and the creatures jumped out of the tall grass and all ran back towards the water, hooves thudding and raising dust, and they dived into the lake, disappearing under the waves.

Although overwhelmed by horror and fatigue, he gathered cigarette butts with one hand and the remains of the food with the other. There was a lot of food, but he was more concerned with the cigarette butts. When he had gathered a handful he heard a rustling in the bushes, got scared and ran from the lake shore, frightened for his soul – but even more by the prospect that someone might take his haul.

And then – he leaped out from behind the bushes. He wouldn't have called him a man, because he didn't look like a man, more like a ghost. Filthy, covered in rags, growling and brandishing a weapon that looked like a trident, like a sharpened, seven-branched candlestick attached to a pole. The candle spikes had been sharpened, and, even though they lacked the barbs that there would have been on the tines of a trident, he was so alarmed that at first he couldn't make out what the ghost was growling, *essen, essen,* shouted the creature, but Vincentas had barely any food left, in one hand he held the cigarette butts, in the other a crust of bread he hadn't yet swallowed, he didn't have the energy to fight the armed madman so he tried to skirt around him, but he slipped, fell on one knee and then suddenly felt a dull thud against his side, and then, now on his back, he saw the white clouds and couldn't understand why his body suddenly felt so heavy, like lead, that he couldn't get up, as though he were an insect pinned down by a giant needle, as though he had suddenly become an injured and powerless giant beetle.

When he finally sat up the creature had disappeared, and it was only then that he realized that his – the creature's – voice was somehow familiar, that it was probably Aleksandras's, yes, it was definitely him, the same Aleksandras who should have been dead, who couldn't have risen from the dead, and yet if he had somehow risen from the dead he had disappeared, and with him his entire treasure – the handful of butts, the crust of bread and all that was left was a stabbing pain and blood gushing from seven little holes, but luckily he found one cigarette butt in the grass, it had fallen from the sleeve of his jacket, the jacket he had at some point taken off a corpse when he had needed to replace his ruined clothes, he had told him you don't need this any more, but I could really use it, and it did come in handy, as a cigarette butt had become stuck in the sleeve, and so now he could have a smoke, he could savour the moment, and then, he could no longer remember what happened next, he came to in a basement wrapped in strange rags, a doctor was telling him that he had been at death's door but that the critical days had passed and everything that had been worth living for was in the past, all that was left was the hope that Our Lady of the Gates of Dawn and the memory of Judita would take care of him and protect him.

It had probably been Aleksandras. He was supposed to have died at the beginning of the war, but he hadn't gone anywhere. His shadow constantly hounded Vincentas and would not let up. It didn't matter what people called it – a ghost, a spectre, guilt. Oh, where is my beloved Judita now, he wondered, lying in a dark basement somewhere in Germany, far from home, from light.

THREE KINGS

He should have died three times by now.

The first time was before he was even born. His father, a construction engineer, was driving while drunk; as his mother tells it, they had been to a party celebrating the completion of a building. His mother had been seven months pregnant, but that hadn't stopped her from being the centre of attention, and after one especially passionate dance with a tsarist general his father had made a scene, drank more than he should have and then they had left.

They argued as they drove, his father apparently castigating her, suggesting that the child might not even be his. At a turn the car slid off the road and into a pond. His father, a tall man, was stuck behind the wheel, the car sank, his mother had struggled out of the vehicle but couldn't make it to the shore. She lost consciousness and was pulled out by some nearby fishermen. He was born in an old wooden rowing boat among worms and dead, freshly caught fish.

When the war started he went out into the streets to take photographs. He was arrested by partisan rebels and accused of spying for the Bolsheviks. They wanted to shoot him on the spot but then threw him in the lock-up. When they led him out and stood him against a wall he was spared by an SS officer.

The third time he had escaped death had been quite recently. He had gone out to gather cigarette butts and might not have returned. He couldn't have sworn on his life – and life was worth so little in those days – that it had been Aleksandras, Judita's husband, but he suspected that it had been him. And that he had wanted to kill him, something that Aleksandras would have had every right to do.

He knew that Aleksandras was dead, or that he should be dead, but after everything that he had seen he wasn't surprised that the dead were more alive than the living, that the living were more dead than the dead.

But was he still alive?

He wanted to die. He felt weak, helpless and useless, he wanted to end it all because he saw no point in going on. But then, from somewhere very deep, from the darkest corner of his unconscious, came the realization that the only reason for which it was worth living and suffering was his son. He didn't care any more what future generations might think of him; he didn't know those generations and never will. The most painful thing was that he would probably never know his son either. And then a strange desire arose in him, took hold of him – the desire to explain to his son who his father was, who *he* was. This simple, clichéd thought had saved his life. He began to resist death, and death withdrew a little. Sometimes he felt its presence, sometimes he even imagined it standing in a corner, but in its hand it held not a traditional scythe but a seven-tined harpoon. When he felt better he thought about his life; he couldn't blame the way he had behaved on the times he had lived through. To him it was as colourless as developing fluid. Only individuals can dilute an era with the colours of their own various emotions and experiences. But over the last few years most people had done their best to soak that strip of time in blood. He did not want to ask for forgiveness. He wanted to see his son, to touch him, smell the warmth of his skin, talk to him. Adults speak to children as if they are halfwits. He didn't want that kind of conversation. He imagined a reserved conversation between two men . . . Of course, he was not sure what he could speak about with a son he had never seen, with whom he never spent even a damned second. People hide the truth from children, not because they want to spare their delicate minds but because they want to conceal the truth about themselves for as long as possible. The only person Vincentas had been able to speak to as he lay on his deathbed was the doctor. In his thoughts he had referred to him as 'the butcher', but he was a good doctor, who had listened to him, nursed him, believed him. He was so perfect that Vincentas sometimes wondered if he wasn't a figment of his imagination. That there was no doctor, that there had been no war, that he was still waiting for Judita to walk through the door, undress quickly, slip under the covers and press her icy feet against his warm calf.

CHRISTENING

He's sitting in the kitchen, day is breaking, Judita is asleep. He suddenly has a strange feeling of déjà vu: all of this has happened before. As if he is looking at a photograph taken by someone else. He knows that it's just his mind playing tricks on him, but at the same time he's rather enjoying the deception – as though someone is responsible for it all, for what is happening to him, to everyone.

Judita is asleep; he's sitting in the kitchen looking out of the window. The sky is gradually brightening. The summer nights are short. He can't sleep. Here and there an occasional shot echoes. Something is happening that would have been unimaginable even a few days ago. That night, just a few days into the war, he suddenly understands, and it takes his breath away. Something is happening that will alter all of their destinies. Perhaps not everyone's, but most people's. Everything will be different. It is not clear whether for good or bad, but people living in this city, in this country, perhaps all over the world, will never again return to their homes the same as they left them. And how many will never return. Such thoughts are dizzying, overwhelming – they at once terrify and challenge and intrigue. A dark excitement, as terrifying as a dream from which one cannot awake. He sits and looks out of the window.

*

That night, when they began to make love, when he entered her, he thought he heard a noise, a cracking sound that threw him off his stride. As though a joint had cracked, but it wasn't exactly a sound . . . He might have felt it more than heard it.

'Did you hear that?' he asked Judita.

'What?' she asked.

Of course she had not heard anything, because it had only been in his head.

For the first time, he stopped just as they had begun their lovemaking. An unpleasant feeling. Something that had never happened to him before. Twenty-six is too young to have problems of that nature. To start and not finish is at the very least unpleasant. That is a universal principle of harmony. Like with a composition – if it is left unfinished one feels a lack, a deficit, a frustration. To make love and not be satisfied – it's not right. He reached over to the chair next to the bed, grabbed a packet of cigarettes and lit up.

Judita ran her long fingers over his ribs.

'We haven't finished yet, and you're already smoking.'

'Yes,' he mumbled, 'I just . . .' And he fell silent.

'I'm scared, too,' she whispered.

'Don't be afraid,' he said. 'As long as you're with me nothing bad will happen to you.'

'Don't be afraid . . .' she repeated, staring at the ceiling.

'Yes, don't be afraid,' he said once more. 'It's something else. I must be tired. I overdid things today. We'll sort it right away.'

She leaned her head on her hand and looked at him.

He liked looking at her.

He liked it when she looked at him.

'It's really nothing. I'm just tired. Honestly.'

'Silly boy,' she said. He feels pleasure when she calls him 'silly boy' – it feels like someone is caressing him. Judita says that he did not get enough attention from his mother. That is why he is like this – still immature, agitated, egotistical.

For a few moments he lay there smoking, slowly blowing smoke towards the ceiling.

'Aleksandras disappeared,' said Judita, breaking the silence.

'Disappeared? Seriously?'

'He said he was going to dig a trench.'

'What do you mean, dig a trench?'

'Stop repeating everything I say.'

'I'll stop.' He turned towards her. Aleksandras and war sounded ridiculous together.

'His neighbour served in the First World War and convinced him that you have to dig a trench so that you'll have somewhere to hide if you need it.'

'Has he done it?'

'I don't know. I saw a hole, but only a child could hide in it. Aleksandras was also planning to stop by the telegraph agency . . . And I haven't seen him since.'

He did not know what to say. His heart rejoiced. His heart quivered and rejoiced. He didn't listen to his heart, because his heart was crazy. He was afraid that Judita would not like that joy. He was afraid that Judita would not like how he was getting excited from all this fear and joy.

'I think he's gone east.'

Judita raised her head. 'He couldn't have.'

'Why not?'

'He would have told me. We spoke about it.'

'Could there have been other reasons?'

'Like what?'

'I don't know.'

'You think that he knew?'

'I don't know.'

Vincentas was telling the truth. He didn't know if Aleksandras suspected anything about him and Judita. About him and Judita. About the two of them. How sweet it sounded.

She didn't say anything, then sighed heavily. 'Maybe it's for the best. For everyone.'

'Someone I know . . . we worked as guards together . . . he said he saw Aleksandras at the station, that he got on a train.'

It didn't sound convincing. He had never worked as a guard, although he had known one guy who served as a paramilitary naval guard. Judita sensed the lie.

'Why were you talking to your friend about Aleksandras? Tell me. What do you know?'

He didn't know what to say. He didn't know anything. Just what everyone knew, that there was chaos in the streets, that the Reds and the Jews were running.

'I'm sorry. I didn't manage to come up with a convincing lie.'

She gave him a light punch in the ribs.

'I don't think he would do anything like that,' Judita eventually said. Then she laughed quietly. 'I kept hesitating about leaving him, felt sorry for him, thought he wouldn't survive on his own . . . And what if he did actually go east? What if he knew about us? Oh, shit, he knew about us!' She leaned on her elbows and looked at him carefully. 'I feel like such a slut,' Judita moaned theatrically and hugged a pillow.

'You are the most wonderful slut I've ever known,' he said and kissed her.

Judita again punched him in the ribs, harder this time. 'And just how many sluts *have* you known?'

'I've often been told I'm the son of a whore.'

Judita moaned once more. 'This war will tear off all our masks,' she said, still lying back and hugging the pillow.

When she arrived that night he'd meant to tell her what had happened the day before. He didn't want to frighten her, but he knew that it wasn't right to hide the truth. Now he was no longer so sure.

His hands continued to shake and his heart pounded madly. It was the first time he had felt such overwhelming tension. It was somehow like making love but different. Like its opposite – its dark, brutal side.

They lay in silence for a while, Aleksandras's name still hanging in the air.

Then she pressed against him, her bare skin slightly goosebumped from the cool evening air.

'Do you love me?' she asked in a whisper. 'Have you seen what they are doing with the Jews?'

'I've seen,' he said.

'They spit on them, beat them, curse and kill them. What has happened to this peaceful, hard-working nation? Maybe they have never been so peaceful, so devout?'

'I don't know. I don't want to think about the nation, only about you. I will protect you.'

He embraced her and once again felt the blood rush to his groin. Such a good feeling. In that moment he believed he could do anything. That he was all-powerful. That he could create. Embark on grand works, change lives, divert rivers. Build socialism and then tear it down. He pulled away from her slightly and ran his palm over her breasts, abdomen, the curve of her hips.

'What?' she asked, a bit self-conscious.

'Why didn't you have children?'

'Aleksandras didn't want to. At least until now. So he wouldn't lose his freedom.'

'Children don't limit freedom – they broaden it.'

She smiled slightly.

He fell silent, again caressed her shoulder, then her hip, thigh, drew his palm over the barely perceptible bumps on the skin of her thigh.

'It's a strange machine, the body. Such a strong but powerless machine. It reminds me of a camera – it lets in and preserves different forms of light.'

'It preserves what?'

'Light.'

'What does it look like in there, inside?'

'I don't know – maybe like thoughts, memories, dreams. It's all light.'

He caught her eye.

'You're looking for light in me?'

'I can't get that cracking noise out of my head.'

'What cracking noise?' asked Judita.

'As though it wasn't real, just in my head.'

She sighed heavily, closed her eyes and crossed her hands over her chest, as though she were trying to emulate a bas-relief on a tomb.

'Right now you're my only reality,' she said almost inaudibly.

Her spectacular body. He could see it from a distance, he never mistook her for another woman when he waited for her at the Žaliakalnis funicular. She would come down from the top, from the hill, and he would say, you are an angel descended from Heaven, and she would smile and laugh, showing her white, even teeth and would laugh and say, 'Why?' Once she asked, 'What kind of an angel could I be? An angel comes down from Heaven only for two reasons – either he has been expelled for his sins or he comes down to this vale of tears to rip a soul from some poor body. What kind of an angel am I?' And he embraced her and they walked on together, his nose nestled in her thick, fragrant hair, and he whispered, you are every kind of angel, I like both types, no, that's not right, she objected, you have to choose. It isn't that easy to choose between a fallen angel and a murdering angel, he said, and Judita triumphantly raised her hand in the air, you see, she said, you don't know, you can't choose, I can't, he replied, because I don't want to be that stupid God who banished such a beautiful angel out of jealousy or that poor wretch whose soul is about to be ripped out by such an awfully pretty angel.

Fine, she said, you've wriggled out of it. This time I'll leave your soul alone, let it continue to ripen.

He drew closer to her. Judita continued to lie there, her eyes closed, lips slightly apart; if he had not felt the warmth of her body she might have been dead.

He had not had his camera with him. Before everything that happened he had carried it like an item of clothing, like a part of his body. It was better that he did not have it – if he had tried to take a photograph he would have been shot. Killed along with the rest of them. He found this scene: they lie there with their bloody mouths agape, half naked, some completely naked in pools of blood and that sound . . . that cracking sound. That splintering. He had never before heard the sound of human bones cracking. Of a skull splitting.

Vincentas had been walking home along Vytautas Prospect. It

had not been that long ago, but he couldn't remember if it had been sunny or cloudy that day.

He had looked at his watch; it had been around ten in the morning. Or had it been evening? No, morning. By the cemetery he was stopped by an armed soldier.

'Don't go there,' he said. 'Better not go there.'

He looked over towards the cemetery and saw people digging pits. There is a lot of death in the city, so a lot of pits are needed.

He had gone out to fetch the doctor, but no one had come to the door. Juozapas, his stepfather, was bedridden. Some retreating Russians had stopped by his carpentry workshop and demanded a length of rope. Juozapas had insisted that they pay. The Russian officer had scribbled something on a piece of paper, but Juozapas had shaken his head and demanded money, shove your paper up your backside, shouted Juozapas, I wouldn't even give you a coffin for free, what do I need your paper for, you're never coming back, for the love of God let's hope you never come back. A few unpainted coffins stood in the corner of Juozapas's shop, the Russian officer understood that Juozapas was offering them a coffin and was about to shoot Juozapas, but his pistol jammed, or maybe he had run out of bullets, because some of the Russians had run from the city not only without bullets but some without guns. So the Soviet soldiers beat Juozapas up, kicked him unconscious, ransacked the shop full of completed work, shat in a freshly built coffin and took off.

Vincentas's mother had reproached Juozapas, 'Bloody hell, Juozapas, be happy that you're still alive – they could have shot you on the spot. They're savages, those Asiatics!'

'You can't blame everything on the war. So, what, if it's wartime there's no decency or anything?' muttered Juozapas in a thin voice as he lay there. Vincentas's mother had waved her hand and then opened the living-room sideboard, pulled out a half-empty bottle, poured herself a shot, taken a deep breath and thrown back the vodka. She drank like a common worker – no food, quickly, no ritual, not wasting any time with niceties on such an insignificant act.

His mother sent him to fetch a doctor they knew, Bluzonas. Juozapas had recently built him a medicine cabinet, and the doctor had yet to pay for it.

Vincentas was not allowed in. The maid said that no one was at home. She was frightened or maybe just half asleep. Her eyes swollen. As he walked from their building he saw a curtain twitch on the second floor. Bluzonas's beard was unmistakable. It was him. They simply had not wanted to let him in. Out of fear, or just to be safe. There was a lot of fear in the city, many people peeking out from behind curtains. Shots popping here and there. The Germans were already in the city; they had started to hunt down any Bolsheviks who had not managed to get away in time.

He returned to the door and knocked again. There was no answer. Not even the maid appeared this time.

Even though the soldier – actually he was not a soldier but a partisan; he was wearing an old army jacket but civilian trousers and shoes – even though the partisan soldier had advised him not to go there, Vincentas did not take any notice. He did not want to argue with an armed man, so he circled around and once more entered Vytautas Prospect. A group of people had gathered by the garage, around the fence, and were looking into the yard. He couldn't see anything through the crowd, so he went over to Miško Street and entered the yard of the former Polish high school, which bordered the garage yard. Here, too, spectators were hanging off the fence.

'Is there a game of football going on there?' he asked a man with a crumpled hat. The man grinned oddly and shrugged his shoulders. Looks like it, he replied. A crumpled hat and rotted front teeth: it's easiest to remember ugly images. Why is that? Maybe because he was not raised properly.

He had not found the doctor, so there was no need to rush. Juozapas would manage somehow, and, if not, there was nothing he could do about it. Death was now a frequent visitor; no one would be surprised. Maybe it's easier to die when everyone's dying. When so many are dying. Or maybe the opposite is true: it's no big deal to die in a crowd of corpses.

He pushed through the crowd, the excited, whispering, waving people.

People were being brought to the garage yard in twos and threes, evidently from the cemetery; some young men without jackets were beating them with rubber truncheons and crowbars.

'They're being led from the graveyard to be sent to their graves,' said a voice behind him.

The crumpled hat's voice, Vincentas thought.

The paving of the garage yard was strewn with mutilated bodies and swimming in blood. Those being brought in were dragged by the hair, shoved, their heads smashed with crowbars, sprayed with a hose. The same hose that was used to wash cars. The hose writhed like a long, shiny snake.

A huge, shaggy-haired, bearded old man in a camel-hair coat held the hose in both hands and shouted, 'You scum. So you think you can escape what's coming to you?'

The crowd gradually pushed Vincentas forward. Perhaps the

sky went black or he closed his eyes, but suddenly he realized he was right next to the old man, who had now thrown down the hose and was standing with one hand tucked into the wide leather belt girding his waist, the other clutching a long iron rod.

The old man handed him the rod, smiled, slapped his back and then his cheek. As if they knew one another. He looked like a shepherd. It was June, the middle of summer, the old man was dressed so warmly, sweat poured down his cheeks, his hands were sticky, as if he had been eating pears, his fingers sticky from pear juice, and Vincentas felt it when the man clapped his cheek. Like priests do or men who like children. Or maybe shepherds or gardeners.

And then it felt as though the rod were alive, pulsing in his hand; he glanced down and saw a man lying there, twisted, his face distorted in agony, the rod poking out of his back like a wing, like what is left of a wing when the feathers have been ripped off. That's what a fallen angel looks like, he thought, and he couldn't move, didn't know what to do. It struck him that it would have been good to have had his camera with him. That he could have hidden behind it. What he felt floundering in his hand was the man's life. The last vestiges of it. But you can't photograph things like that. And he didn't want to photograph them. He had got so used to being on the other side of a lens, to hiding behind his camera, to separating himself from reality with a thin strip of film. The rod gradually stopped pulsing.

Vincentas stood in the crowd and felt his extremities slowly melting, as though they had been cast in ice. As though he had, in fact, grabbed the rod sticking out of the dead man's back and that piece of iron had turned him into a pillar or a block of ice. He began to retreat slowly and then bolted; he wanted to run as far as he could from that yard to wipe out the feeling of the pulsing metal. Iron is never weak. You can never hear it beat. An iron heart beating in his hand. And that imaginary and yet horribly real feeling made him want to throw up.

Judita began to moan, kneading Vincentas's torso with her feet as though trying to squeeze all she could from him, and they were falling together . . . plunging . . . two angels, two wingless angels with rods of sin . . . sticking out from their backs . . .

He lit up once more. Now with some relief.

'I want some, too.' Judita reached out her hand, carefully took the cigarette from his mouth, pursed her lips around it, took a drag, then another, placed the half-smoked, smouldering cigarette back in his mouth, leaned back on the pillow and blew the smoke out loudly.

They always smoked after making love, often sharing a cigarette. It was like an extension of pleasure, a distant echo of orgasm that returned now to the chest, then escaped with the smoke to freedom.

She lay on her back, her legs crossed, the dark tuft below her abdomen looking like a wound, like congealed blood.

He thought he knew every centimetre of her body, but did he know anything of her soul? Could he have said anything about even the tiniest part of her soul, he wondered to himself, but said nothing.

He placed his palm on her breast. Drew his palm across it as though across sand. As though he were smoothing out ridges in the sand. Warm gentle sand, glistening in the sun.

He had barely closed his eyes and the old man once again leaped out before him, grabbed the hose and turned it towards the two still, lying bodies and shouted, 'I christen you with water – so that you will convert, but another, more powerful, will come after me. I'm not worthy even to kiss his shoes, and he will christen you with fire!'

Fire. Better the smell of burning meat than rotting.

Then the old man suddenly turned the hose around and lashed at Vincentas, as though whipping him, and then laughed, tilting his long, sweaty, blood-flecked beard up to the sky. Then the old man set off at speed, and Vincentas ran, too, his legs heavy, as though stuffed with wadding, until he lost his breath and again felt like throwing up.

Judita is asleep; he's sitting in the kitchen looking out of the window. The sky is gradually brightening. The summer nights are short. He can't sleep. Here and there the occasional shot echoes. Who were those men? Why were they killed? Communists? Secret police? Who was that old man, that bearded lunatic? Why did the old man look at Vincentas as though he knew him? And that very real feeling of metal: in his mouth, his hands. The taste of iron, the taste of blood. He did not tell Judita about it. There's enough talk about it already. The Jews are being rounded up, being beaten and shot in the streets.

He's sitting in the kitchen, watching the light outside the window grow gradually. Like a photograph brightening in developer fluid. You never know what you will see in it. It's like dreaming the same dream a second time. You've already seen it, that image, that piece of reality, but when you see it again now it will be different. The same but completely different. Like it has tasted a bit of you. A moment that only you saw, only you, and now you want to show it to others. When photographs of this day are developed – who will be on the other side of the lens, who will come to christen us with fire and water? Whose body, which poison, will this era taste of? He doesn't show it, but he can't deceive himself – he, too, is frightened; he sits half naked in the kitchen while Judita sleeps, smoking, quivering like an aspen leaf. He's frightened, he's very frightened, as though he were really holding a metal rod in his hand, a rod that had skewered a man like an insect on a mounting board, pinned down his existence like a butterfly on the page of death. May Our Lady of the Gates of Dawn protect me, most Holy Virgin, pray for us now and in the hour of our death, amen, whispered Vincentas through stony lips and felt a little better.

Judita went home in the morning. Although he tried to convince her to stay she was determined – she would go and wait for Aleksandras to return.

'It's awful to get home and find it empty,' she said and left.

He scanned his empty room, took a deep breath, filling his lungs with air that was still full of Judita.

PONTIUS PILATE

When they came to get them the Russian was in the corner of the cell, shitting. The man had lain there all night facing the wall; it had occurred to Vincentas that he might be dead, but then morning came, and he just got up, pulled down his trousers and began emptying his bowels. Jokūbas the Elder and Simonas, who was called Petras, because there was another Simonas – Vincentas would learn their names later – stood in the entrance to the guard-house and looked mockingly at the Russian. The prisoner was barefoot, his filthy trousers pushed down over his bent knees, his shirt bloodied. His face was swollen, with the kind of black eyes that come from heavy blows to the nose.

Vincentas reckoned he couldn't look quite as bad as the Russian.

'Bloody hell, he's still shitting!' Simonas Petras was in a good mood. 'Come on, Ivan, let's go. And have pity, oh Lord, on your shitty soul. And you, too, Mr Photographer. We're going to take one last picture.'

The prisoner wiped his backside with a handful of straw in a leisurely fashion and pulled his trousers back up. Simonas Petras marched out holding his weapon before him; Jokūbas the Elder had stuffed his pistol into his belt.

'He was a lieutenant in charge of a cannon,' explained Simonas, who was called Petras, to Jokūbas the Elder. 'They were supposed to cover boats travelling down the river Nemunas. Only one bridge was left standing, the others had been blown up. The stupid Russians were shooting all over the place. Sometimes the anti-tank cannon went off, but it wasn't much of a threat. On the other hand, if those German aeroplanes hadn't shot out of the clouds who knows how it all would have ended? The Russian was probably knocked out by a shockwave. A bomb must have fallen near him. Do you have any idea how that feels? It's like having the flu with a fever of forty-one. There's a buzzing in your head, you see double, you lose your coordination. The Russian was the only one left by the overturned gun. At first he tried to right it, but it takes more than one man to do that. What the hell, we stopped the Russian units from crossing the river, but it looks like they went upstream instead, towards the east.

'We watched him and waited to see if any others would turn up. Nobody wanted to go near there. He was crawling around that wrecked cannon like an insect . . . Like my grandmother used to say, a castrated beetle. Then I leaped towards him and shouted "*Ruki vierch*", but he just stared at me with his mouth open like a dying carp.'

'How about you shut up?' interrupted Jokūbas the Elder. 'Men died there, and you're coming out with all this bullshit.'

'I know, I know men died there, and I could have died there,' Simonas Petras shot back but then stopped talking. He liked to talk. There are people who, when they start talking, you can't stop them. They will talk about anything – anything to avoid being silent, like they are afraid that silence might lock their jaws for all eternity and they might never open their mouths again.

Simonas Petras glanced at Vincentas and, without saying a word, hit him in the ribs with his rifle butt. Vincentas doubled up in pain, and Simonas Petras hissed, 'Take that, you Bolshevik bastard! Forward!' he said, shoving Vincentas before he had a chance to catch his breath.

During the first days of the war the radio had broadcast news incessantly. He sat, still sleepy from the night before – he had slept badly, had dreamed of the bearded old man in his shepherd's clothes, then Judita had insisted on going home to wait for Aleksandras. Vincentas went to his mother's for breakfast, sat in her kitchen barefoot in an undershirt, picking at some black bread with butter and pressed cottage cheese and chewing on some spring-onion leaves as he read the paper.

> Lithuanian brothers and sisters!
> The fateful moment of our final reckoning with the Jews has arrived. Lithuania must be freed not only from bondage to the Asiatic Bolsheviks but also from Jewry's long-standing yoke.

The bearded old man in his shepherd's clothes, the glistening black hose in his hands, flashed through his head.

> The ancient right of sanctuary granted to the Jews during the time of Vytautas the Great is now completely and permanently rescinded.
> Each Jew, without exception, must hereby withdraw from Lithuanian lands without further delay.
> All those Jews who are clearly guilty of betraying the Lithuanian state and persecuting, torturing or harming Lithuanian nationals will be held individually accountable and will receive the appropriate punishment. If it emerges that during this hour of Lithuania's reckoning and rebirth Jews guilty of severe crimes find ways to escape, it will be the responsibility of every loyal Lithuanian to take personal action to detain said Jews and, if necessary, to punish them.

And again he saw before him the previous day's scene of execution: the bloody pavement, the dead bodies, the people watching the act of vengeance, the faces filled with horror and secret satisfaction, enjoyment, confusion, and fear, and disgust, and the thrill of vengeful retribution.

> The new Lithuanian state will be restored through the strength, effort, heart and wisdom of members of the Lithuanian nation. Jews are banished completely for all time. If a single one of them should dare to think that he will find some sort of sanctuary, let him be aware from today of the irreversible verdict upon the Jews: in the newly restored Lithuanian state not a single Jew will possess either civic rights or the possibility of earning a living. In this way the mistakes of the past and Jewish baseness will be corrected. In this way a strong foundation for our Aryan nation's future success and happiness will be laid.
>
> Thus we must all prepare for battle and victory – for the sake of the freedom of the Lithuanian nation, the cleansing of the Lithuanian nation, an independent Lithuanian state and a bright and happy future.

His mother entered the dining-room from the bedroom, turned up the radio and went back to the bedroom where the moribund Juozapas lay. The dictator's elevated voice reached his ears.

> The Provisional Government of the newly awakened Lithuania hereby proclaims the restoration of the free and independent Lithuanian state.
>
> Before the clear conscience of the entire world, the young

Lithuanian state enthusiastically pledges to contribute to the reorganization of Europe on a new foundation.

Battered by the savage Bolshevik terror, the Lithuanian nation is determined to build its future around principles of national unity and social justice.

He had heard this from the very first days of the war, as German bombers conducted night raids on Alytus, Kėdainiai, Šiauliai, Kaunas and Riga, all of which had Soviet army garrisons. German army units were attacking Russian border posts and penetrating the Lithuanian border. It all looked very serious. It was war. Germany against the Soviet Union. The biggest explosions could be heard from the direction of Aleksotas Airport and the suburb of Šančiai, where the Reds had established a garrison.

'Battered by the savage Bolshevik terror, the Lithuanian nation . . .' he said to himself under his breath, his mouth full of cottage cheese. These words were not inspired solely by ecstatic joy. The Bolsheviks had indeed earned the hatred of several generations. Terrifying news was constantly circulating about people who had been arrested or shot – sure, at first the Soviets had left things as they had been, people said it was so their victims would stop being vigilant, but by autumn they had begun to close government offices, reorganize, arrest and persecute. Commissars, usually Jews, had turned up in every organization and pestered people with their pledges, socialist contests and other nonsense. With such unqualified people in charge life began to break down, shortages of clothing and other essential items grew and then the mass arrests and deportations had begun. Most people worried that they might be on the lists. You couldn't be sure of anything. People were saying that sixty to eighty thousand people had been arrested. The charges were usually trumped up – counter-revolutionary activity or enemy of the people, although the secret police didn't bother explaining what that meant.

The radio played the Lithuanian national anthem, shots echoed throughout the city, a machine-gun hammered near Vytautas Bridge. The Russians were withdrawing from Užnemunė, Lithuanian territory to the west of the Nemunas, and were trying to cross the Nemunas in small boats. They had destroyed the bridges themselves and were now caught in their own trap.

In the end Vincentas gave in, grabbed his camera and went out into the street.

It looked as though the Great Flood had begun, and all those who could were rushing to save themselves in Noah's Ark. It was mostly Jews – they ran down the streets clutching suitcases and boxes, as though they were not people carrying burdens but burdens carrying people, caught up in the swirling current of time. Those who were not planning to escape stood in long lines by the shops. People pressed against the buildings because a bomb could go off anywhere at any time, leaving plumes of smoke and injured passers-by.

A soldier on horseback appeared unexpectedly in the street; he looked as pathetic as he might have a year ago, when hordes of filthy, scruffy Bolsheviks occupied the country. A Russian bomber flew over, and the soldier raised his arms triumphantly and began to wave, but the bomber crew did not have time to take note of what was happening on the ground. Two German fighters shot out of the clouds, and a few seconds later the Russian bomber disappeared beyond the river, trailing a black line of smoke, followed by a dull explosion.

Vincentas raised his camera and took several photographs. The young cavalryman smiled sadly at him and waved gallantly – it wasn't clear whether he was encouraging himself or saying goodbye. Then suddenly he drew his sword and waved again, but now more threateningly and aggressively, as though challenging someone. Gunshots popped, and the cavalryman galloped off down the street followed by several armed men.

'Let him who is without sin cast a stone at me, shoot me! I am not God, and I cannot take another man's life because it is not I who gave him that life, but nor can I allow that man to take my life because he did not give me mine!' shouted a long-haired man in a black suit from the middle of the street. The madman was barefoot and wore an enormous wooden cross around his neck. He kept waving his arms in the air as he repeated his litany, 'Let him who is without sin cast a stone at me . . .'

Vincentas wanted to photograph the madman, but he suddenly ran off after the disappearing horseman and his pursuers. All of this was rather strange and alarming. At the end of the street the horseman swayed to the side, fell across the horse's neck, then slowly leaned back as the horse disappeared around the corner.

Vincentas saw a group of men in a bizarre mix of clothing, military and civilian, the only thing identifying them as a unit being the white armbands that most of them were wearing. They were hurriedly dragging someone to a dark alley off Donelaitis Street between the ironmonger's and the cobbler's.

He wondered what was going on. He walked as far as the alley and stopped by the corner of the building, looked in but did not see anything. He stepped into the alley, looked around cautiously and did not see anything suspicious, except that somewhere, further in, he could hear muffled men's shouts and the short but deep cries of a woman. Vincentas took a few more steps. The day was cloudy, and dusk clung to the alley, which wasn't even a street, just a gap between buildings, a narrowing gap with a large lilac bush growing at the end of it. The voices were coming from behind the bush. He approached as close as he could, saw the backs of two men and through their legs a woman's white calves raised high, the soles of her feet bare and filthy, one bleeding slightly, then he saw a man's bare buttocks between the raised calves, banging furiously, the woman's moans weakening with every movement.

A shard of glass must have cracked under his feet because one of the men turned and looked him straight in the eye.

'What kind of a whore are you?' asked the shorter, crop-haired man, aiming his gun and taking a few steps towards him.

'I'm . . .' replied Vincentas, thrown off track, as he suddenly realized this would not end well for him. 'I'm just a photographer . . . I . . . I'm leaving, I thought someone was crying for help, but it seems not. Forgive me.'

'On whose orders?' asked the other man, who was wearing a faded Lithuanian army uniform.

'What do you mean, on whose orders?' replied Vincentas, confused.

'On whose orders are you photographing?'

'Nobody gave me orders,' he replied. 'These are historic days. I want to immortalize them.'

'Are you a Jew?'

'I'm a photographer. I take pictures.'

The rest of the men had approached to check out the unexpected photographer.

The rapist stood up, slowly buttoned his trousers, pulled out his pistol and looked angrily at Vincentas, his eyes so strange that

Vincentas's anus clenched up in fear. Still staring at Vincentas, the man suddenly aimed his pistol towards the ground and shot the girl as she lay there. She had not had time to cover herself up, so she was left with her legs spread, naked up to her waist, her dead eyes staring at the lilac bush that had long since bloomed.

'I'll immortalize you, you communist whore,' said the man, approaching Vincentas. He was bigger and taller than the others, auburn-haired, blue-eyed, a few days' stubble sprouting on his cheeks. 'Why are you wasting your time with him?' he angrily upbraided his accomplice. He punched the photographer in the face, took his camera. The historic days had turned into a nightmare. They could have shot him on the spot.

From the first time Vincentas saw him he thought of the SS officer as the Artist. He did not yet know anything about the man but could tell intuitively that the German took a lot of care over his appearance. Perfectly cut clothes, a small, almost delicate build, a distinct profile, somewhat angular but graceful movements. He simply liked to look good, and he knew that he did.

It was he who had ordered that the arrested men be brought in. The Russian stood by the formation, looking haggard: in his underwear, emaciated, with several days' beard growth. He was smiling slightly, and not just any old way but with contempt. But it was probably the concussion. Vincentas wasn't sure how he looked himself but doubted whether it was any better than the Russian officer.

The officer in charge of the partisans gave a command, but the SS officer revoked it. Apparently, execution was not his intention. He slowly circled the Russian prisoner, inspecting him up and down, then turned away from him and waved his hand back in his direction.

'Clothes are not natural accessories for animals,' said the SS officer. 'And man does not merely use clothes to protect himself from the cold. Over time they have become part of his identity. He fuses psychologically with his clothes, they complement him, are an extension of him, they provide not only warmth but an illusory sense of security, a space between his exterior and the imaginary borders of his personal territory. Undress him.'

Two of the partisans quickly ripped off the man's clothes so that the Russian officer now stood completely naked. Before he had stood erect, had looked almost scornfully at the SS officer, but now he gradually became hunched and covered his groin with his hands, his eyes fixed on the ground.

'Do you see what a marked difference that makes?' continued the German officer, in the voice of a fascinated, curious researcher. 'Stripped of his clothing, an individual will also lose some of his confidence, especially if he is before others who are clothed. Therefore, if you want to gain the upper hand, undress your opponent, take away his ability to hide – and I am not only talking about clothes. Take away his family, his hope, his future, his sustenance and so on – what is most important is that he be unable to hide. Then you will defeat him.'

The SS officer gracefully pulled out his revolver, took a step forward and shot the Russian prisoner in the back of the head.

The prisoner crumpled noiselessly, simply collapsed on the spot where he had been standing. The lecture was over.

Vincentas was struck by the grace of the German's movement. The SS officer had pulled out his gun as though it were a sword, a rapier in a contest that could have only one victor.

He remembered the young Russian cavalryman who had waved his sword so gallantly and then disappeared around a corner, leaning helplessly back in his saddle, most likely already dead.

His bowels filled with a cement-like weight. A feeling of cold froze his breast, spine and thighs so that if someone had knocked into him he would have shattered into pieces. His mind was empty. The image of some strange glass figurines he had seen the previous Christmas near the Cathedral of St Peter and St Paul flashed in front of him. The sun shone, people sauntered past with hot breath steaming from their mouths, while the figures, which represented the Holy Family, sparkled as if cast in silver.

They stood him against a wall and blindfolded him. He had not slept all night, had imagined that if they should want to blindfold him he would ask them not to, but now he said nothing. As much as he had tried to convince them that he was not a communist agent, no one had listened to him. When he had demanded to be taken to the commander they had laughed. At first he had thought that it was all a joke, but then was overcome by horror at the thought that it is possible to kill a man for fun and that in wartime no one cares, no one will ask how or why. Or for what.

Then he heard the German commander's voice ordering that his blindfold be removed. Which was better than being stripped naked.

'Of what are you accusing this man?' asked the German.

'Of working for the communists.'

The German nodded. Then addressed him. 'Why do they call you "the Photographer"?'

'Because I am a photographer. Before the war I had begun to work in a studio.'

'Do you know anything about artistic photography?'

'Yes.'

'Do you have any photographs?'

'I do.'

'Did you learn to speak German in school?'

'My mother taught me.'

'She is German?'

'No.'

'Jewish?'

'She is a singer. And a dancer. A former one.'

'That sounds very Jewish.'

'I don't know. I don't know how Jews dance.'

'Is it true that you are a Bolshevik agent?'

'These days truth is in the hands of whoever holds the biggest weapon.'

Somehow the conversation with the German was having a calming effect on Vincentas.

The German once again looked him up and down. 'Come and see me this evening at this address. Be sure to bring some of your photographs.'

And he handed him a slip of paper with an address.

And then it all ended very suddenly. He had felt as though his bowels were full of bloody Christmas icicles, but now the joy of an Easter morning flooded his breast. His knees were buckling, he longed to collapse and bury his head in something soft. In Judita's breast. But he tried not to show any emotion. Especially not to those bastards who had been ready to blow his brains out.

Jokūbas the Elder, the same tall, heavyset man who had raped the girl in front of him and then cold-bloodedly shot her, approached him and whispered angrily in his ear, 'Get this into your head, you piece of shit. I don't like you. I don't care that the German is standing up for you, that he wants to make you his slut. Just understand one thing – I'm watching you! Sooner or later you'll slip up, you'll make a mistake. You'll try to show off, contact your people, get away. Just one slip, and I'll strangle you with these very hands, you filthy Bolshevik. Just one slip!'

NIGHT WATCH

He was assigned to stand guard by some kind of warehouse on Daukšos Street. The battalion was in the process of being put together, and Vincentas showed no enthusiasm about serving in it, but Jokūbas the Elder had made sure that he would be part of it. I'll make a man out of you, he had said, and if you get up to any bullshit, you're done for. Vincentas did not quite understand what 'a man' meant in Jokūbas the Elder's lexicon, but it was clearly nothing good. So he stood by the building, not knowing what it contained, maybe timber or bricks, without a weapon. Only his partner Tadas was armed; Vincentas's sole means of defence was an armband with the letter T.

'What's the point of guarding this warehouse? No one's going to rob it,' he said to Tadas a few hours later, by which time it had become deathly boring loitering on a street corner and staring at the occasional passer-by with their suitcases, straw hampers and bundles, lost and frightened and looking around them.

'Jokūbas the Elder warned me to keep a close eye on you.'

'And what else did he say?'

'That you're a provocateur. Are you a provocateur?'

'Go to hell.'

'Only after you,' said Tadas, adjusting his weapon on his shoulder. 'Some of the others were assigned to guard the water-supply station at Eiguliai – we could be riding around on bicycles – or the ammunition and military warehouse, or the radio station. But here it's just furniture – dirty Jewish and communist furniture.'

Tadas ordered him to look around carefully so he didn't miss any uniformed government representatives, while he himself observed the passers-by. He finally picked out an elderly Jewish couple. The man and woman were dragging two heavy suitcases each.

'Come here,' Tadas said to them, waving his rifle. 'Over here, by the wall.' He led the husband and wife further away along the warehouse wall and ordered them to open the suitcases.

The husband wanted to obey the order, but the woman suddenly protested, 'You have no right to act like some thug. Why should we show you what's in our suitcases? Who are you anyway?'

'I . . .' Tadas faltered, blushed and glanced at Vincentas, who turned up his palms helplessly, and then Tadas cocked his rifle, shoved the muzzle next to the man's mouth and snarled, 'Open it, you piece of shit!'

The man opened his mouth, and Tadas stuck the muzzle into it. Vincentas heard the metal knock against the man's teeth.

'What was that?' he said, turning to the stunned woman. 'I can't hear you! What did you say, you old slut? Say it again, you old hag, say it again. What did you say? What am I?'

The woman did not say a word and opened the suitcases, staying by them.

'Turn away! Face the wall! Faster!' ordered Tadas, and he bent over the suitcases. He rummaged through the couple's belongings, pulling out shirts, underwear, tossing them right on to the pavement. People walking past glanced into the alley without saying anything, only quickening their steps.

'Get out of here!' shouted Tadas, and the couple quickly packed up their things and disappeared down the alley.

Tadas came up to Vincentas and showed him a watch, a coffee mill, a Zeiss Ikon camera and a several tins of food.

'Want some tinned food?' he asked.

Vincentas was hungry. His stomach felt like a bottomless pit after the hours of standing; he even felt a bit nauseous. But he shook his head. He thought that this tinned food would make him feel worse.

'Who took my camera?' he asked Tadas.

'I don't know. I wasn't there. Jokūbas the Elder was in charge of the group that arrested you. They probably sold it and split the money.' He turned the camera he had stolen from the Jews in his hands. 'How much would I get for it in the market?'

Vincentas did not have any money. Nor did he have a camera. He did not want to ask Tadas to give it to him for free. Maybe out of timidity, or because of the scene he had just witnessed: the image of the couple being robbed.

THE ARTIST

'Have you ever seen a severed head?' He paused, then without waiting for an answer, clarified, 'More precisely – the process of separating the head from the body? Of course you haven't.'

He had just been silently looking over a stack of Vincentas's photographs, which included several nudes of Judita. He had brought them to show the German but now regretted doing so. When he saw those photographs in the SS officer's hands he suddenly realized that had wanted to show off to him, that there would have to be some compensation for the image that the German had seen: Vincentas powerless, crushed, condemned. In bringing the photographs of his naked lover he had evidently wanted to prove that he, too, had some worth, that he was a man – a man before whom a beautiful woman would bare herself. But when he observed the German perusing the nudes he began to feel even worse, even more pathetic and demeaned. And the SS officer spent more time looking at his lover's body than at the other photographs.

'A pig,' Vincentas finally said.

'A pig?' replied the German, surprised. 'What about a pig?'

'I have seen a pig's head being cut off.'

The officer laughed. 'That would be a vulgar brand of naïvety, no? How different Christian iconography would be if instead of

John the Baptist's head on the platter it had been a pig's. It would be playful, but weak. Although, if we're thinking about the origins of Christianity . . .' The German fell silent for a moment and then began to laugh loudly. 'That would certainly be a swinish, a truly swinish prank!'

When he finally calmed down, he stood, moved to the door and turned around.

'Would you like some coffee? Or something stronger?'

Vincentas nodded. He would like everything. He would have some cognac and then press three grenades against his stomach and blow himself to pieces.

'I'll trust you to choose,' he added politely.

The officer left. Vincentas looked around. The SS officer had established himself in a spacious five-bedroom apartment. Its previous residents had clearly been wealthy. The apartment was furnished with expensive furniture, a solid round table with five chairs stood in the drawing-room; there were tall, wide windows, not less than thirty square metres of woven carpet, and the office to which the German led him contained a small, polished Empire table and a three-seater sofa covered in green silk. Only one detail of the apartment was unusual: every single wall was covered with paintings. In the office almost all of the paintings depicted a decapitated head. Vincentas was not an expert on biblical subjects, but that was exactly what they showed: Saint John the Baptist's head on a platter.

'An interesting collection, don't you think?' he heard the SS officer say from the doorway.

Vincentas nodded and went back to his place at the table. The officer was followed by his aide, who carried a silver tray reminiscent of similar items in some of the paintings he'd just been looking at, only this tray held not the prophet's bloody head but two cups, a coffee pot and a sugar bowl.

When the aide left, the officer took a sip of coffee and began to speak. 'Beheadings and other subjects exist in art for a number of reasons. One is to present a particular story that matters to the artist, to viewers, the society and audiences of that time. A simple purpose – to present a story, a narrative.'

Vincentas picked up his coffee cup, breathed in its aroma deeply and put it back on the table. Coffee like that had become hard to find lately. The officer looked at him in silence, as though expecting some kind of reaction.

'Hmm,' he mumbled. 'Stories . . . should they entertain the viewer or . . . ?' He did not know what more to say. He had never looked at paintings as stories. In truth, until then he had had little interest in paintings.

The SS officer perked up. It seemed that it was enough for him that someone was listening to what he said. 'Not necessarily. For instance, Giotto's fresco cycles, which depicted the story of Christ's life – such narratives introduced people to certain events. You've heard tell of the Poor Man's Bible? They were paintings for ignorant, illiterate people. They would come to church, see paintings of the saints – characters from the Scriptures about whom they had heard from their parish priest, and the characters would be familiar. In effect, churches, temples and other places of worship were the equivalent of today's cinemas. In that sense, if we're referring to the Renaissance or the Enlightenment, the artist was fulfilling a fundamental desire, or duty, to tell a story. And that is not related to the specifics of art. History or stories are told by art, cinema, literature and, of course, works of music. In addition, different narratives offer different possibilities for one or another artistic genre to display its tools, to demonstrate its language, its capabilities. If we're looking at beheading, it's a desire to tell the stories of Judith and Holofernes, Salome and John the Baptist, David and Goliath. They are all stories, and people like to tell stories, do they not?'

The German looked at him reproachfully, as though perhaps he did not like to tell stories.

Vincentas shrugged. 'I don't know, perhaps. I'm not very good at it myself. Maybe I don't have enough experience. One would need to have something to tell.'

'Well then. A photograph is also a kind of story. And I'm not talking about photographs documenting specific narratives: celebrations, parades, people playing football or some other sport. Even a woman's naked body can tell us a lot. For instance, looking at the woman you have photographed I can tell that she feels a lot of trust for the individual on the other side of the camera. And perhaps even more. Her eyes are full of passionate longing. She is baring herself not before the lens or an invisible audience that will (or more likely will not) see her image, she is baring all before a man to whom she is attracted. And she knows that he is attracted to her as well, she can see this, feel it, and I can see it in the photograph, in her eyes, in her pose. So the two of you must be lovers.'

Vincentas could feel his cheeks burning. He could remember clearly that after that he and Judita had made love. He had photographed her and then . . . passionately, greedily, on the floor. His cheeks burned, but he felt a chill pass through him.

'A woman in love – that in itself is a story. Like any body is. When instinct wells up from our depths, when it becomes visible, we become more open to an attentive gaze. On the other hand, bodies that are already dead – which have no more passion, no spark, which have extinguished all of their feelings and desires – such bodies are usually indecipherable, hard to read.'

'I never thought about that,' admitted Vincentas.

'It doesn't matter,' said the officer, waving his hand. Another matter is that these beheading stories offer many possibilities for art and painting to display their capabilities. Other topics don't offer such possibilities, possibilities for showing the body. If an artist is painting a beheading he has to imagine how to represent the body. He would not be able to represent the body in the same way if he were painting, for example, a corn harvest, cherry-picking or people eating.'

'Do you mean that the intention is to instil fear?'

'Why?' replied the SS officer.

'Well, is that the effect the artist is aiming for? Is that the message?'

The German sat in silence. It seemed he had said everything he wanted to say, and his guest had become utterly uninteresting and unnecessary. Once again Vincentas felt a chill. What could it all mean? Perhaps some obscenity lay behind it all. Why had the SS officer invited him here? To give him a lecture on art, on severed heads? On the Poor Man's Bible? It was hard to imagine that a German would be so concerned with an unknown photographer's educational lacunae.

'I can imagine that this seems a bit unusual,' he finally said. 'I hope that I did not make a mistake in selecting you. One way or another it's a question of an exchange of services.' Then he fell silent again.

'Will I have to do anything?' Vincentas asked and immediately regretted it. It could have sounded like an offer. On the other hand, he felt he owed the German his life. Had it not been for the SS officer his own people would have shot him as a communist spy. His own.

'Yes,' the officer replied immediately. 'You will be given everything you need. A camera, film, you will not have to do any dirty work. Unless you want to, of course . . . You will have to photograph.'

'Photograph?'

'You will work for me exclusively. You will receive a permit, so do not worry about that. You will have to hand in any film you shoot right away without delay. Do you have requests, questions?'

Vincentas thought for a moment and remembered Tadas, how he had shoved the rifle muzzle into the man's mouth. He said quietly, 'I don't want to be part of the battalion.'

'You can continue living as you do, but you will have to travel to all of the assignment locations with the battalion. A special group has been formed for operations in the provinces; Obersturmführer Joachim Haman will be in charge. You will sometimes have to go out with them.'

'But . . .' he tried to protest, but the German simply waved his hand.

'It is not negotiable.'

He stood up, unbuttoned the collar of his uniform, undid his belt with its holster, then turned and said in an irritated voice, 'Go! My people will find you when we need you.'

Vincentas turned towards the door without saying anything, agitated, terrified.

'Sleeping with a Jewess these days – not very smart, although perhaps quite romantic,' he heard as he opened the door. He closed it as fast as he could from the other side.

THE CROSS

Vincentas sat in the kitchen, sipping tea and reading an excerpt of a document the SS officer had given him:

> The photographing of executions for official purposes is permitted only upon orders from a strategic unit or special unit commander, an SS military company commander or a war correspondents' group commander. If under exceptional circumstances it is necessary to carry out such photography and it is not possible to gain permission in advance from a strategic unit or special unit commander, SS military company commander or war correspondents' group commander, they must be informed about it immediately.
>
> The operative unit or special unit commander, SS military company commander or war correspondents' group commander is responsible for ensuring that plates, film and photographs do not remain at the disposal of any of the staff of the operative offices . . .

The document was signed by someone named Heydrich. Why had the SS officer given Vincentas this document? He had told him to familiarize himself with it. That must be the procedure. Vincentas understood perfectly well that he would have no freedom in his actions.

'What are you reading?' asked his mother, coming into the kitchen.

'Nothing,' replied Vincentas, folding the paper and sticking it in his pocket.

The word 'executions'. He did not know what to expect, but this word alone horrified him. Maybe he should have tried harder to resist, to refuse? To run? But where could he escape to with an alcoholic mother and a bedridden stepfather? And what about Judita? What would happen to her? The reports of what was happening to the Jews were increasing in number and horror. At the same time news of the ghastly crimes being committed by the retreating Bolsheviks was coming in from the provinces. Even as they ran from Lithuania they had managed to brutally torture maybe hundreds of innocent people. Would the Germans surpass them?

Juozapas could barely speak any more. He complained that his mouth was dry, that his tongue was tangled, that it was getting harder to breathe. Doctors and medicine were unavailable. And that smell, that constant smell of piss and rotting flesh. It's hard to get used to that, although one can get used to anything, even the smell of death. When a person is healthy he doesn't think about such things, those smells don't irritate him, people don't even notice them, and if the nostrils pick up a whiff of death coming from somewhere, everyone turns their noses away, pretends that it's just a minor fact of life, an unnecessary fragment of existence. That's not mine, it has nothing to do with me. What's important is the present.

When there is a very ill person at home such smells and such thoughts are an inevitable consequence. His mother nursed Juozapas patiently, but she sometimes left the bedroom wrinkling her nose. She had an antidote to those wretched smells and scenes of illness, however. A bottle of alcohol of one kind or another always stood in the kitchen cupboard. In better times it was even a bottle of the Lithuanian honey liqueur, *krupnikas*, but these days she was very fond of vodka.

Before the war Juozapas had cooked up glue from animal waste. The smell had been disgusting. When Vincentas had asked where Juozapas had found the bones, the latter had smiled, stroked him with his heavy, calloused hand and said, these are infidels' bones, then would look around him, squinting furtively, and whisper, as though he was telling the biggest secret, I did away with a few Jews, that's where the bones are from. Seeing the child's expression he would throw back his head and laugh.

He laughed rarely. Perhaps because he was constantly working at something – carving, hammering, planing. A tired man does not have the energy to laugh. Either that or he had simply been of a dour disposition.

If life is made up only of memories and a person remembers only what he needs to, what's the point of life? Juozapas liked to say this, and would then offer the answer himself: life is a mystery, just like faith. Vincentas had always wanted to ask what he meant when he talked about memories but never did. Juozapas had always been a bit of a stranger to him, someone without a past, and Vincentas was not interested in that past.

When Juozapas laughed he emitted a high-pitched sound; sometimes it seemed that he was not laughing but squealing, like a rat caught in a trap.

And he looked like an animal. A long, pointed nose, thin lips, ears stuck against his skull, his neck always thick with greying down, a balding crown, shiny and uneven like the bottom of a tin pot; his mother used to take milk in a pot that looked like that and leave it for the stray cats who gathered in the neighbouring stairwell.

His stepfather had always smelled of wood, even when he was cooking glue from animal bones and gristle. It was the smell of dead wood, but at the same time it was a festive, exalted smell.

Juozapas had once received a commission from a farmer who wanted a cross for his land, to greet those arriving and send off those departing. When the cross was almost completed – there was only the figure of the crucified Christ left to be attached – Vincentas had lain down on the cross, spread out his arms and closed his eyes. He had tried to imagine how the Redeemer felt when the Roman soldiers crucified Him on the Hill of Golgotha. They stand by the cross, sharing out his clothes, while He, suffering a hellish agony, hangs on the cross. Vincentas was disappointed: he experienced nothing remotely mystical, only the uncomfortable hardness of the wood.

Then everything happened very fast. The cross lay on two beams, about a metre above the floor. Juozapas came into the workshop and pressed down on Vincentas's chest with one knee, then quickly tied first one and then his other arm to the cross. Vincentas was not the strongest of teenagers, and he was unable to resist. Then Juozapas did the same with his legs. He tightened the rope so that Vincentas would not slide down, raised up the cross, leaned it against the wall and left the room.

Juozapas did not reappear for an eternity, and no one apart from him ever went to the workshop; Vincentas's wrists ached horribly, the ropes cutting into his skin, tears running down his face. A few times Vincentas tried to call his mother, even though he knew she would not hear him. The longer he hung there the more frightening were the thoughts that entered his head: maybe

Juozapas had lost his mind and had left Vincentas there to die? At first he was overwhelmed by an intense hatred for Juozapas, then he began to curse all the arseholes who think of planting enormous crosses by their homes and, finally, almost unconscious from the pain, Vincentas became completely indifferent. The only thing that he knew for sure was that his real father would never have behaved that way. The father he had never known and had longed for his whole conscious life.

'Do you understand now that a cross is not something to play with?' Juozapas asked as he untied the ropes.

Vincentas never forgot that lesson, and now, as Juozapas lay suffering, smelling of decay and faeces, helpless and repulsive, he sometimes thought that it was something of a punishment for the nasty old man. Even if Vincentas had not delivered the mortal beating himself, he now felt somehow avenged. He sat in the kitchen looking at his mother, who had just drunk another one of her doses – a small shot glass she referred to as a 'bunny's palm' – and now sat calmly at the table flipping through a newspaper. He looked at her and thought about how illness is the heaviest cross anyone ever has to bear, that a serious, incurable illness is a cross from which one is taken down only after death, and then one's clothes are divvied up, one's body hidden away for all time until the Resurrection, until the Final Judgement.

'Poor Juozapas,' said Vincentas, turning his eyes towards the window. His mother sighed but said nothing.

JUDITA AND ALEKSANDRAS

Judita and Aleksandras lived in the suburb of Šančiai, in a wooden house that could be reached only by passing through a large, poorly maintained garden of overgrown grasses and shrubs. Judita and Aleksandras lived in one side of the house, the owners in the other.

Vincentas had met Aleksandras the previous evening, and now he was going to visit the couple at home.

Vincentas liked to go for walks along the river, especially in the evening when the fog begins to swirl over the water and the trees to wade into it like desperate suicides. That was when he would get the best photographs. With atmosphere, as his teacher Gasparas used to say. An atmosphere that was probably created simply by that suicide motif.

'Trees trying to commit suicide – isn't that great?' said Aleksandras gleefully when he heard Vincentas's explanation of what he was doing there when there was not another soul around.

Aleksandras had been riding a bicycle that evening. He had stopped near Vincentas because his chain had fallen off. It fell off and got stuck between the back wheel and the frame; the wheel suddenly stopped turning, the bicycle toppled over and Aleksandras crashed to the ground, rolled a few metres down a slope and lay there unmoving.

Vincentas ran over and helped him up.

'Did you hurt yourself?'

'No, but thank you.'

Aleksandras spoke Russian. He gestured towards the camera. 'Did you manage to get a picture? It would be a great shot – a helpless intellectual falling to his end . . . or something like that.'

Aleksandras was short, small-boned and a bit overweight, with tousled black hair and widened eyes.

'No, I didn't have time. Forgive me,' Vincentas, for some reason, answered apologetically.

'Don't be silly. But if you could help me find my glasses – I'm like a mole without them.'

The two of them began to crawl around the slope searching for the glasses. Aleksandras was crawling not only for show – his eyesight was genuinely poor.

'Thank you,' he said to Vincentas again after the latter found the glasses. 'And what do you photograph?'

'Suicidal trees,' said Vincentas, pointing at the trees that were gradually becoming enveloped in the evening mist, even though it was clear that it was by now too dark to take a photograph.

'Trees trying to commit suicide – isn't that great?' For some reason Aleksandras rejoiced when he heard that explanation. He paused, then asked, 'And what do you think about opera?'

'Do you sing in operas?' Vincentas asked cautiously.

'No, I create them.'

'I'm not too fond of opera. Those fat women pretending to be desirable lovers and princesses get on my nerves. It's just silly.'

'Fantastic. Everyone thinks that, but no one says it out loud. And least not in decent company. Thank you!'

'Not at all.'

Aleksandras picked up his bicycle and smacked the seat angrily.

'Bloody chain. It keeps falling off. What do I do now? Throw it in the river and walk – that's what I *should* do!'

Vincentas turned the bicycle over, gave the chain a couple of pulls, rotated the pedals both ways, pulled once more and then the chain slackened. He hooked the chain on to a tooth, turned it, caught his finger between the chain and the sprocket and some blood oozed out.

Aleksandras went pale, turned away and held out a handkerchief, still not looking.

'Tie it up,' he said, still turned away. Then, still not looking at Vincentas, he quickly told him his address and insisted that he visit them the following evening. He said he had an opera ticket and wanted to thank the man who photographs suicidal trees and fixes strangers' bicycles. And he rode off still not having even glanced at Vincentas's injury, which, although wrapped in the handkerchief, was still bleeding.

Vincentas passed through the vestibule and knocked on the door, then knocked again. Not getting a response, he stepped inside. The room was empty. A table, chairs, piano; modest but tasteful, tidy, clean. Except for a pile of papers on the piano.

'Hello,' he called, then, louder, 'Good day!'

He heard a sound in the room. He entered the room and almost froze in astonishment. A woman was sitting at the table. He gasped a few times and had no idea what to do. The woman was naked to the waist. She looked relaxed, one hand resting on the table, the other holding a large plum. She had just taken a bite of the fruit; the juice was running down her cheek, and a single drop hung from her nipple. Maybe that drop, maybe that drop was what so threw him because he could not pull his eyes away from it; he stared and stared and stared, unable to say or do anything.

'It's beautiful, no?' she asked in a strong, low voice that was at once pleasant and soft.

'Hello,' he said automatically and turned his eyes to a cupboard with a large butterfly on the door. His throat dried up completely for a moment. He felt his blood flowing both up and down – to his cheeks and to his groin.

'I . . . he . . . Aleksandras . . .' he mumbled, trying to swallow.

'Aleksandras? Your name is Aleksandras?'

'No, Aleksandras told me to come by . . .'

'Oh yes. He's in the bedroom. Putting on a tie.'

'A tie,' he repeated automatically.

'Yes, it's one of those male rituals. He calls it a date with the gallows. Do you know each other? Do you play together?'

'No . . . Yesterday we . . . by the river . . . I fixed his bike.'

The woman smiled. 'Typical Aleksandras. Yesterday he met someone; today he's taking them to the opera. You know, one time he brought home this blind beggar whose voice apparently reminded him of Caruso's singing!'

'No, I don't sing,' said Vincentas.

He unconsciously brought his hand to his neck. He had not put on a tie.

She extended her hand, her fingers sticky from plum juice. 'Judita,' she said, looking straight at him. He had turned his eyes to the side.

For a second their palms were stuck together.

'Are you blushing?' the woman asked in mock surprise.

'No, it's because of my waistcoat.'

'Ah . . . But it isn't red.'

'No.'

'Then it isn't about the waistcoat.'

'It's just very warm.'

Although he desperately wanted to look at her he did not dare, but, squinting, he could see, or perhaps rather feel, her nakedness, her warmth, her attraction. He was self-conscious about looking at her directly, but the image he had seen upon entering the kitchen was still right before his eyes.

Judita said, 'I feel warm, too. I'll go and get ready.'

Then he finally raised his eyes towards her. It seemed to him that now she was blushing, too. She carefully covered her breasts with her left hand. Earlier she had been sitting without any shame, but now was blushing.

She got up, shook her light, shoulder-length hair, lowered her hand and smiled. He could still feel her sticky fingers in his palm, could still feel them. She was so close, he could see his reflection in her large eyes, two flustered, speechless men – that was just how he felt, split in half – and he held his fingers, sticky from the plum juice, before him as though not sure where to put them. It felt like those fingers were slowly beginning to burn.

'I'll just be a minute,' said Judita quietly, almost in a whisper. 'You can wash your hands,' she added, nodding towards the corner of the kitchen where a pitcher of water stood next to a shining white basin.

And she passed by him – standing there in the kitchen doorway – almost brushing him with her round, dark nipples.

He stood still for a moment, then stepped towards the table and sat down in her place. Her smell lingered around the chair, juicy like the plum, an uneaten piece of which lay before him on the table. He picked up the piece of fruit, sniffed it and popped it in his mouth.

'Hello there. I didn't hear you come in,' he heard Aleksandras say from the living-room. 'So, shall we go?'

'Where?' he asked in surprise, hurrying to swallow the last of the plum.

'What do you mean, where?' countered Aleksandras with even greater surprise. 'To the opera.'

'Oh, yes.' He felt as though his brain were a blackboard from which someone had erased all the important marks, leaving only a black, empty rectangle.

He couldn't concentrate. He stared at the hundred-kilo gypsy Carmen throwing herself around on the stage but saw only Judita's hand as it rested on her knee. He had thought that Judita would not join them at the opera, but it turned out there were three tickets.

'The way things have turned out, Aleksandras has been feeling quite lonely,' Judita said to him when the chance arose during the intermission. 'We lived abroad for some time, and since we came back it has been hard to make friends. Especially since Aleksandras speaks only German and Russian, so you can imagine . . . Not just friends, it has been hard to find work as well. No one will take him. Aleksandras thinks it is because of his background, but I think he just needs to learn Lithuanian.'

'Yes,' agreed Vincentas.

'I can see that the two of you have found something to talk about,' said Aleksandras as he approached them. 'I was just speaking to a colleague. It looks like I might be able to make some money this weekend. They need a pianist. It's just a wedding, but why not, don't you think, my love?' And Aleksandras squeezed Judita's hand in joy.

Feeling awkward just standing there, the three of them slowly began to walk.

'I don't like opera for two reasons, neither of which has to do with singing. First of all, most people who go to the opera have no intention of listening to the music. They go only because it is high culture; they feel like eighteenth- or nineteenth-century characters, from a time when honour and dignity and titles still meant something, when a person was assessed not by what he did but how he looked. Secondly, all this ghastly walking in circles; how here in Kaunas during intermissions everyone shuffles around in a circle as though they were prisoners let out of their cells to exercise in the yard. Looking at all these puffed-up peacocks it's easy to imagine that this walking, the intermission, matters more to those attending than what happens on the stage.'

He spilled all of this out to Aleksandras when the latter once again asked what he thought about opera. The funniest thing was that the two of them were, in fact, just at that moment shuffling along in the circular promenade, as it was the first intermission. Although Vincentas had rehearsed his speech all evening, when he finally expressed his views on opera he did not feel entirely confident – he had heard a visitor to the photographer's studio say something similar. Some people like to philosophize when they are sitting before a camera lens. Of course, there are also those who are completely stunned and don't say a word, even after the photograph has been taken.

'Did you hear that?' said Aleksandras, smiling and glancing at Judita.

She nodded.

Aleksandras wriggled, as though someone had poured ants down his back. 'But that is not what is needed,' he said.

'What is not needed?' asked Vincentas, confused.

'Protesting against the bourgeoisie – it needs to be destroyed, not complained about.'

'That's Bolshevism,' said Judita.

'Better Bolshevism than opportunism,' replied Aleksandras.

For a while they walked on in silence. Judita excused herself and disappeared into a crowd of well-dressed ladies. The two of them continued walking in the circle with all the others.

'What do you think about *Don Juan*?' Aleksandras asked suddenly.

He was not sure what to reply. 'I thought we were watching *Carmen* . . .'

'Well *Carmen* . . .' muttered Aleksandras.

'I don't know much about opera. The other day an acquaintance was talking about how, during *Aida*, one of the trumpet-players was completely drunk. It was a fantastic show. It seems there were four trumpet-players, and one of them . . .' Again the 'acquaintance' was a client at the studio, a lively poet who had just published his first collection of poems. He had told the story of the drunken trumpet-player so humorously that Vincentas had not been able to concentrate on his work.

'I'm not asking about Mozart,' interrupted Aleksandras, 'and not about today's performance, which is quite adequate apart from Carmen herself, who looks a cow being led to the slaughterhouse.'

'Some men like heavy women.'

Vincentas immediately thought about Judita. She was not heavy, even if she was slightly plump. A figure of gentle, even lines rather than sharp contours. It was the gentleness of those lines that gave her an air of true, appealing femininity.

Aleksandras looked at him seriously through his round glasses, which made him look like an ageing owl. 'I recently read that the character of Don Juan embodies the male desire to sleep with all the women of the world. And only because that man is very insecure, so Don Juan can be said to be the embodiment of male fear.'

Vincentas felt unsafe. He still did not know why, but clearly sensed that it was something to do with the plum. With the sticky palm. With Judita. A sweet weakness filled his chest. 'It's human to fear. One should be wary of people who aren't afraid of anything.'

Aleksandras looked at him in silence. It seemed as though he was expecting concurrence but was not getting it. Vincentas shrugged.

Then Aleksandras explained, 'All of his sexual adventures, his desire to sleep with all women, merely reveal that he is driven by a constant fear of incapacity. He embodies the fear of impotence.'

The couple walking in front of them exchanged glances, the woman whispered something in the man's ear, the man turned around and looked at them with contempt. 'Stinking Bolsheviks,' he muttered under his breath and turned away. Vincentas and Aleksandras slowed their pace somewhat to increase the gap between themselves and the couple.

'You know, that Don Juan . . . maybe he just had certain abilities or attributes . . . For example, maybe his cock was such that women just couldn't resist.'

'That's just another legend created by men – that women are obsessed with the size of men's instruments.'

'Yes, but what if it really was . . . impressive?'

'Women don't care about that. It's the emotional connection that matters most to them.'

'Aleksandras, how many women have you met who have told you that nonsense about emotional connection? How many women have told you that in all honesty, without being pushed into it?'

He once again saw opera lovers' concerned glances directed at them and nudged Aleksandras. 'We should talk more quietly, or they'll be ripping off their own trousers right here.'

Aleksandras laughed merrily. He laughed loudly, but as if he were laughing to himself, did not want to share his joy with anyone. Then suddenly he fell silent, as though that joy had never existed.

They walked on in silence. Vincentas did not give a damn if an awkward silence hung between them. He felt good because he was thinking about Judita. He thought of her sitting at the table with the half-eaten plum in her hand. He moves towards her, she places the plum on the table, pulls him to her with his belt, then puts her hand in there and holds him with her fingers all sticky and sweet from plum juice, and he becomes harder and harder, is bursting out of his fly, and . . .

'What's with you?' he heard Aleksandras's voice reaching out to him from somewhere far away.

'Nothing.'

'Thinking about Don Juan?'

'No!'

'You don't feel well?'

'I couldn't feel better.'

'Forgive me, then. I'm especially good at getting on people's nerves.'

'Maybe it has something to do with that Austrian doctor . . .' Vincentas could not remember his name.

'Mr Freud? No, I don't know,' said Aleksandras, shaking his head. 'Although Freud is a very popular subject of conversation in certain circles, barely anyone has read any of his books, even though they have strong opinions about them. It's strange, don't you think?'

Because Vincentas belonged to the camp of the non-readers, he shrugged his shoulders – nothing strange about it. Very human.

Aleksandras clasped his hands behind his back and began to speak, looking straight ahead.

'I'm more interested in the Commander, the Stone Guest in Pushkin's version of the story, a man who has lost love, whose passion has died. Why was Don Juan successful with women? Is it because all women are whores? No. It's simply because they're married to old men who are both physically and creatively weak, because women live with men who have turned to stone, who have died. In times past that was common. So Don Juan, who was the embodiment of the youthful drive to fertilize everything, did not have much difficulty getting close to those women.'

'Yes, but not all women are married to much older men.'

'No, of course not. But a few years of marriage often make someone an old man. They suck out the passion, it vanishes. It all vanishes.'

Vincentas looked more closely at Aleksandras's face and noticed that he was much older than he had seemed yesterday. He may be much older than thirty, could even be forty. And then he suddenly thought about Judita – poor Judita! She was living with a stone man.

'What's vanishing?' he heard Judita ask, and Aleksandras waved his hand.

'Let's go. The intermission is over. If we get in quickly now we

won't have to push our way past those bags of mothballs in hats.'
He turned to Vincentas and whispered, 'It would be good to continue these pleasant discussions.'

Although Vincentas nodded he was thinking about something else.

For a few days he didn't know what to do with himself. Wherever he went, whatever he did, all he saw before him was that drop of juice hanging off Judita's right nipple.

They did not meet often. He worked in the studio so was free only after work. The owner of the studio, Handke, let him leave during work hours only reluctantly and then threatened to dock his pay or to shop him to Juozapas.

The three of them went to a concert together, returned once to the opera, then went for a bicycle ride outside the city. Having found a quiet glade near a small lake they settled down for a rest. Judita took cheese, vegetables, fruit and a bottle of wine out of a basket. Vincentas felt quite ambivalent. On the one hand he had unexpectedly gained new, interesting friends, but on the other the friendship was compromised by his powerful attraction to Judita. He felt increasingly that he could barely control himself. He was further agitated by the fact that he could not tell from Judita's behaviour whether or not she felt anything similar towards him.

'When we lived in Paris we would drive out to the Bois de Vincennes,' she said.

'It isn't as dull as Bois de Boulogne ... It's wild, real, mysterious,' added Aleksandras as he tried unsuccessfully to uncork the bottle.

'Yes, mysterious,' said Judita without looking at Aleksandras. It seemed to Vincentas that he could detect a note of disappointment, even reproach, in her voice. He looked first at her then at Aleksandras, who was still struggling with the cork.

'Pass it here,' said Vincentas, opening the wine with ease.

Aleksandras lay down on the grass, his hands locked behind his head. 'I like to watch the clouds floating by. If I look at one for a long time it feels as though it's not the cloud that's moving but that I'm flying. It's like dreaming with your eyes open, although some Buddha worshipper would say that it's simply meditation. Ugh!' he cried suddenly and sat up. 'How disgusting!'

With a movement full of revulsion Aleksandras swept an insect off his sleeve, stood up and began to pace up and down.

'Aleksandras, stop it, sit down,' said Judita.

'How barbaric – as though I were some piece of carrion,' sputtered Aleksandras.

'He would like nature to be like a musical score,' said Judita to Vincentas with a smile, making excuses for her husband.

'Nature's order and man's order are two very different worlds. Even though there are always points where they intersect, concord. Birth, death . . .' Aleksandras said, agitated. 'I recently read a story by Franz Kafka about a man who one day wakes up as an insect.'

'A real insect?' asked Vincentas. 'That's pretty good.'

'Yes, an insect. Not bad, eh? You wake up and you're an insect. Enormous, the size of a man. Well, maybe a little smaller, but still – gigantic.'

'And is everyone else an insect?'

'No, the rest are still human. But they behave terribly, like rats. Do you read German? You must read it, you really must. One's imagination needs to be challenged. And I don't think that it's funny. It's tragic to feel like an insect among men – or the reverse.'

Vincentas nodded, but he was thinking about something else. He saw Judita's hands cutting vegetables, the neckline of her dress, could feel the smell of her skin, maybe it was only an illusion, but he was sure that he could detect the scent of her body, feel the taste of her skin on his tongue.

When they returned to the city and were saying their goodbyes, Vincentas proposed that they go to watch the military parade the following week.

Aleksandras frowned, but Judita laughed. 'I would be happy to,' she said, 'but definitely not Aleksandras. Soldiers make him nauseous.'

'Spare me,' said Aleksandras, waving his hands. 'There's nothing more ridiculous than watching people showing off their skills at killing.'

THE LOST SHEEP

He and Judita agreed to meet near the bus station. The buses were packed, so they walked.

'I like walking,' said Vincentas. He wanted to add 'with you', of course, but did not dare.

'Me, too,' smiled Judita, and their hands inadvertently touched.

He could have walked like that for a thousand kilometres.

At least twenty thousand people had gathered. The mood was elevated, women admiring the soldiers, and the soldiers, feeling their gazes, standing even taller. Mass began, said by a bishop surrounded by a bevy of priests. From a distance they looked like insects: one of them finds something and the rest scurry to carry off a little piece of it.

'The priests are like ants,' he commented. 'Each one carries a tiny piece of Christ's body.'

Before that he and Judita had been silent. He knew that he should say something, but his desire to say something was so great that he was speechless. And his head was as empty as yesterday's paper.

'The people are like ants, too. They bring all of their sins to the church,' he continued. 'The priests collect them, all of those horrible, mortal sins of ours, and take them to God.'

He felt that he had overdone it. Priests, sin – he was talking complete nonsense, not at all what he wanted to say, but he couldn't help himself.

Judita laughed. 'And what does God do with them? Wash them out?'

The idea of God doing laundry made Vincentas laugh, too. 'He soaks them in a huge bucket and waits until they become soft and clean and turn into virtues.'

Judita did not say anything. Once more he tried to get her to talk. 'No? Maybe not. But what do you think – what happens to those sins that have been forgiven? Are the priests like holy tea-strainers of mercy and forgiveness through which the sins pass before going back into to the world in the form of virtues? After all, sin and virtue are related – they are both born of man.'

'I'm not religious,' Judita said suddenly, 'but your theory is nice. I like ants. Quite a bit more than I like priests.'

Vincentas fell silent and felt an icy regret within his chest. He didn't dare say anything else. And yet he had to say something. 'I don't like the Church or priests, but as for God . . . I like to feel His presence. I like to think that there is something greater than me. If He didn't exist, the politicians and bankers would be very quick to call themselves gods.'

'"Oh, leader of our nation – your thoughts are our deeds" – is that what you had in mind?'

'Yes, I suppose so.'

He wondered if their president was in any way like God and quickly decided he was not. He lacked gravitas. He was not convincing. God is He who has no equals, who is unsurpassable, swifter than the wind, thought, death.

She took his hand and squeezed it hard. A fever pierced through him from his heart to his feet. He could think about nothing, only that she, for whom he longed so intensely, was there beside him.

The troops were lined up in three echelons at the airfield, some distance from the honorary grandstand. The president, together with General Raštikis, heard mass. Then the president, riding in a carriage drawn by two black steeds, began an inspection of the units, with Generals Raštikis and Adamkevičius accompanying him on horseback.

From a distance they could hear President Smetona greet the army regiments, 'Good day, men,' and then a thundering, unified reply, 'Good day, sir!' A large infantry band passed by them playing a pounding march. The band came to a halt in front of the grandstand where all the dignitaries were seated, and then the parade began – the officers' academy, two infantry battalions, the communications battalion and then the motorized units: the anti-aircraft artillery, the anti-aircraft machine-gun unit, the pontoon battalion, several Vickers tanks and armoured companies and a hundred aeroplanes or more darkened the sky.

But the people – and it was being said that at least twenty thousand had gathered – the great audience of spectators, and especially the women, were waiting for the cavalry. As soon as the artillery display, their tanks also pulled by horses, was over, the crowd stirred. The entire Lithuanian cavalry was participating in the horsemen's parade: Grand Duke Jonušas Radvilas's First Hussar Regiment, Grand Duchess Birutė's Second Uhlan Regiment, the Third 'Iron Wolf' Dragoon Regiment, two Riflemen's Union Mounted Squadrons and a Mounted Artillery Division, and the people's eyes glittered from the horsemen and their mounts, from the hussars' red hats, the uhlans' white ones with raspberry trim and the dragoons' bright-canary-yellow, from the little flags on the lances, and the ground thundered from thousands of hooves, and the weapons clanged, and it seemed that the air itself hummed from the mass of moving animals.

Judita, standing half a step in front of him, turned back to Vincentas. 'Isn't it great?'

'Yes . . . bloody hell.' And suddenly he realized that he was jealous. And did not even know of whom. The horses, the flags, the handsome young men sitting as though nailed to their saddles and flying by to who knows where – to a grand future, to glory, as if to a greater and more noble joy than the assembled viewers, whom the apostles had only granted legs, whom nature and the laws of destiny had locked to the ground.

They were walking along the river. Judita suggested they sit down right by the water as she wanted to have a cigarette.

'Why is it that women don't like to smoke while walking?' asked Vincentas, wanting to hear her voice. For a while Judita remained silent as Vincentas tried to start a conversation. She seemed to be trying to figure something out.

'Only whores smoke while walking,' Judita explained.

'So that's it. So if I see a woman who is smoking while walking, I can assume that she –'

'But don't forget that there are exceptions,' she interrupted him. 'Give me a light.'

He lit her cigarette.

'And you?' asked Judita.

'I smoke only occasionally, most of all I like to . . . after making love,' he said, watching for Judita's reaction out of the corner of his eye.

She said nothing and smiled. More to herself than to him. He was flirting, and it was going well. At least he had not been openly rebuffed.

They silently observed the flowing river.

'I recently had the opportunity to circulate among diplomats and a war attaché. Interesting crowd,' Judita finally said.

'Were they the kinds of stuffed shirts that we saw today at the parade?'

'I mainly make money working as a translator. Either through a bureau or by contract.'

'Interesting work.'

'Not really. You know, maybe it's all those images from the military parade . . . You see something and it suddenly triggers very different memories, sometimes completely unrelated . . . Does that ever happen to you?'

'Sure.'

'I recently heard the German war attaché Köstring speaking about the Red Army, about how it is now like a giant strongman whose head has suddenly been lopped off. That gigantic torso miraculously survives, it's capable of striking out at those directly in front of it but not of more complex actions.'

'You could be a spy. A female spy can turn a man's head in a second.'

'Certainly.'

She continued to smoke in silence, then suddenly threw the cigarette butt in the water, turned to him and said, 'We are right in front of that giant – Lithuania is. Right under its feet.'

He so wanted to kiss her, to hold her, to press her hard to his chest. For a moment it seemed that she wanted that, too, but as he hesitated she suddenly turned away, stood up, took several quick steps, turned around and said, 'Do not accompany me. Not today.'

'All right. Whatever you say.'

He stood there, flustered, a lump in his throat. As in childhood, when he had wanted to cry following some upset. His chest was about to explode from a strange feeling he had not felt for a long time, perhaps not ever.

He began to walk slowly along the river. It was deserted, barely one or two passers-by were visible in the distance. A broken branch floated along the current, a faded whitish rag caught on it. Just as he felt a flag of surrender raised above his tiny state of 'I'. Priests as ants? What a disaster – what kind of idiotic nonsense had he been coming out with all day? To be with a woman like that and go on about cassocks. He should be shot.

Suddenly he heard steps behind him.

She approached him, her head slightly cocked, smiling guiltily, as though confused. For a while they continued to walk side by side in silence. Then, without turning her head, she said, 'I would like to smoke . . . together with you.'

When they reached his home Judita stopped, took his hands, looked him in the eyes and said, 'Let's say that I stopped by looking for my cat. After all, it isn't decent if a woman comes to a man's house when she barely knows him, no?'

'This is already our fifth meeting,' said Vincentas.

'Really? That must be a record.'

He put on a concerned face, clasped his hands behind his back and tilted his head so that he would look like a concerned old man. In a thin, shaky voice he asked, 'What kind of cat are you looking for, madam?'

Judita laughed. 'It isn't very big, sir. A female, white with a black spot by one ear.'

Vincentas lived in a basement flat. It had once been his stepfather's workshop, but Juozapas eventually moved up to the first floor, where he also received clients. Some rope, a little bit of metal, some nails, horseshoes, horseshoe nails, wooden spoons, ladles, rolling pins, salt cellars, door and window furniture, locks, shovels, rakes, scythes, whetstones, hammers, axes, augers, saws, butcher's knives, kitchen knives and various other treasures. Vincentas would sometimes cover for Juozapas, but it was mostly his mother who helped out in the shop. She liked to chat with the customers. Not only liked to but knew how to. Especially the men. She had still not lost the charm she had developed as a dancer and singer. Of course, she had danced and sung mainly in public houses, but when a woman reaches a certain age her past gives her a kind of dignity, while minor details become so small as to be invisible.

It was not so easy to get to his flat. First one had to climb several steps from an entrance in the yard, then go along a corridor, go back into a yard and only then, after circumventing a strange, buttress-like protrusion in the wall, did one come to the steps leading down to his dwelling. During winter a permanent dusk hung over the space, but in summer there was always enough light, even though the windows faced a blank wall just a few metres away.

Vincentas often saw cats in the yard. They loitered, waiting for pigeons to land. They slunk, froze, then slunk again. Perfect photographic models.

He rummaged through a stack of photographs, found a few with cats lying in wait for their prey.

'Here, madam, take a look. Is the one you're looking for among these good-for-nothings?'

She laughed. She did not want to play the game any longer.

'Can I smoke?' she asked.

'You can.'

She smoked again, but he did not. He rearranged the photographs from one stack to another.

'I like them,' she said. 'But there aren't enough people – why aren't there more people?'

'People like to look at mirrors not photographs.'

'That's strange,' she said. 'I've never thought about a photograph being like a mirror.'

'A mirror is a moving photograph.'

'Like film?' she laughed.

'Except that movement spoils everything.'

'Really?'

'I think so . . . Maybe. I don't know. Maybe all true things have to be simple, clear. And things that are complicated, tangled, always changing form and shape . . . Truth is as simple as a stone. A stone doesn't move.'

Again he felt uncomfortable. It wouldn't have taken much for him to start going on about priests and ants again.

She said nothing in reply. A moment later she reached out her hand and stroked his cheek, his neck, his shoulder. She moved closer, leaned over and kissed him.

'And I think that moving objects can also be very nice. Even rather pleasant.'

She nestled against him and for a moment sat there unmoving. He did not know what to do. They had known each other barely a couple of weeks. They were still strangers – and at the same time surprisingly close. She was a few years older, married, experienced, but it seemed as if he had known her for a very long time, not externally, but from the inside, that he knew by heart everything that she was behind those dark deep eyes. It was hard to explain, and he didn't try. She sat there, nestled against him, he could feel her warm, barely quivering body through her thin dress. Once, she had been somebody's wife, lived somewhere without him, lived her life – unknown, forbidden, unreachable to him – and in that second he felt that she was now here. That she was right next to him, that there was nothing preventing him from touching, embracing, taking her. He could feel her scent, her quivering transferred to him, or maybe it was his trembling that was being absorbed by her and he was feeling the echo of his own excitement, they were like a single vessel in which tiny ripples suddenly become huge waves. He felt strong and helpless, all-powerful and paralysed by uncertainty, as though he were a glass boxer; as a child he had seen one in a shop window, a boxer who could be shattered by the slightest blow, and yet blows were his trade, his life, his fate, and he had to enter a fateful ring and face the greatest demon, his greatest foe – himself.

He took her hand, searching for those same feelings that had overcome him when he had first seen her, half naked, plum juice running down her cheek, a single drop, almost invisible but caught by the light, shining on her dark nipple.

He was still lying in bed smoking; she was collecting her clothes in silence.

'I would like to photograph you.'

'I'd rather you didn't,' she said, shaking her head.

'Just as I saw you in the kitchen, the first time we met.'

'And what if I should be embarrassed?'

'You wouldn't be.'

'You couldn't show them to anyone.'

'That wouldn't be the end of the world. Just like sin. If you don't reveal it, it gnaws at you from the inside, like a worm . . .'

There they were, the ant-priests once again flashed through his mind.

'Those Catholic jokes bother me a bit,' she said.

What could he have expected.

'I'm sorry, I didn't mean to. I've got a thing about priests. My stepfather, Juozapas, was very religious. Now he's dying.'

Even better – now he was going to start talking about sick people and death.

'I understand,' nodded Judita. 'Aleksandras and I . . . how can I explain it to you? Do you remember when we went on that picnic?'

'Yes.'

'There was talk about Vincennes . . .' Judita sighed. 'He's been acting strangely of late. He doesn't want to make love any more. Or rather . . . In Paris he would talk me into making love in those kinds of places . . . dangerous places . . . the Bois de Boulogne, for example.'

'I don't understand,' he said.

'So, near a path where people would be walking. He feels bad about being much older than me. He thinks that he doesn't satisfy me any more. When it's him who is unsatisfied by everything lately. He'll be forty soon, and he's still just a promising musician.'

He said nothing. Then he took Judita's hand, brushed his lips against it.

'Well, I'm not so very mature . . .'

Judita laughed. 'Well, I'm not a saint, but I'm not quite ready to undress in front of a camera.'

'It's not quite the same thing.'

'No, it isn't. But there's something. An association.'

'Getting caught with your knickers down by the side of the road – and a photograph?'

Judita laughed so hard she held her stomach. Then she lay down on her back and stretched her arms out to the side.

'OK, give me a cigarette. That's what I came for after all.'

'For what?'

'To have a cigarette with you.'

Her voice was as sweet as – as what? When you eat a pear and the juice runs through your fingers, then your fingers become sticky, as though they have been soaked in blood. It's pleasant while you're eating, but after you have swallowed the last bite that stickiness begins to bother you and annoy you.

After her steps had faded away Vincentas tried to grasp what had happened. His head was empty, his stomach muscles were sore. He had not been with a woman for a long time. He stood up and slowly began to gather the photographs that were scattered around the room. He felt as though he were gathering shards of himself. A giant with clay feet. That curse – of feeling infinitely happy and infinitely unhappy at the same time. That curse.

TALITHA CUMI

The word 'angel' was scrawled on the blackboard in chalk. The rest of the sentence had been erased. Angel of vengeance, angel of redemption – it could have been either one.

He got up quietly so as not to awaken the other men and went out into the yard. He couldn't see the guard, who was probably off dozing somewhere. The Germans were staying at the local police station; the brigade was sleeping in the town's school. After a night of festivities at a local restaurant, most of the men were indistinguishable from the mattresses spread on the floor.

Vincentas stuffed his camera into his coat and headed off in the direction of the forest. He looked at his watch and saw that it was five in the morning. The sun was just coming up – the best time of the day if you wanted to catch the light. To capture the idea of light, as Gasparas would say. Where could he be now? Underground, probably; still wearing his thick-lensed glasses. Lying in the dark, trying to see the essence of things with his myopic eyes. His grey beard sticking up, his thin hair pressed to his forehead in a black band. Although short-sighted and ailing, he had been a strange and interesting person. His photography students called him by his first name, Gasparas. The photographer Gasparas. It was from Juozapas that Vincentas had first heard about photography, that miracle of light. While still a teenager he had read a few articles and a small book called *The Amateur Photographer*, and then, when he turned eighteen, he had bought his first camera, a used Kodak Retina. But it didn't go well, so he had found Gasparas. Without his thick-lensed glasses Gasparas couldn't see a thing. He would take them off, look straight ahead with his strange, empty eyes and say, 'Now I can see the real world.'

Vincentas liked studying with Gasparas, who did not talk only about technical things – distance, focus, exposure, making prints – but also liked to philosophize and was good at it. A frozen image, Gasparas would say, raising his finger and then pausing, is not an image, because a photograph is a frozen idea. Whose idea? He didn't know. The world's, God's, man's. Nature's. When you are photographing a tree and there is no one else around, whose idea could it be? If the world is God's idea about goodness, beauty and truth, then the tree is also God's idea about the tree. And man is God's idea about – about what?

Gasparas was talking about Plato and his cave. About how people are like the prisoners squatting in that cave, underground, chained up so that they can neither move nor turn around. There is a crack behind them, and all they can see is the shadows on the wall before them. If someone walks up there, behind them, the prisoners see moving shadows and their own shadows, but they do not see the true light. People never see the true light because they do not understand its source. It emanates not from the heavens above nor from electric lamps. It is there, inside. Socrates knew that, and Christ knew that, and when they spoke about love they were talking about that very light.

But if the world is made up of God's bad ideas – if we are ideas about falsehood, malice, envy – then there is no hope for us, no hope for our souls.

Gasparas often talked about Plato's allegory of the cave and liked to say that Plato was the first theorist of photography. People cannot see the beauty of this world with the naked eye; they generally see only the shadows, not the essence, of things. But photography can do that – it can show us what an object really is. Because photography is not just the object itself; it is always above it, beyond it.

He would speak about the world of ideas and constructs, but Vincentas best remembered the image of people sitting chained in a cave, able only to see shadows. Who are the ones walking by – philosophers? Or prophets, warriors, or perhaps rich men who can purchase anything they desire, even truth?

Feeling somewhat nauseous and light-headed, Vincentas strode down the country road. He wasn't sure if he felt that way from the alcohol he had drunk or from what he had seen the day before. He remembered Gasparas and his cave, because now he felt as though he were in a cave himself. Everything that was happening around him seemed to be happening somewhere off to the side, as if behind a transparent wall. He felt ill. The invalid's world is like living in the cave, where one can only see shadows and reflections of the living, the well.

He thought he saw some movement in the pit. The ditch-diggers, in their haste and laziness, had not finished burying the dead – they had just sprinkled them with lime and thrown on a few shovels of earth. The contours of the bodies were sharp in the morning sun, and here and there the sparkling layer of lime looked like snow fallen in midsummer. How many were down there – a thousand, fifteen hundred? He had not managed to photograph anything yesterday. Although he had known and had prepared, when the bullets began to spray and the people, struck by them, to collapse dead, he was overcome by a paralysis that held him until the very end. He had pressed the button a couple of times but doubted that he had captured anything clearly. He had been standing too far from the ditch, scared to go any closer because Jokūbas the Elder had threatened him: If I see a lens pointed at me I'll shoot you! After that he hadn't tried to raise his camera to his eyes, had just stood and watched.

Vincentas approached the edge of the pit, pulled out a cigarette and lit up. Now he would have to get used to smoking not just after sex but after death. Below, by his feet, lay a little girl. Her slight body was half covered with lime and earth; she lay prone, and you could tell it was a girl only from the stiff braids. He kneeled down on one knee, looked around and stretched out his hand and whispered, '*Talitha cumi* . . .' Get up, little girl. He was echoing the words said by Jesus to the daughter of Jairus.

He looked around again and was overcome by a feeling of shame and despair. It was all so unexpected – at once horrific and prosaic. As though it were not the thousand people killed yesterday lying there in the ditch but mannequins, or extras in a film, who would soon get up, dust off their clothes and return to the village until the next session.

His hands trembling, he pulled out his camera and tried to find the best angle. One side of the girl was lit up, the other in shadow. Her body is trapped in a cave under the earth, while her soul – or perhaps only its shadow – walks around above. As the sun rises, shadows are long, just as when it sets. It is the best time of the day to take photographs. The best time to become light.

*

He liked photographing Judita. She would leave work early, and as the sun slowly went down she would lie on the bed by the window, one side of her lit, the other in shadow. Her pubic bone also cast a shadow, as did her breasts, nose, a hand raised slightly or placed under her head, a bent knee, a hip – everything casts a shadow and everything seems to be only a reflection, as though it were not the real thing but only a suggestion of it.

Once Judita said, 'You look at me as though I were an object.'
'When?'
'When you are photographing me.'
'No,' he replied. 'I see you differently.'
'How?'
'As a very precious object.'

Here, by the pit full of freshly slaughtered Jews, he felt as though he had betrayed Judita. He will never dare to admit what a mess he has got himself into and will always feel guilty. Even if he did not kill. Yes, he is only a witness. Like Him, that Other. He hangs on His cross and watches as villainy is committed in His name. It's a good excuse – I would do something, but my hands are nailed down. With nails of guilt on to the post of shame. Vincentas felt like he would throw up.

He wiped his mouth with the back of his hand, and something like the flash of a blade caught his attention. To the right, down the slope, the surface of the lake rippled, and a few pine trees stood awkwardly alone, as though they had escaped from the forest or perhaps the opposite: they could not return to it. *Talitha cumi*, he whispered to himself again. Everyone wants a miracle. Even the smallest, most pathetic miracle. And then he had a real scare. The camera fell from his hands, made a hollow thud at his feet, and he began to back up from the edge of the pit.

There, below, someone had moved. The girl in the pit. Her hair was like the whitest wool or snow, and her legs looked like cast brass. Instinctively he looked around for some object – a rock or a stick – with which to defend himself. But there was nothing like that near by. The girl moved again. And she moved as though not by her own efforts but by a force coming from somewhere else, from outside, from the depths. His mouth burned as though scalded by sulphuric acid; he tried to lick his lips, but his tongue would not respond. He took several steps forward, picked up the camera and approached the edge of the pit. He stepped carefully into it. It wasn't deep, with gravel edges and sand below. Afraid of stepping on a buried corpse, he carefully tapped the girl's back with his shoe. She stopped moving. If he had a weapon, would he dare to shoot a child? To shoot one who had already been shot. To finish someone off, so she wouldn't suffer. Or maybe she could still survive? If he were able to save at least one life, would his guilt be less? Vincentas looked around feebly. I was dead, but here I am alive for ever and ever, holding the keys to the world of the dead.

The little girl's body moved again, turned slowly on its side, and a bloodied, chalky hand emerged from under it. The world of the dead was speaking to him. Unable to resist, he gave into temptation and pressed down several times. He liked that sound. Like little guillotines, as Gasparas used to say. Click, click, click – listen, you hostages of darkness, to the decapitation of reality. It dies so that it can be born again on film. The same but now different. Light struck down and light resurrected.

Then he stretched out his hand, firmly grasped a childish palm and pulled.

The boy, no older than ten or twelve, was bloodied but uninjured.

His oversized underclothes were full of holes. He had lain there all night, perhaps unconscious or perhaps out of fear.

A miracle, he said to the boy or to himself. You have a chance. We all, always, have a chance. Go, just get out of here, he said, although he could not hear his own voice.

The child understood. He ran through the dewy meadow towards the lonely pines. The sun had risen over the tips of the trees. He ran towards it unevenly, staggering to the sides on his wobbly legs, leaving a messy trail in the grass. Vincentas focused and pressed once more: click. Here in my hands are the keys to the kingdoms of death and life. The sin of false pride, but it's so sweet. The plum juice runs through my fingers; the blade of death dissects the soul.

Suddenly a shot thundered over him, somewhere close to his ear. Startled, frightened and briefly deafened, he once again let the camera fall from his hands. The child stopped, took a step to the left, then one to the right, and fell on his side, one leg briefly sticking up and shaking slightly, as if blown by a strong wind, although the morning was so still that not a branch quivered.

Tadas was standing behind him.

'Bloody hell, you frightened me,' said Vincentas, rubbing the ear deafened by the shot.

'He would have got away,' said Tadas. 'You wanted to let the little bastard go.'

Vincentas bent down, picked up the camera and checked to see if it had been damaged, dusted it off and once again looked towards the child lying in the meadow. 'I didn't want anything. He's just a child, for God's sake, just a little child.'

Tadas leaned his rifle against his leg and pulled out a cigarette. 'He's better off there, believe me. There was no point pulling him out of the ditch.' Tadas carefully scanned the buried bodies. 'Those stupid peasants – they couldn't even bury them properly. They're just in a rush to sit down and get drunk and then stuff their bags with Jewish rags.'

Vincentas was still looking at the dead boy lying in the meadow. 'If I were you, I wouldn't want to meet him at St Peter's gates.'

'I'm not in a rush to get there.'

'Next year in Jerusalem. That's what they say to each other. When they're saying goodbye.'

'There you go,' said Tadas with a grin. 'He won't even have to wait for next year. He'll get there today after lunch.' Pleased with his joke, Tadas laughed loudly. He was drunk. After a moment he added, 'He fell beautifully. Like he was dancing.'

Vincentas was still rubbing his stunned ear. 'In my childhood I learned a poem about the dead dancing,' he finally said. 'They were dancing in a meadow. Girls rocking dead babies in their arms. Do you have children, Tadas? Do you? Children, a wife?'

For a while they both looked down at the bodies covered in lime and dirt. Nobody moved. The silence was making Vincentas uncomfortable. If he were shot now, no one would care; it would mean nothing. They would tell his mother it was an accident.

'He fell beautifully,' Tadas repeated.

Vincentas looked up at the sky. There were no birds, no aeroplanes. He turned away from the pit and stuck his camera back into his coat.

Tadas threw his rifle over his shoulder and scratched his cheek. 'That Gestapo officer of yours – he pays well?'

'He doesn't pay me.'

'Why do you work for him?'

'I don't know.'

'Idiot.'

'Which one?'

'Both of you.'

'I guess so.'

It had never occurred to Vincentas that he could be asking the German for payment. And he didn't want to be paid. Because he knew that he owed him his life.

'You wanted to let a little Jew-boy get away,' said Tadas, teasing him again.

'But you didn't let him get away.'

'No, I didn't. I'm not you. If I told Jokūbas the Elder he'd get you for it.'

'I'm not a soldier. I don't have a weapon.'

'You want to stay clean? You work for an SS officer, so you'll go with us.'

'And where will you go?'

'To the end.'

'I don't want to go anywhere. I want to go home. I want it all to be over.'

'You want so many things – but Christmas is a long way off,' said Tadas.

Vincentas looked at him. The rolled-up sleeves, the thick, blond-bristled paws. 'Stop – I'll take a picture of you.'

'No, I don't want you to. Not here.'

'What's wrong with here?'

'I can't stand being photographed near the dead. It's a strange fashion these days – everyone wants funerals to be photographed. It's disgusting.'

'People need proof that they're more alive than the dead.'

Tadas looked at him as though seeing him for the first time. 'What's with you?' He shook his head, sat down on a mound of earth, pulled out a bottle and took a swig. He offered some to Vincentas, who grimaced but then took it.

The alcohol burned in his dry mouth, and at first he was overcome by a hellish feeling of nausea and almost threw up. But then everything calmed down, the warmth in his stomach started to spread through the rest of his body, and he felt an easing.

Squinting, Tadas looked at him. 'Death is death. It's disgusting. I was a teenager when I first understood that. Her name was Marija. She died at seventeen. She was very pretty, with thick black hair. I could watch her washing it, brushing it, for hours. She would be wearing this sheer linen slip, and drops of water would fall on the fabric, and the more drops fell the more shone through. You can imagine – big, round, firm. She would be smiling, sometimes singing, and would look at me with such eyes that my head would spin, you know . . . My sister Marija.'

Vincentas didn't reply. He just wanted to get out of this place and as far away as he could from the pit. But instead of leaving he sat down with his back to the lime-filled hole.

Tadas continued his story. 'It's wrong. She died, and no one even knew what she died of, although they talked about some mysterious blood disease. She was so pretty, so young, and when she died I didn't even understand that that was it, that she was gone, that I'd no longer see her brushing her hair, that I wouldn't hear her singing in the morning, you know. I was alone at home the day she died. I sat by her deathbed and cried. She was so young, so pretty.' His eyes glistened, and it looked like he might suddenly break out in sobs. He paused and then sighed. 'And I've never met a girl as beautiful as her.'

Tadas fell silent. Vincentas tried not to look at him. He sensed that Tadas was very agitated, very vulnerable. There are people who can't forgive those who witness their moments of weakness.

'I've never told anyone about that,' Tadas murmured.

Vincentas nodded slightly.

'And you won't tell anyone about it either,' Tadas continued just as quietly but now in a harsher tone.

Vincentas nodded again.

Tadas jiggled the lock on his weapon.

It was a threat. Wordless but convincing. He had a weapon – and power – in his hands. Pale, red-haired, freckled Tadas with his oversized paws. With his bloodshot drunken eyes.

'I don't have any choice,' said Vincentas.

Tadas suddenly let out an unnaturally loud laugh and then a wide yawn.

'We need some breakfast. I saw a hen-house. An omelette would hit the spot on a morning like this.'

Vincentas didn't want to eat. His head now hurt less, and he no longer felt nauseous, but he had no appetite.

They both stood up.

'Just don't go too fast – I have a blister,' said Tadas.

'New shoes?'

'New.'

'Go barefoot.'

'It's all right. I'll manage.'

'Take your shoes off. Give your feet some air.'

Tadas did not reply but kept his shoes on. Vincentas started moving slowly in the direction of the village. Somewhere on the outskirts a cock was crowing. Maybe that was the hen-house that Tadas had in mind. Vincentas turned back and stopped. Tadas was standing and looking at the dead boy lying in the meadow. Then he sat down on the ground and pulled off first one shoe and then the other. There was a large broken and oozing blister on his right foot.

'What a pain,' he said, frowning.

'Put a bandage on it,' Vincentas suggested.

For a moment they stared at the injured foot.

'You see? What did I say?' Tadas continued in an uneasy voice. 'Goddamned Jewish shoes!'

Vincentas picked a couple of plantain leaves and handed them to Tadas for his blister and continued slowly towards the village.

Tadas, limping and with his shoes back on, quickly caught up with him.

They found Jokūbas the Elder sitting on a knoll, smoking. He looked at them ironically. 'Communing with the dead, were you?'

'Yes,' chuckled Tadas. 'The photographer was in a hurry to get to Jerusalem. He was looking in the pit for a suitable beard.'

Jokūbas the Elder sneered. 'So, Mr Photographer – you went to mourn your mates?' He turned to Tadas. 'Why didn't you shoot the Bolshevik bastard?'

Tadas looked at the ground, jangling his weapon. Vincentas looked at Tadas. So he didn't just happen to be following Vincentas. It looked like Jokūbas the Elder had wanted Tadas to shoot him. He shot the boy instead. The child had saved his life.

Jokūbas the Elder looked into the distance, in the direction of the crowded, dirty pit.

'I used to come here often, on summer afternoons – the kind of day when large white clouds float by in the sky. From the top of the hill I could see their huge dark shadows crawling over the earth, the ploughed fields, the meadows, the hills and the valleys. Sometimes a bigger cloud would glide over, and its black shadow would cloak the entire field up to the very edge of the valley, and on the other side everything was shimmering in the sun so that it looked like something out of a fairy tale or another world. Now it will never be like that again – never. This obscenity has ruined it,' said Jokūbas the Elder, gesturing towards the pit.

'Are you from around here then?' Tadas asked him.

'What difference does it make where I'm from? We're all going back to the same place. I'm starving,' said Jokūbas the Elder. 'Let's go and get some breakfast.'

Tadas inhaled deeply through his nostrils. 'Some eggs.'

'Yes,' nodded Jokūbas the Elder.

'You know, you slice some smoked ham, a pinkish band of fat along the skin, and fry it up.'

'Now you're talking!'

'Then the eggs – three of them.'

'Maybe even four.'

'So that the yolk doesn't break but doesn't set either.'

'Of course. So that when you start eating you can dip your bread in it.'

'And some chopped dill on top.'

'Oh yes.'

'And some fresh finely chopped spring onions.'

'And white bread.'

'And freshly pickled cucumbers.'

'And some garlic, too.'

'But not too much!'

'Sliced paper-thin.'

'A symphony.'

And the two men ambled off towards the village.

*

From the top of the hillock Vincentas turned back once more. A light wind tousles the tall, uncut grass of the meadow. At the edge of the forest a woodpecker taps, in short bursts, at an old pine tree. A child lies in the grass with one leg thrown out to the side, his head unnaturally twisted back. From higher up he might look like a large bird or an angel, with bloody wings, a chalky face and glassy eyes overflowing with emptiness. But apart from Vincentas there is no one looking – the morning is calm, the sky cloudless, and neither aeroplanes nor birds nor angels fly overhead.

THE FATHER

Vincentas entered the church, kneeled by the central altar and turned towards the men's side. A few years ago this had all been flooded, as if the river had wanted to pray. Its waters rose and entered the sanctuary to rid itself of its sins. As if water could be sinful. The only holy river is the river of faith that flows through me. Vincentas felt a stab of guilt – in truth, his faith was rather weak. Fortunately the stab had not been deep – in fact, it had not even left a wound.

The church didn't give a damn about his feelings or his wounds – it was like Noah's Ark holding a cross up to the sky, floating towards the highest light, sheltering all those who are tired and rejected, all those who need comfort and hope between its walls.

The organ drones like the engine of an ocean liner slicing through the waters, the sounds rising and stretching like fluid willow branches, weaving into the discordant but passionate voices of the choir. As a child Vincentas had a stereoscope containing a multitude of small colourful pictures; through the magnifying glass they looked wonderful – cars, people, scenes from nature, even images of New York, Krakow, Warsaw and Paris, motorcycles, horses, aeroplanes. And one picture contained an enormous boat that made Vincentas think of a church floating across the waters.

The organ and the choir were the best part of the service. The priest droning on with his back to the faithful, the homily, confession and Holy Communion – the familiar routine failed to move him.

The first time he went to confession he asked Juozapas, 'Why is the priest locked up in prison?'

Speaking through a grate. Through a grate, into God's ear. The priest sits in the prison of his body. Dispensing advice to the free. Teaching about life when he himself knows nothing of life. Of lives of sweat, moaning, intertwined limbs. Or perhaps that which is forbidden is best seen from outside? Vincentas always had a lot of questions while in church, and they would seem important and solemn, but back out in the sun, in the light, those questions somehow faded and getting answers to them became less important. Only God knows, as Juozapas used to say.

God, shut up in a church and never getting out. All questions are important to Him. And He does not care about a single question. Because He knows everything.

And it will never be known whether it is He who is closed off from the people or whether it is the people who are behind the grating and will never see His face. Like in Plato's cave. Some see the light, others only shadows, only illusions. And all will become clear in the light of the Last Judgement.

What struck Vincentas most was that great feeling of release when he would confess his childish, naïve sins to that indistinct being who sat shining behind the grate in the dusk, that ear connected straight to Heaven. He would leave the confessional trembling, trying his hardest not to forget the penance he had been assigned – three 'Our Fathers', five 'Hail Marys', five 'I believe in one God, the Father Almightys . . .'

Vincentas sat down close to the confessional and closed his eyes.

His mother had asked him to hurry, but he was dawdling. He could fail to ask the priest to come and Juozapas would pass away without having received the last rites. Without having waxed his skis, as the boorish workers who liked to drop by Juozapas's workshop to share gossip and dirty jokes would have said.

Our Father, who art in Heaven, my father, where are you, I never saw you, thy name come, thy kingdom be; as a child he used to say that his father had died in a car crash, his mother used to tell him that the car had skidded off the road on a bend. His father had died, and she had been pulled out by three fishermen, on earth as it is in Heaven, give us this day our daily bread . . . She had been pregnant and Vincentas was born that very day. Hail Mary, full of grace, the Lord is with thee . . . was my father handsome, he used to ask his mother, and she would tell him about a very good-looking man. Conflicting feelings, looking at Christ. A feeling of relation. Did his mother invent the story to raise him a good Christian, or was it her idea of a joke? Three fishermen. Three kings. Oh Christ, King of Heaven, they are both fatherless, they were both raised by stepfathers, they each have a hole in their psyche that can't be filled, only He was King of the Jews, while Vincentas is the Jew-killers' handyman, a pawn, a servant the masters will discard once his services are no longer needed. This thought weighed on him. More and more. As much as he tried to console himself, tried to convince himself that it was all transitory, that he owed the SS officer his life and couldn't back out now . . . But why couldn't he back out? He's afraid for his own life . . . And for Judita's . . . Now she is in his hands, she depends on him, on his will, on his love . . . And if he only wanted . . . but he doesn't want to . . . Oh yes, he wants her, he wants her, but that desire . . . that desire can betray a person, for out of desire one person can betray another . . .

People in the countryside are horrified at the slaughter of the Jews; they say that the Jews who are communists and committed crimes against Lithuania should die but let the rest work and in that way redeem their guilt . . . But what guilt? He who does not have a home is guilty . . .

If the Son of God was King of the Jews that means He was a Jew himself. Or could it be that the Son of God has no nationality?

A newborn does not care about nationality . . . All he wants is food. Then he starts to soil himself . . . to scream, to demand . . . Food, air, attention . . . A dead man does not care about nationality; he doesn't demand anything any more. He gets as much as he earned while alive. As much as others decide he is worth . . . Six boards and a handful of sawdust.

Death is purifying, it cleanses us of our earthly habits.

For, after all, He cared not about His son but for the descendants of Abraham . . . that is why He had to be made like His brothers, so that He could atone for the sins of men . . . but for what? For Himself. What nonsense. I am the father and become my son, so that through the son's lips I can pray for the forgiveness of the sins of the world, for people I do not know but whom I created and set free in the world . . . to ask myself for forgiveness . . . Why did I create them? So that they could worship me. Why do I kill them? So that they will fear me. If I kill them, then they will fear and worship me. I cannot kill them all at once; I can only kill one people at a time. First the Jews, then the Poles and then the Lithuanians . . . The Nazis will never recognize Lithuania's independence; they see the Lithuanians as their servants . . . Why did I kill my only son? So that they could all see what can happen and therefore fear me. If I could kill my only son, and in such a violent way, it means that I can do whatever I want with people

I don't know – burn them, hack them up, cut, strangle, whatever, whatever I want, whatever I want . . .

Vincentas once again thinks that what he wants is Judita.

She is the only sinner who could also be a saint, he thought to himself as he looked at a painting of the Holy Virgin.

A few days earlier he had kissed her crotch; he hadn't shaved so she suffered at first, but then she carefully took his head in her hands and said, it's prickling me, and it slipped out of him, just like Christ's crown, imagine what it would feel like to have your scalp pierced by thorns . . . That angered her, and she didn't want to carry on making love . . . When a man and a woman are in bed together there's no need for a third, even if that third person is God . . .

Where could he have disappeared to? Why did he abandon his only son? Did he never think about him, or was it the opposite – he watched and followed his every step . . . ? He thought every tall, handsome man was his father, even though he had never seen a photograph of him . . .

His mother said that they only had one picture taken of them together, and it had disappeared . . . it was lost . . .

She could have lied . . . She had sung in restaurants, would come home late. She would sleep in late, and he would sometimes smell the stale alcohol on her breath. Juozapas suffered it all with good grace. He felt inferior. She was a singer; he was a carpenter. At first Vincentas had thought that Juozapas was his father. When he learned it was not the case he was relieved. He didn't want his father to be like that . . . Ugly, obsequious, a man who spends too much time in church . . . It was he who constantly dragged the young Vincentas to mass . . . At first his mother went very occasionally and unwillingly and then stopped going altogether. Every time she seemed to be suffering from some kind of unbearable pain.

'I can't take a man in a dress seriously,' she would say.

Vincentas stood up, went to the door, kneeled quickly, made a cursory sign of the cross, walked out of the church and towards the presbytery. The priest was not there, and the housekeeper invited him to sit down and placed a glass with a cold cranberry drink in front of him.

When the priest entered the room Vincentas stood up and kissed the outstretched hand.

The priest adopted a sorrowful expression.

'Are you not Juozapas's son? Such a devoted member of our community. But you, it seems, are a rare visitor to the house of God . . .'

'The war,' muttered Vincentas. 'And I'm not his son, I'm his stepson.'

'I see,' the priest replied then sat down, took a packet of cigarettes out of a drawer, lit up and only then thought to offer one to Vincentas. He refused.

'These days people need God even more than in peacetime.'

'Perhaps people do need God, but does God need them?'

'Well, well,' said the priest, nodding his head. 'God is not a movie theatre – you can't go and see Him just when you feel like it. You have to approach Him slowly, patiently. If someone begins to see God as entertainment it means his heart is empty, that his soul is empty, moribund.'

'It's a good time to commit sins.'

'An adult must answer for his actions and confess his sins, whatever they may be.' The priest wiped his lips, a bit of foam had collected in the corner of his mouth as he spoke. 'God's mercy is unbounded.'

'Then why was He so merciless towards His son?'

'His son? You are referring to Christ the Redeemer?'

'Yes.'

'That only demonstrates his boundless mercy for us, for human beings. Love does not mean that we grew fond of God and He grew fond of us and sent us His son. God is love, therefore he who remains with God remains with love, and God remains in him.'

'Yes, that is great mercy and love. But what if in loving God you harm someone close to you . . . someone who is closest to . . .'

'God's ways are mysterious. On the other hand . . .' The priest sighed. 'I have thought about that quite a lot myself . . . Jesus Christ is God in human form, correct? In other words, Our Lord is like a king, a ruler, who, unknown to all, disguises himself as a beggar and wanders the streets with all the other beggars, living their lives, experiencing their pain and hardships, the hunger, poverty, humiliation, loss . . . and then dies such a horrible death to prove that He drank the human cup to the dregs . . .'

'So when Christ says, "My God, my God, why have You forsaken me?" and "Take this cup away from me," who is He appealing to? Himself?'

'No, you see everything too rationally, too humanly. He's only trying to show that human life and God's existence are two separate things. Two completely different dimensions, if you will. It's philosophy. Appealing to His Father and according to His Father's will, Jesus Christ shows us the path that we must follow. We are mortal, and that is irreversible; we are vulnerable, and that is reality, but as Christians we receive a great gift – a path we can follow towards the light, the path of love and salvation.'

'What would you say to a woman who sees her infant hacked in two with a spade, and then . . . then she meets a similar fate?

What would You, Father, say to such a mother? That all is love, that the horror and hatred that she feels towards the executioner are also love?'

The priest shakes his head. 'You should not talk like that.'

Vincentas understood – there was talk that a good third of all priests had been recruited by the NKVD and then re-recruited by the Gestapo.

'You are right, I shouldn't. It's just that sometimes questions arise for which I can find no answers.'

'Hatred is the reverse side of love,' said the priest. 'You know the expression about turning the other cheek? That's what it means – by turning the other cheek you turn away from hatred and towards love. It does not take much. One only has to want to do so. One only needs to turn the other cheek.'

'That seems too simple.'

'Yes, everything that makes us human is simple. And that's what is hardest. Because man tires of simple things, he gets bored. And then he complicates life so that everything becomes as intricate, as complex as possible. Ultimately those simple things become inaccessible, can no longer be experienced.'

Outside it seemed to darken, perhaps a cloud passed in front of the sun, and the priest began to speak more loudly. 'The war against Bolshevism is meaningful not only as a battle for the survival of nations or human freedom this war is also a crusade, a crusade for man's spiritual beliefs and his freedom of conscience. If someone is destined to captivity then he goes into captivity, and if another is destined to die by the sword he will die by the sword; it is an awful battle, but then it is said, "Put in your sickle and reap, for the time to reap has come, for the harvest of the earth is ripe, and the angel left Heaven's slaughterhouse, and swung his sickle, and harvested all the grapes on earth, as the fruit was now ripe, and he poured all the grapes into the great press of God's wrath, and out of the press coursed blood . . . a great deal of blood."'

The priest fell silent, raised the glass with the cranberry juice to his lips, and the liquid in the glass became dark and thick, and it looked as though the priest were drinking darkness, that his lips were dyed the colour of blood.

'From Heaven's slaughterhouse?' Vincentas asked quietly.

The priest blinked several times. 'You are overtired, my child. The temples of Heaven, it is said, the temples.'

Vincentas nodded.

They both sat in silence. The priest sighed. 'I do understand what you are talking about. It should not be this way. Even if it is retribution, an eye for an eye and so on, it should not be this way. We can only pray.'

'For what?'

'For the victims and the executioners. For their souls.'

Vincentas nodded once more. 'I understand.' Then he remembered why he had come there. 'As it happens, Father, Juozapas is very weak. If you could . . .'

The priest raised his hands, palms upwards. 'Why did you not say so right away?'

'I don't know. After all, it is said that the dead should bury the dead, while we need to worry about the living.'

'Wait a moment, I'll get ready.' Then, as he left, he turned back and said, 'The quote is inaccurate.'

Vincentas did not reply. He realized that now he would have to walk home with the priest, and he did not want that at all. He did not want ever again to see that thoughtful, well-groomed, plump face with its saccharine smile more suited to Heaven's slaughterhouse than to a temple.

While the priest heard Juozapas's confession and gave him the last rites, Vincentas and his mother sat in the kitchen. His mother had grown old – she rarely went out any more. One evening she had put on her best clothes, a hat, black shoes and gloves, and had gone out for a walk on Laisvės alėja. She returned angry and disappointed.

'Laisvės alėja is full of Germans. Who do they think they are, the arrogant bastards! I wanted to go into a restaurant – and they called me an old whore. Can you imagine? The food shops designated for the Germans have everything: white buns, butter, vodka, vegetables. I met a neighbour. Do you remember Mrs Julija from the second floor?'

'The one who didn't know how to ride a bicycle?'

'Really?' asked his mother, surprised. 'I had no idea.'

'Her husband bought her a bicycle, but she never learned to ride it.'

'It doesn't matter. Her husband died during the June Uprising trying to protect the bridge from the Reds. She said she had stopped by the department store, and it's full of wonderful goods: toys, balls, wooden goods, handbags. It appears all of them were made by Jewish craftsmen.'

'The Jews are a skilful people.'

'The poor Jews,' said his mother.

They sat in the kitchen in silence.

'Juozapas was a skilful person. And he loved you like a father.'

'He's still alive,' Vincentas reminded her.

'Yes, yes, alive.' His mother stood up with difficulty and approached the kitchen cupboard that Juozapas had made. He had built all of the furniture. He had even built his own coffin. Vincentas watched his mother open the cupboard door as though she were opening the lid of a coffin, then reach her hand in to pull out a half-empty bottle of some coloured liquid.

'Cranberry vodka. Would you like a drop?' she asked Vincentas.

'Yes.'

In the rectory he had drunk water with cranberries, and now it was vodka. What next? Hell's tar with cranberries?

His mother poured them both shots. She was drinking more and more. He had no idea how she had got hold of any vodka, but the bottle in the cupboard was never empty.

'Where did you get it?' asked Vincentas.

'Old connections,' winked his mother.

'How old are you, Mum?' Vincentas asked suddenly.

His mother looked at him carefully. 'Surely it isn't as bad as that?'

She pulled out her compact and inspected her face, drawing a finger over the fine wrinkles radiating from her mouth.

'There it is, not much more to hope for, not much at all.' Sighing heavily, he sat back down.

'Did my father look at all like Juozapas?'

'For God's sake, child, don't you understand how annoying that is? And being annoying is one of the most awful human traits.'

'For a long time you told me a story about my father. I think I should know who he was, what he looked like. Shouldn't I?'

'I envy the birds,' said his mother. 'Parenthood lasts only a few months for them.'

'Why won't you talk about it? Did he mistreat you in some way? Did he hurt you?'

'Well,' she said, raising her glass, 'I suppose you're old enough now. You're making your own living . . . By the way, what is it that you do? Judita said that you sometimes get called out by soldiers.'

'Yes, I guess I am. I do some photography.'

'Ah yes, photography. You should be grateful to Juozapas for that.'

'I am grateful.'

'Judita is a nice woman. But you know, you do know how it is . . . I heard that people get sentenced to death for hiding Jews. The whole family could be shot.'

'I know.'

His mother sighed. Then she took Vincentas's hand. 'You see, it's all terribly boring. I didn't want to tell you, but . . . I don't know who your father is. I can't remember. There were a few men around that time . . . There were many men, and there's no way I can say which one it was. I didn't even know all of their names.' She looked at him carefully from under slightly lowered lids. 'See, you don't like hearing that your mother's a slut. Nobody likes that kind of thing – I wouldn't like it myself. But nothing is that simple. I loved life, didn't sell myself, I just liked . . . I liked it, and I just don't understand why it's forbidden and sinful to enjoy the pleasures that life has to offer . . . Understand one thing, son, youth doesn't last long, and then those pleasures simply become inaccessible. Today I was kicked out of a restaurant and called an *old* whore. If I were *young* no one would call me that – the German officers would invite me to join their table and would offer me food and drink. That's the difference. While you're young you don't realize the gifts you have and when you're old you realize what you've lost, but that doesn't help much.'

Vincentas said nothing. In the next room lay the dying Juozapas, his stepfather, and next to him sat a representative of the Heavenly Father, while his real father was *unknown*, someone or other, but who? A random stranger, a criminal, an artist, a baker, a swindler, a gambler? Whoever.

Juozapas died that very night.

CHILDHOOD

Juozapas had built his own coffin. Vincentas hired a truck, he and the driver lifted the coffin into the back and then, together with his mother and Judita, they drove to Juozapas's home town. That had been the dying man's last wish. It was not a long drive. Juozapas's sister had made arrangements with the local priest. During mass Judita wandered around the cemetery. She joined Vincentas and his mother when they accompanied the coffin to the freshly dug pit.

There were many birch trees in the cemetery. Vincentas had been five when they had buried his mother's sister Gema. Or maybe eight?

'How old was I when Aunt Gema was buried?' he asked his mother.

She gave him a dirty look and whispered angrily, 'Ten', then turned her head back towards the priest. For you are dust and to dust you shall return, said the priest to Juozapas, who lay there in the coffin he had built himself, on sawdust he had made himself, preparing to become dust once again.

You couldn't disagree with him. With either of them. They had done everything correctly, Juozapas, the priest. Death had taken on a different role. Before, it had been an actress, the most important person on the stage of life. Like his mother, when she was still singing and dancing. Now death had grown old, had lost her leading role and become an extra, was only given roles in crowd scenes. So many people died every day that death had become banal, decorative, background material, a minor character.

They held the wake at the home of Juozapas's sister, Julijona, who kept glancing and glancing at Judita until she couldn't hold back any longer. 'Isn't she a Jewess?'

They said quick goodbyes and drove back to the city, making the excuse that the driver could not wait any longer, that they had already paid him fifty marks extra to wait.

Sitting in the cab next to Judita and his mother, Vincentas again recalled Aunt Gema's funeral. Wandering around her enormous garden, he had found a pile of ampoules and medicine bottles under a tree. He stuffed his pockets with them, even though he had no idea what he was going to do with them. He smashed a few against the shed wall. The bottles exploded, the liquid running down the wall; it had been summer, so the stain quickly dried. Disappearing, just like a person who yesterday had been speaking and eating but today was no longer speaking or eating and tomorrow will not be there at all; the photographs will yellow, and in time those who might have looked at the photographs will be gone, too.

Back home, Vincentas lay on his bed and stared at the ceiling.

'But you didn't love your stepfather, did you?' asked Judita, sitting next to the mirror. His mother had invited them to dinner. She was suddenly feeling lonely.

'I'm not talking about love,' he replied.

'It just seems like you're grieving.'

'It doesn't matter. It doesn't matter what it seems like. I gathered some pieces of birch bark, the kind that curl up, arranged them by the wall of the wood shed and walked along it proudly, imagining that I was some sorcerer or healer with a great collection of ancient texts and medicines that could raise the dead. I can't remember where I found some matches, but in the end, disappointed by the failure of my spells and healing, I stuffed all the ampoules into the birch-bark curls and set them alight. The bark crackled merrily and the ampoules and the little medicine bottles exploded even more merrily, frightening the funeral party.'

'What a little monster.'

'My mother said that I was already ten.'

'Boys mature later.'

'A crowd of black-clothed men and women ran over and explained that I shouldn't behave that way, that there was a deceased woman in the house. "What difference does it make?" I asked. "I won't wake her up."'

'And you didn't wake her up.'

'I remember now that Juozapas was the only one who laughed. They were all angry, and he alone laughed and then said that I was right, only the trumpets of the Last Judgement would wake the dead.'

Judita turned around and looked at him briefly. Then she got up from her chair by the mirror, approached the table, took a cigarette out of a pack and lit it carefully.

'I think your mother can wait a bit.'

'Her room was always full of all kinds of thread. Because she only worked at night, in the daytime – after she had had enough sleep – she liked to sit there and sew, embroider. She told me about how she had learned that craft from her mother's sister Serafina. Aunt Serafina was a nun, and in the convent she and the other nuns sewed and embroidered church vestments – mantles, chasubles, stoles. She taught my mother to work with many kinds of fabrics and threads. An embroidery stand and frame stood in the corner of my mother's room by the window – two wooden rollers on which the fabric could be stretched by turning cranks at the ends of the rollers. After the First World War, when the country was getting on its feet, my mother had supplemented her meagre cabaret-dancer's and singer's salary by sewing – often refashioning old clothes.'

He had liked to sit in her room and smell the rustling fabric, to watch her lay a piece of carbon paper over the stretched fabric and then draw an entire garden, a garden with shimmering stars, and then how those drawings would gradually turn into colourful blossoms and fountains.

Vincentas also liked those nights when she didn't have anyone to leave him with and would take him to work. The pianist Dinas, a round-faced, chubby man – if asked how old he was he would snap back that it was rude to ask dames that sort of thing – taught Vincentas all sorts of card tricks. Once he asked him and his mother to hold the ends of a willow switch with her ring threaded on it, then threw a handkerchief over it, shouted 'Abracadabra!' and pulled away the handkerchief, and there was the ring in his hand, even though Vincentas held the willow switch so tight that the tips of his fingers went white.

His mother was always surrounded by cheerful, carefree people who all loved Vincentas, would grab him in their arms and hug and caress him, especially the intoxicatingly scented young women.

His mother would disappear into the back room with different men, saying that she had to 'discuss the conditions of the deal', and then he would be taken care of by one of her girlfriends or the homosexual Dinas.

Life really was like a holiday, even if they were often short of food and didn't always have firewood. Everything changed when his mother lost her job. It wasn't clear why. She would say that it was because she had lost her love of singing, but more likely she was simply discarded to make way for younger and prettier women.

Then Juozapas appeared on the scene. His mother married him without even consulting Vincentas, and he never forgave her for that. Juozapas was a dried-up, balding, short-haired man with a thin moustache under his nose. Vincentas thought that he had flippers like bat wings under his armpits. His mother scolded him for such fantasies, but he had the right to dislike the man. His life changed dramatically: before he had been surrounded by a cheerful, colourful company of dancers and singers, but now he had to obey the orders of a man with an axe in his hands. Juozapas was a carpenter, but in his heart he was a Prussian officer, always issuing commands, ordering him and his mother about. He cut Vincentas's hair in a brush cut and made him make his bed like a soldier – quickly and strictly, creasing the corner of the blanket on a stool using a hammer. Vincentas would be punished if he spoke at the table or was late for breakfast, lunch or supper. Once he was ordered to leave the table because he had grabbed a piece of bread without asking – even worse, before Juozapas had finished saying grace. Prayer was more important to Juozapas than bread. Vincentas had to study the truths of the catechism, would be woken in the middle of the night and forced to recite all the prayers, and sometimes, even at the table, Juozapas would turn to Vincentas with piercing eyes and ask him to name the mandatory holidays, and he would have to answer – all Sundays, Easter, Pentecost, the Feast of the Holy Trinity, the birth of Christ, the revelation of Christ, Christ's ascension into Heaven – and he wouldn't be allowed to eat until he had named them all.

At first his mother had tried to defend her son. Then she tried to sing again – Juozapas did not oppose it – but bit by bit she succumbed to the alcohol and eventually gave Vincentas up to Juozapas's control. Strangely, the man seemed more interested in his stepson than he was in his new wife.

Vincentas would think about his father the engineer, would build tall buildings with him in his mind, inaccessible castles on steep river banks; they would travel together to Paris, Krakow and America, sailing across oceans or taking an aeroplane.

Vincentas soon began to doubt his mother's stories about his father and his birth. A car would have been a great luxury in those times and not something every engineer could afford. His mother dutifully replaced the car with a horse-drawn carriage. And then once, when she was very drunk, she began to cry, and stroking his head told him about how his father had died from the treacherous Spanish Flu that had come from Asia in 1918.

'Do you miss the stories?' Judita asked.

'Yes, I do,' said Vincentas.

'You know what I think – damn the stories,' said Judita. She said it passionately, almost angrily.

'Damn the stories,' agreed Vincentas. 'When I started going to school one of my classmates, big-nosed Jurekas, offered me a better explanation of my origins: your mother is a whore; you're the son of a whore; a bastard. Because his nose was such a convenient target, that time I managed to pay back the insult, but the story of my father was spoiled for ever.

'Juozapas was a black cloud that darkened the bright and colourful skies of my childhood. But he also taught me lots of interesting things – woodworking, for example, and, most importantly, photography.'

'And what about your mother?' asked Judita.

'She only admitted it recently.'

'Poor boy,' Judita teased him.

'Yes, I really felt like a poor boy,' acknowledged Vincentas, turning to the wall. He felt as he had that time Juozapas had tied him to the cross. Helpless, in pain, unable to do anything. Nothing at all. Not even move a finger. Wrapped in a piece of birch bark and tied to a cross. All that was left was to set fire to it all, and he would explode.

Judita stood up. 'I'll go and help your mother. I hope you'll join us soon.'

TEST OF FAITH: BALTRAMIEJUS

The engine of the bus droned. Some of the men were dawdling. They'd woken early and had a trip of several hours ahead of them.

'Faster, faster,' the lieutenant urged the brigade members as the men climbed sluggishly on to the bus. 'It's going to be a hard day. Lots of work to do!'

The bus drove out of Kaunas under a cloudy sky. The air smelled of dust and rain; it looked like it was starting to drizzle, but then the clouds dispersed, suddenly, as though they had been wiped away by a gigantic, invisible hand.

Jokūbas the Elder pulled out a packet of cigarettes, put one in his mouth, then took it out again and started turning his head, inhaling loudly through his nostrils.

'What the hell is this stench?'

'It's an internal-combustion engine.' Tadas stretched and gave Pilypas a punch. 'Give me a sandwich. I didn't have time to have breakfast.'

'You're always hungry,' grumbled Pilypas, and he bent over his knapsack.

'OK men, what the fuck, something really stinks,' said Jokūbas the Elder, drawing heavily through his nostrils. There were two Jokūbases in the brigade, so one was called the Elder, the other – the Younger. There were two Simonases as well. One was simply

Simonas, the other, too, although everyone called him Petras. A Simon who is a Peter. Jokūbas the Elder had come up with the joke. He had studied at the seminary but never became a priest, was kicked out before his ordination. He, however, claimed that it was his own decision to leave.

Jokūbas the Elder lit a cigarette, then turned his head towards Baltramiejus, who was snoozing next to him. Once again he breathed in through his nose and then bent over the man's chest.

'For God's sake, Jokūbas the Elder, I didn't know you were so attracted to men!' shouted Andriejus, turning towards him and laughing. A few of the other soldiers chuckled in agreement.

'Go to hell,' said Jokūbas without raising his eyes. Then he punched Baltramiejus. 'Baltramiejus! Get up, you spawn of the Devil. You've shat your pants!'

Baltramiejus opened his eyes and looked around, alarmed. 'What? Are we there?'

'You stink.'

The confused Baltramiejus blinked a few times and looked around. 'Bloody idiots,' he said and once again leaned his head against the window, intending to sleep some more.

'Wait.' Jokūbas the Elder suddenly grabbed Baltramiejus's shirt pocket firmly. The man waved his hands angrily.

'Jokūbas! What are you doing?'

'What do you have there?'

'Nothing.'

'Show me.'

'It's none of your business.'

'That shit you have in your pocket – it stinks.'

'No.'

'I'm telling you.'

'Don't be ridiculous.'

'Show me.'

Andriejus got up from the front seat. Matas and Pilypas also looked at Baltramiejus with curiosity.

'OK, OK, if that's what you want,' said Baltramiejus, raising his hands. 'Do you know the story about why Jews don't eat pork?'

'There are a lot of stories about why they don't eat pork,' said Jokūbas the Elder. 'Show me what you have.'

'Fine, right away,' said Baltramiejus calmingly, then suddenly shot back, 'Why should I show you anything? Can't I have a bit of privacy, it's my own business what I –'

'Show me. It's an order!' interrupted Jokūbas the Elder.

'Fine, right away, but it's a whole story –'

'He who has ears to hear, let him listen . . .' interjected Jokūbas the Younger.

Baltramiejus glanced at him, then began to speak. 'So it is written – I haven't invented or added anything. Christ came to a seaside village. Not far from the market where he planned to buy himself some food for supper He was blocked by a gang of aggressive local youths. They were looking for trouble and wanted to mock the Redeemer. Everyone says that you're the Son of God, they said to him, everyone says that you can raise the dead, that you're a prophet, that you . . . I am the light of the world, Jesus interrupted, he who follows me will no longer walk in the dark and will have the light of life. The Jews laughed, and one of the them, the most forward, said, here's an overturned barrel, if you are such as you say you are, tell us what's under it, and then we'll believe you. I know where I have come from and where I am going, but you know nothing, said Jesus, wanting to continue on His way, but the Jews wouldn't let up. You're a coward, you make claims about yourself and your claims are false. Fine, said the Son of God, if that's what you want, under the barrel there's a pig with her piglets. The youth laughed at and mocked the Son of God. Before He had appeared they had hidden a young Jewess there with her two small children. You pretend to be a prophet, they shouted, you speak about the light of the world, and you can't even say what's right under your nose. But what horror, what a shock befell them when they turned the barrel over – there was no Jewess nor her children there, only a pig and two piglets!'

Jokūbas the Elder finally lit his cigarette, while Andriejus turned away to the front and said, 'That's just a story. Jews don't eat pork because Christ drove all the evil spirits into pigs.'

For a while the men were silent.

'And what is it that stinks then, great lover of old wives' tales?' demanded Jokūbas the Elder, breaking the silence. 'Show me or I'll take it out by force.'

Baltramiejus reluctantly unbuttoned his shirt pocket and pulled out an object wrapped in a handkerchief.

'Just what I thought. Carrion,' nodded Jokūbas the Elder.

'It's a bone,' Baltramiejus said shyly, unwrapping the hand-kerchief. In fact, it was a piece of pork rib. There was no way anyone could have detected it unless they had already known it was there, so it looked like someone had snitched on Baltramiejus.

'Throw it out,' said Andriejus, opening the window. 'It's unhygienic.'

'I . . . it's just . . . These days people are saying all sorts of things . . . You hear that sometimes they rise from the dead . . . from under the ground . . .'

'You're an idiot, Baltramiejus. I told you yesterday that's all just gossip, and you're like a little kid!' Andriejus spluttered.

Baltramiejus glanced at him reproachfully. 'Jews. Sometimes they rise from the dead.'

'Nonsense.'

'The photographer said so.'

'What did he say?'

'That he saw it.'

'And you think that this bone will protect you?' asked Jokūbas the Elder in exaggerated surprise.

Baltramiejus said nothing in reply, turned away and stared out of the window. The whole bus broke out in laughter.

'Mr Photographer, I still haven't figured out if you're an idiot or a genius,' said Jokūbas the Elder. 'So it was you who advised him to protect himself from the dead Jews with a pig's bone?'

'No,' said Vincentas, shaking his head.

'Holy Jesus,' said Jokūbas the Elder, waving his hand dismissively. '*Obscurum per obscurius*, explaining the obscure by means of the even more obscure!'

There were quite a lot of Germans at the site, two of them walking around with film cameras. Seeing Vincentas with a camera in his hands, one of the German cameramen came up to him.

'It is strictly forbidden to take photographs. Strictly! Understood?'

Vincentas showed him the SS Sturmbannführer's permit. The German let him be, but soon after a stony-faced first lieutenant approached him and said that he was forbidden from photographing today. He did not explain why. Vincentas guessed that there were too many senior German officials present. They did not want to end up in the frames – they only photographed and filmed the bloodthirsty Lithuanian barbarians.

'This nation lacks rigour,' said the German as he walked off accompanied by a sergeant who reminded Vincentas of Juozapas.

Seeing Vincentas returning to the bus, Jokūbas the Elder waved for him to come over.

'So many gentlemen, and they're all so handsome,' he said mockingly. 'I have some work for you.'

Vincentas tried to resist, but Jokūbas the Elder took no notice.

'A lot of people lack rigour. They're rushing all the time. They want better lives, right away and without putting in any effort. They barely lift a finger and then ask for money,' Juozapas used to say when Vincentas asked him for money. He didn't ask for handouts – he worked as Juozapas's assistant and had, in his opinion, earned it. But each time he had to listen to long lectures and advice. Juozapas liked to do everything slowly, carefully, thoroughly. Once they had a job covering the roof of a shed in the outskirts of the city. A minor structure, minor work, for very little pay. Vincentas got bored with the monotonous hammering of nails and was hurrying to finish faster. He had saved some money to go to the cinema. The Metropolitan cinema had just started showing the first American talkie, *The Jazz Singer*, and Vincentas was dying to see and *hear* it. Greta Garbo, Marlene Dietrich, Ramon Novarro, Lilian Harvey, Clara Bow, Brigitte Helm, Maurice Chevalier – the actors' names sounded like spells to him, like secret codes for entering a magical world of light and splendour. Maybe that was why Juozapas, having seen Vincentas's passion for film, began to teach him about photography – he helped him buy his first camera and then even set him up in a studio where his Jewish friend Maksas Handkė worked.

Juozapas grabbed him hard by the wrist, yanked him towards him and said, 'Look me in the eye.'

His eyes were brown and watery and bulged somewhat. They reminded Vincentas of a fish, of a dead carp.

'If you do something, do it well or don't do it at all,' said Juozapas, then told him to hammer down the nails that had come through the inside of the shed roof.

'You can't see them and no one will ever reach them –' replied Vincentas.

'God will see them,' Juozapas cut him off and squeezed his wrist so hard that the skin was bruised for days.

Vincentas often thought about Juozapas after he died. Or maybe Juozapas was thinking about him from the beyond?

With a local lorry driver he loaded ten smallish barrels of lime, eight boxes of vodka and a few cases of beer. The driver was drunk, but not so drunk that he couldn't drive. Vincentas felt thirsty.

As though reading his thoughts, the driver grinned. 'There's nothing worse than getting a thirst when you're working hard.'

Vincentas sat in the cab next to the driver and thought about thirst, about the Redeemer's thirst. Andriejus had talked about how in those times the Romans soaked sponges in vinegar to alleviate thirst. According to him it was some kind of narcotic solution, so that the crucified would suffer less. Who knew if he could be believed – Andriejus had done time in prison for trading in contraband. He had been caught moving cocaine from Latvia, and he was partial to the fine powder himself. He was frequently in a good mood, cheery. He often asked Vincentas if he didn't want to try some of his magic powder.

'You won't need any more photographs,' Andriejus tempted him. 'There'll be a lot of pictures, and not boring ones like yours: everything moving like in a film, and even better – in colour.'

The Redeemer's thirst was something altogether different. Maybe it was a desire, a very strong desire to find out what awaits you when the dark is descending over your eyes. Thirst is fear, and even He felt fear, He must have been frightened. When He had asked His Father to withdraw that cup, He had been frightened. Nobody wants to die. Even God, because who else, if not He, knows truly what death is?

The airport appeared in the distance. A few kilometres from the small town, to the left of the road on the banks of a brook, they finally saw a long trench. Perhaps a hundred metres long, about four metres wide and approximately two metres deep. Soviet soldiers – POWs – had dug the pit and were still gathered by the edge, and when Jokūbas the Elder waved at them they ran up to him like miserable, filthy, hungry little dogs.

Jokūbas the Elder looked disdainfully at the prisoners. 'People degenerate very quickly. Just give them the opportunity to become animals and it happens just like that. They make excuses about how circumstances made it happen. But no circumstances can force someone to lose their humanity – to neglect to wash or shave or comb their hair. Animals.'

The prisoners unloaded the barrels of lime, and Jokūbas the Elder ordered them to carry the vodka and beer a bit further away, near a fresh but already drying pile of loamy soil with a few wilting branches stuck into it. It was still well before midday, but the sun was already very strong. It would be a hot one.

Jokūbas the Elder told the driver to carry on to the stud farm. Vincentas asked what he should do.

'Go with him. He might need some help, and you're not much use here.'

On the way to the stud farm the driver pulled a small bottle from his pocket and took a swig. The smell of vodka filled the cab.

'Soon we'll load up some dying nags,' said the driver, looking at Vincentas, who did not reply, so the driver spat angrily out of the window and shut up.

Near the stables stood several German cars, along with police and farm trucks. A German military commandant and a local police chief, a little man with short legs and a huge belly that barely fitted under his jacket, were in charge.

Uniforms transform people. Yesterday Vincentas was an insignificant and powerless city-dweller; today he has metamorphosed. He belongs to a group that has power. People value power. They respect it and fear it. To some degree Christ, too, is a uniform. His suffering is a uniform. His Father is a uniform. His threats are a uniform. People don't even know if they believe out of love or fear. A person who loves is weak; he is ruled by feelings. A fearful person is always alert, cautious, focused. Responsible. I should drink, thought Vincentas, I should drink because it isn't going to be good. When you see a pit that size it can't be good.

The men were being held in the granary, the women in the barn. The doors of the granary were ajar, and the commandant was explaining to the Jews that he was going to lead them to a work site. That he would first take the old men and those that could not walk. The Jews listened, hanging their heads like horses.

'What are we doing, boss?' the driver asked Vincentas, who flinched. In truth he had no intention of being in charge. He shrugged his shoulders.

'I don't know, don't know.'

The driver once more spat angrily out of the window. 'Everybody wants to be in charge.'

He drove up to the doors of the granary, got out of the cab, lowered the side of the bed and stood leaning against the vehicle, watching the old men struggle to climb up in.

'You could pull up the bench,' Vincentas suggested to him, and the driver assented, went over by the granary where a small bench stood and brought it to the side of the truck so that the old men could step on it to get in.

'Everybody wants to be a boss,' the driver once again stated gloomily.

'What's your name?' asked Vincentas.

'Michael the Archangel,' the driver shot back. Then, a bit more quietly, 'Mykolas.'

The Jews sat down on the truck floor; those who could not climb in were assisted by their own.

The co-op truck drove ahead of them, thick dust rising from under its wheels. The road was almost invisible; Mykolas the driver slowed down a bit, fell behind and then stopped completely.

'Damned engine,' he said, slapped the wheel angrily, then got out and opened the bonnet.

Vincentas paused for a moment, opened the door and got out, then stepped back up on the running-board, pulled his camera from under his jacket and aimed at the Jews sitting in the truck bed. The sick, elderly men sat there looking straight ahead with unseeing expressions. They neither talked nor asked anything, didn't even complain. Judita had once said she found it strange that there were no people in his photographs. Now there were people – people who would soon no longer be. Vincentas photographed these people who would soon meet their maker, whom he would never see again. Indeed he had often photographed people he never saw again, but this was different. He would soon witness these people's deaths, and they would remain only in his photographs. He pressed the shutter-button mechanically, advanced the film, pressed again and felt as though he were looking through a crack into an alien world, a world that was incomprehensible and unreachable to him, as if he were peeking through a keyhole at a world that would soon disappear for all time and he could do nothing about it. What unsettled him was that he felt something intensely – maybe it was fear, but something else, too – something terrifying and incomprehensible that shook the darkest depths of his soul.

'Let's go,' the driver shouted irritably, and Vincentas jumped back into the cabin.

When they arrived at the pit the Jews became agitated, praying loudly and shouting unintelligible words. The pit was already lined by the old men who had been brought by the co-op truck. The driver opened the side of the truck, and a few Russian prisoners climbed up and began to throw the sickly old men into the pit. Two of them would pick up an old man like a bag of rubbish and throw him into the pit where other unfortunates lay moaning.

Jokūbas the Elder stood by the pit holding a sub-machine-gun.

'Now we'll splatter the guts out of these pieces of shit.' He fired along the length of the pit. Laughter could be heard; the moaning in the pit died down. Vincentas got back into the truck and tried not to look in that direction. The Germans filmed and photographed Jokūbas the Elder, who neither threatened them nor objected.

The old men were driven in two trucks. After four trips they had all been ferried, and each time, as the trucks drove away from the pit, Vincentas and the driver could hear the shots.

After all the old or infirm had been taken, the younger men

were driven out of the granary. They stood in rows of four with their hands behind their backs. They were not put in the trucks, which were ordered to follow the procession. Vincentas did not understand why the empty trucks were needed. To catch anyone who tried to escape? Even though the men were supervised from all sides by local policemen and some German soldiers, Tadas climbed into the back of the lorry with a sub-machine-gun. Two rows of guards also stood around the execution site: one contained Lithuanian policemen, the other German gendarmes with sub-machine-guns. The Jews had to undress and kneel down in the pit with their heads lowered. A dozen or so men from the battalion stopped by the edge of the pit, as well as several Germans with automatic weapons. Suddenly three of the condemned got up and took off down the pit, jumped over the edge and tried to escape towards the river, but a burst of gunfire was heard and all three collapsed.

Jokūbas the Elder had ordered that the boxes of vodka and beer be left not next to the pit but by the mound of excavated earth. Now someone took the initiative to bring one box closer. It may have been Baltramiejus. At first everything went smoothly, in an orderly fashion. A row lies down, is shot, the Russian prisoners sprinkle on some lime and few shovels of earth, then another row, and again, and again. And then everything went wrong.

One tall, broad-shouldered man did not want to undress; there was a tussle, Baltramiejus began to wave his pistol in the man's face, a German commandant ran up and there was a struggle. Baltramiejus stumbled over a box of vodka and fell into the pit, then a Jew jumped in after him and began to strangle him, then grabbed his gun and shot at the German military commandant, who was standing by the edge of the pit, but missed. Then the commandant jumped into the pit and immediately got hit over the head with the pistol. The man tried to shoot again, but the weapon jammed. Jokūbas the Elder then also jumped into the pit, and plunged a knife into the Jew's back, and the man fell dead. The first to be pulled from the ditch was the military commandant, who only had a scratch on his forehead and a sore head. Baltramiejus was pulled from the pit barely breathing.

The Jew had crushed his neck. At first the lieutenant ordered that Baltramiejus be taken to hospital because there was no doctor there, but Baltramiejus died shortly after being lifted into the truck. Several men from the unit carried him away from the pit, and he lay there until the executions were finished.

During a pause in the shooting Jokūbas the Elder came over to Vincentas.

'You and the driver aren't doing anything, so here's a job for you – gather up the Jews' rags and go to the town. Trade it all for some bootleg booze; the vodka is finished, and there's still a lot of work to do. Now it's time for the prettier part of it.'

As the truck full of clothes began to roll towards the town they met a column of women who were being marched to the execution site. There were fewer guards, but the empty co-op truck was still following behind them.

The driver knew what to do. He drove into the yard of the police station, stopped and looked at Vincentas.

'Dump all of those rags out the back. I'll be back in a minute.'

Vincentas opened the side of the truck, and without rushing began to throw the clothing out. It was mostly jackets and trousers, some shoes. To touch the clothes as little as possible he pushed them off with his foot. Not long before the old men and the sick had been thrown from the lorry. Now all that was left of them was a pile of clothes. Vincentas wanted to photograph that pile, but the driver came out of the police station with two enormous bottles of bootleg vodka, followed by a policeman who also carried bottles containing a few litres apiece.

'I don't have any more, honest to God,' swore the policeman. Then he saw the pile of clothes and began to shout. 'Are you all stupid, or what? Bloody hell, what did I say? The clothes go in the barn, in the barn.'

Vincentas and the driver, who swore the whole time, threw the clothes back into the lorry and followed the policeman, who trotted along in front of them to a barn a short distance away.

They drove back in silence.

By the time they reached the execution site the column of women had arrived. When they saw the bloodied men in the pit they began to shriek and pull their hair. A couple of men who had not yet been covered over stirred slightly. One even tried to get up, and then Tadas, Jokūbas the Younger and Pilypas jumped into the pit and smashed their skulls. Brain matter splattered everywhere, eyeballs flew out of sockets, the men were swimming in blood. They were all thoroughly drunk, rushing to finish and shooting inaccurately, urging the Russian prisoners to sprinkle the corpses with lime and without even letting them finish began to drive the women into the pit and to shoot them still standing. The earth in the pit rose and heaved as though an earthquake were taking place.

A woman with a child in her arms stopped at the edge of the pit, looked around helplessly, stood her three-year-old boy on the ground and pushed him, so that he would move away from the pit. What could she have hoped for? But she still hoped for something, maybe a miracle. The child tottered towards Jokūbas the Elder, who was holding a leather whip in his hand. At first he wanted to strike the boy with the whip but then changed his mind – he kicked the boy, and the child cried out in pain and flew several metres. Jokūbas the Elder continued kicking the boy towards the pit; the child whined hoarsely as he rolled along the ground like a ball until he fell into the pit next to his dead mother.

Vincentas stood next to a bucket of water. It looked like it was filled with blood. Jokūbas the Elder had bloodied his hands while stabbing the man who had strangled Baltramiejus. Blood and brains had splashed on to the men who had walked along the edge of the pit and shot at the backs and skulls of those lying there. And blood had sprayed on to the men using shovels to finish off those who tried to jump out of the pit. They had all washed in the bucket, and the water became thick with blood. Where was the priest who could say that he who worships the beast and its image and receives a mark on his forehead or on his hand, he, too, will drink the wine of God's anger, poured undiluted into the cup of His wrath, and will be tormented in fire and brimstone; where is that do-gooder priest who forgives everything, that priest so full of grace?

Vincentas took a half-finished bottle of bootleg spirits and threw some back. The strong drink scalded his throat, and for a while he could not catch his breath. He grabbed his chest and unsuccessfully tried to take a few breaths. By the time he finally succeeded his eyes were full of tears, his face very red.

'What – not feeling too well?' said Andriejus, clapping him on the shoulder.

Vincentas pointed silently at the bottle of alcohol.

'So the first time you need to take a deep breath, and breathe out as you drink, then it won't go down your lungs,' Andriejus advised.

The execution site was now still. The Russian prisoners finished burying the dead. The last to be shot had been children; it looked like they were burying broken, bloody dolls.

The local police and Germans drove away; only the men of their brigade were left standing by the bus drinking what was left of the alcohol.

'What a fucking mess. That Jewish bastard. Those bastard communists. They're all bastards,' said Jokūbas the Elder.

'Baltramiejus was . . . How old was he?' asked Pilypas.

No one knew.

'He was young,' Matas finally said. 'He didn't deserve to die like that.'

'Right. You saw how everyone was looking at me? As though it was my fault that that Jewish shit crushed his throat!'

'It's no one's fault.'

'Let's go,' called the lieutenant from inside the bus, and they all climbed in. Vincentas was the last, and he closed the door behind him.

Baltramiejus's body lay in the back of the truck, wrapped in a dirty sheet that had covered the barrels of lime.

'This nation lacks rigour,' Vincentas heard behind him. He turned – a huge rat with Juozapas's head sat on Baltramiejus's shrouded body, smiling at Vincentas and baring its long, sharp teeth.

THE MOTHER AND
THE SISTER

It was still light as they drove back, but fog was rising along the river and dusk slowly gathering over the city.

The lieutenant turned back to look at the brigade and asked, 'Who will tell his mother?'

'Andriejus', said Jokūbas the Elder from the front seat without turning around, then added, 'and the Photographer.'

Vincentas was not at all surprised. He gets all the lousy jobs. He has to carry this cross. Even if it is heavy, even if he can barely lift it, he still has to. If that cross were light it would still mean absolutely nothing. Absolutely nothing – not Christ, not prayers, not Easter morning. Absolutely nothing.

Four of them carried in Baltramiejus's now-cool body. Matas and Pilypas quickly jumped back into the bus, and it drove off. Vincentas remained with Andriejus. He looked flustered, and Vincentas didn't feel much better.

Baltramiejus's mother sat on a bench by the wall, silently pressing together her pale lips. Only the sister cried.

'It's your fault that he died – yours!' she shouted, clutching the dirty cloth that someone had taken from a Jewish home to cover the barrels of lime. Once she had calmed down, the mother asked them to help prepare Baltramiejus's body for laying out.

'I would ask my neighbour, she always knew how to deal with

the dead, but she isn't there any more. They took her away on the night of 14 June. Her husband was a teacher, she sold flowers – who could have been bothered by a teacher and a flower-seller? They were arrested and deported by the Soviets, like they had never existed, then some nasty strangers moved into the apartment . . . Where is he now? The teacher was good to him, used to take him fishing after his father died. My son liked to fish. He would bring back a fish and say, you cut off the heads, Mother, and would go out again. He would say he had something urgent to do . . . He didn't like blood. He was afraid of blood. My boy . . .'

Vincentas and Andriejus stood there in silence.

Baltramiejus's mother also fell silent, then went to fetch water and clothes.

The dead man lay on a table, his arms resting by his sides, barefoot; next to the table stood his army boots; the buttons on his uniform shone in the dusk like fake coins. There was talk that there were about five thousand Lithuanian army uniforms in warehouses but that the Germans wouldn't let them be used, so the soldiers of the battalion were dressed in a rather haphazard fashion.

She washed her son's body slowly with a white handkerchief, wiping each area several times as if she wanted to fix it in her memory, as if, by saying goodbye, she could still get something from the cold, lifeless body. Vincentas and Andriejus helped her. Baltramiejus was so light, so emaciated, that one person could have easily managed the task, but Vincentas did everything with Andriejus, lifting the cold body gingerly, seemingly afraid that it might suddenly shatter. When some bare part of his own body touched Baltramiejus's own naked one, its icy coldness scalded him. Vincentas thought to himself that a dead person is like ice. It's cold and frozen and then eventually melts – that body, that piece of ice, and then nothing is left of it, the earth takes everything back except the bones, it dissolves the body like ice and sucks out all of its fluids. A chill passed through him.

'What is it?' Andriejus looked at him in surprise. 'It's your first time?'

Vincentas said nothing. Sometimes it's hard to explain what you feel. And you don't need to explain. Everyone has their own worries.

'He had this suit made for his wedding.' The mother took a suit made of black English wool from a hanger and lay it next to her son's body, which they had laid out on the table. The table top was slightly too short, so it looked like Baltramiejus was trying on an item of clothing he had grown out of. 'Boys, you dress him. I'll be right back,' said the mother, and she rushed out of the room. Andriejus went to the door and opened it slightly and the sound of sobbing reached them from somewhere deep in the house.

'Let her weep,' Andriejus said, nodding, then winked at Vincentas. 'Here, I've got some powder.'

Vincentas did not feel the effect of the cocaine at first. He was too tired to feel strong sensations. Nevertheless a strange calm soon came over him, even joy. The day's fatigue and bad mood evaporated.

Baltramiejus lay on the table in his nice black suit, wearing worn but brightly polished shoes, his face whiter than his shirt collar, which, as hard as they tried to pull it higher, still could not cover his horribly bruised neck.

'Why did the sister say that we were responsible for his death?' Vincentas asked Andriejus.

'She doesn't know what she's talking about,' he replied calmly.

'Maybe there's something wrong with her head,' Vincentas said, almost chuckling. It seemed funny to him. 'Maybe she suggested that to her brother . . . Remember the bone? What kind of idiot would think that he could defend himself from the Devil with a bone?'

Andriejus looked at Vincentas with a strange expression, smiling and frowning at the same time, and Vincentas said nothing more.

Then Andriejus went out to smoke and Vincentas went into Baltramiejus's room. His mood had improved markedly, and he wanted to do something. A neatly made bed, a bookshelf – adventure novels, detective stories, fairy tales. A few toy soldiers stood on the bottom shelf. Vincentas bent down – the soldiers wore French uniforms from Napoleon's time. Next to them stood a large book published in 1930 commemorating five hundred years since the death of Vytautas the Great. The nation's grand and glorious past. Grand dukes, knights, honour, bravery and sacrifice. Crowds of patriots, the giant of patriotism crushing the masses with his loathsome ideas, thirsty for victims. Strange to commemorate a day of death, a day of sadness. Someday Baltramiejus's death will probably be remembered by someone. Cannon will fire, honour-brigade soldiers will salute. Albums of photographs might even be published, full of people in folk costumes carrying flags, chanting and singing and praying at Baltramiejus's grave. But he won't care; Baltramiejus will simply never be again. He was now no different from those rags that Vincentas had pushed off the truck with his foot.

Vincentas started to feel strangely happy.

He took a few of the toy soldiers and started playing with them. He placed some on the edge of the album dedicated to Vytautas the Great and others facing them.

'Fire!' he commanded quietly. Then he swept the little toys from the book with his palm and broke off the heads of the ones that had fired. Then, after thinking about it a bit, he broke off the heads of all the toy soldiers he could find. He poured all the little, broken-off heads into his pocket and quickly left Baltramiejus's room.

The door opened quietly, and Baltramiejus's mother and sister entered. They were both dressed in black and wore black scarves on their heads.

'Thank you, boys. We'll manage now.'

'Maybe we can get you a coffin ... If you want, of course,' offered Vincentas. 'We don't charge much.' Then he remembered that Juozapas was gone. 'Actually, I can even do it for free.'

Neither Baltramiejus's mother nor his sister said anything, they just walked around the table where the dead man lay; candles appeared from somewhere in the room, and only when they were lit did they see that Baltramiejus's hands were wrapped in rosaries. In the flickering light of the candles it looked as though his hands were tied up with wire.

'I'll make him a coffin myself,' he promised as he took his leave. 'I'll bring it tomorrow.'

'Thank you,' Baltramiejus's mother said from the doorway. His sister began to sob again and disappeared into the depths of the house.

When they were some distance from the house Andriejus pulled out some cigarettes and offered one to Vincentas. Vincentas shook his head.

'But maybe you could give me some of that . . . powder.'

'You liked it?' Andriejus chuckled. 'What did I say? Everyone likes it. But it's not for free. One dose is fifty roubles.'

'For that you can eat in a restaurant and still have some left for beer.'

'When you use the powder you don't feel like eating. Pleasures aren't cheap.'

'Fine,' Vincentas agreed and began to dig the money out of his pocket.

'I didn't know that Baltramiejus had such a pretty sister,' said Andriejus, taking the notes.

'I didn't know that he had a sister at all. I only met him a few times. And now I'll never see him again. He'll melt. Like ice.'

'You really are strange,' said Andriejus more quietly. 'Jokūbas the Elder thinks you're a Bolshevik spy. But I think you're just crazy.'

'Can't spies be crazy?'

Andriejus said nothing, took a few puffs, threw down the cigarette and gave Vincentas a little bag of cocaine, then he raised his hand slightly to say goodbye and disappeared into the darkness.

Vincentas remained standing there for a while, looking at Baltramiejus's house. A dim light was visible in the windows; the house was surrounded by apple trees, lilacs, cedar. No one could have thought that death had come to such a homely, peaceful place. It was like a guest had taken over someone else's house.

Vincentas pulled the little soldiers' heads from his pocket and threw them into the bushes.

COFFIN MAKING

Vincentas was able to make a coffin easily enough. When he had been about twelve Juozapas had led him to the workshop, collected some of the scraps of birch that lay by the wall, then given him a template to which the pieces should be cut. He took Vincentas's hands in his own, turned them over and inspected them, as though they, too, were carved from wood, then nodded his head and placed a sample wedge-shaped piece of wood on the table along with a sharp, wooden-handled carpenter's chisel. First Juozapas cut up the wood with a saw, then he used the chisel to carve one end so that it tapered and became a small wedge. Those wedges – Juozapas called them *capai* – were hammered into the bottoms of coffins to reinforce them. Vincentas carved a whole box of those wedges. Juozapas was satisfied. Later he taught him the art of planing. The planks came in two lengths – masculine and feminine, sizes one and two depending upon which kind of coffin was needed. First, he would cut the planks down to the standard lengths, then they had to be dried: in winter they would be placed around wood ovens, and in summer he would carry them into the yard and stack them in piles, separating each layer with crosspieces so that the wind could pass between and air-dry them. When Juozapas bought a large number of planks he would work them with the big plane – planed boards dry more easily. Then Juozapas would give him the dried plank to finish with a hand plane. Vincentas liked the repetitive movement of passing the plane back and forth, liked to think about the plank changing, becoming smoother, until, finally, it began to shine – as though that shining had been within the wood already and now, as a result of his efforts, had been liberated, freed to bring joy to our eyes.

It was past midnight when he heard a light knocking on the window of his basement flat. His heart began to beat like crazy. Only misfortune comes to one's home that late at night. Or a beloved.

Judita was sullen; she held some kind of paper in her hand.

He embraced her and pressed her against his breast. He had missed her a great deal; she had not appeared for a few days.

'I've missed you,' he said again and once more leaned towards her lips.

She stepped back, casually pulled the scarf off of her head, sat down on a stool in the corner. Her fingers shook so intensely that it seemed she wanted to shake off the letters blackening the piece of paper, which she still held like an errant traveller with a forged ticket.

'What is that?'

'What am I to do? I should be with them. With all of them . . .'

He took the paper from her hand.

1. Residents of the Jewish race are prohibited from walking on the pavements. Jews are obliged to walk only in the road, in single file.

2. Residents of the Jewish race are prohibited from walking in any gardens, parks or squares or from resting on benches in these areas.

3. Residents of the Jewish race are prohibited from driving or using any means of public transportation, including taxis, coaches, buses, steamboats, etc.

4. Owners of means of public transportation are obliged to display a sign reading 'Jews Not Allowed' in a prominent position.

5. All residents of the Jewish race, of both genders, are required to wear gold stars of 8–10 cm on the left breast and on the back.

6. Residents of the Jewish race are prohibited from leaving their homes between 2000 and 0600.

7. Jews are prohibited from hiring non-Jewish individuals or allowing them to sleep in their homes.

8. Those failing to comply with this decree will be severely punished.

9. Between 15 July and 15 August of this year all Jewish individuals living within city boundaries, regardless of gender or age, must move to . . .

He threw the paper on to the planks prepared for the coffin, approached her, put his arms around her.

'Stay with me. Live with me, and we'll sort everything out.'

'You can't protect me. The deadline will soon come, and they're saying 90 per cent of Jews are already living in the ghetto.' Judita sighed heavily.

'What?'

'I was driven out of my home quite some time ago. I've been staying with a girlfriend, but there isn't enough room.'

'Why didn't you tell me? Why?'

She looked at him silently, her eyes slowly becoming overcast.

'Are you with them?' Judita asked quietly. 'Are you with them? Tell me.'

'I'm with you.'

Vincentas kneeled down and kissed one of her bare knees. Then the other one. He had known about this decree for quite a while, but it had not seemed important. He realized only now that he did not think of Judita as a Jew.

'Don't,' she whispered, then stood up, walked back and forth across the room several times. 'Did I interrupt you? What is this?' She indicated the planks he had assembled to build Baltramiejus's coffin.

'There's something I need to do. For a friend. A last service.'

'Oh.' Judita once more sat down on the stool. 'I really want to smoke. I don't have a single damned cigarette.'

He pulled out a packet, and she carefully took one, her fingers now shaking less. He lit it for her, and Judita inhaled deeply and suddenly broke out in tears. 'Thank you, you're so good,' she finally said through the sobs.

'I'm not actually good. Or if I am, then it's like someone is being good on my behalf. And when I'm bad, I'm being bad on behalf of someone else.' He fell silent. He thought that the powder might be talking for him. He took the plane and began to smooth a plank for Baltramiejus's coffin. The cocaine was still working, he had energy, his head was light and clear.

'I don't understand what you are trying to say.'

'Judita, darling, sometimes I'm horrified that I don't know what I'm saying any more, what I'm doing, why I'm doing it.'

'Come here, I'll look after you.' She stretched out her hand.

He had to build the coffin.

'If I were hungry, would you not feed me? Would you not offer me water if I were thirsty? Don't thank me, because you don't know who you're thanking.'

Judita frowned. She didn't like that kind of talk.

Vincentas thought about Jokūbas the Elder – he might have said something just like that. It made him sick.

He panted as he built the coffin, he stopped talking and just planed and planed the surface of the board, pressing down hard on his tool, and that which had been rough became smooth, and that which had been wood now became a bed, Baltramiejus's last resting place.

Judita sat and watched as he worked, shavings as thin as cigarette paper falling and curling up by her feet.

He finally finished the planing. He sat down next to Judita, ran his hand through her hair.

'It's good that you don't look like a Jew.'

Her face darkened. 'I look like a person.'

'Yes. I'm sorry.'

'Sorry isn't enough here.'

'It isn't enough. I was wrong.'

'You're such a pig.'

Vincentas turned up his hands in helplessness. 'But at least a dear pig?'

Judita was not in the mood for jokes.

Then he painted the coffin. The box would dry overnight; tomorrow Baltramiejus would try it out, and then he would go on his final journey.

When Vincentas lay down next to Judita he could feel that she was tense. He touched her delicate, rounded shoulder. She flinched and withdrew even further.

'You shouldn't be walking around at night. It could end badly.'

'It's all going to end badly one way or another.'

'Believe me, it could be even worse,' said Vincentas and closed his eyes. Children being tossed into a pit. They fall on to their dead mothers' bodies, shrieking, howling, moaning, and they don't stop until the shots silence them. A soldier's boot kicks a child, who flies through the air and squawks like a seagull. Flying and flying and somehow never falling to the ground. One of the soldiers taking part in the shooting looked at the pit and said it was like a cake. Vincentas only now understood what he had meant. Old people, men, women, children – a four-layer cake.

'Look,' said Vincentas and touched Judita's shoulder. She turned around.

'What is it?'

'Magic powder.'

'Cocaine?'

'I think it might do us some good right now.'

'I don't know. Maybe. All right.'

For a while they lay on their backs next to each other. An inexorable feeling of pleasure gradually overwhelmed Vincentas, then the desire to multiply, increase, intensify that feeling.

'Let me take a look at her,' he said.

She's smiling. A mysterious, bewitching smile, and her gaze is more than a gaze, it radiates from a depth, from the past, from unfamiliar latitudes and forgotten times. True, she did not look like a Jew, but only to an undiscerning eye. If you look closer you see her eyes, and they are different, they are not from here, they reflect a very different sky, a very different sun falls and rises in them and different stars shine in them when night falls. The eyes always give it away.

'That's the first time I've had such a request,' she says and turns towards Vincentas. He looks at her, and it's as though he's observing the scene from the outside: Judita, turned towards him on her side, the basement lit by a weak red bulb, which he used to use when developing photographs, a Tino Rossi record playing right there but sounding like it is coming from far away, then he starts to see the view from higher up. He sees the house he lives in, the city full of soldiers, whores, rage, death and oblivion, a Europe overrun by war, black and white, red and brown, everything looks so simple and everything is so mysterious, he feels fear and joy, uncertainty and blessing, and the only real thing is here next to him, before him, reclining on a bed. You are my only reality, Judita had said at the beginning of the war, and she, too, is his only reality, her left leg bent at the knee, he turns her to the side, she brushes the dark tuft of her groin with her right hand, then lowers her fingers a bit further, her index finger barely grazing the dark-brown, almost black lips. Look, she says quietly, and her voice is full of secret joy, for a while they are both silent, breast and groin so full of desire that it takes the breath away, Judita looks sleepy, warm, smelling of earth after the rain, he wants to melt inside of her, to forget everything, everything – Baltramiejus, the photographs, the smell of lime, he whispers, and again that strange feeling won't go away, that he can hear his own words almost as if they were spoken by someone else, that everything that is happening is happening not only here and now but elsewhere, too, somewhere near by, or maybe it has already happened or is yet to happen, but somehow those two images, those two people that he sees, are both here, and also somewhere else. You can't imagine how many men there are in the world who haven't seen her, she about whom they spend so many days and nights dreaming until they can finally get a taste, and they taste with their entire body and all of its fluids, just not their eyes, they never marvel at her with their eyes because they're ashamed that that about which they have fantasized all their days and nights, to all intents and purposes, is just a little hole, A dear little hole, Judita says again with the same voice, a strange voice, at once dear and distant and smelling of distant, exotic lands. Your voice is full of secret joy, he says, is it true, he asks, I don't know what's true, says Judita, I don't hide anything from you, I'm exactly as I have been since I was born, as I have been since the creation of the world, having just left Eden, surrounded by living creatures and fruits, damp and surprised at my ability to feel pleasure and to share it with a man, Brown Eve or Red Eve, or Elena or Beatričě, men themselves don't even know that they have different names for the same thing, the same little hole, he bends over, gets closer, and dives into the damp reddish poppy blossom, it's damp and somewhat cold and slightly salty, like an angel had just cried over it, had descended from the heavens, from heights of brilliant cold and shining truth, had bent over and cried for the entire human race and for them, lying here in this bed where it smells of planed wood and black adhesive paint and the mixture of paint, alcohol and resin that was made to paint the coffin that stands in the middle of the room, waiting for its passenger, like a boat tied to a shore, waiting for him so that it can transport him across the dark waters of forgetting to the shore of eternity. What a nice little cave, he whispers in Judita's ear, we all emerge from that cave, from the dark dampness to the bright light, and then we struggle to get back in, searching for our extension . . . pleasure . . . oblivion . . . the darkness and warmth we lost long ago – birth, the strangest mystery . . . that we die is not strange; the body gets worn out, breaks down, ages, it needs to die off, everything that comes into existence has to die off, but why it comes into being, this we don't know, why does all of it need to come into being, to hurt and to reek, be tortured and torture others . . . Why, oh Lord my God, I ask many days and nights and You don't reply . . . Surely it can't just be because this little hole is sweeter than wine, more fragrant than all perfumes? Yes, it drips honey and milk, tar and fire, blood and pus . . .

'Calm down,' says Judita. 'Calm down and don't agonize over strange questions. I'm here, right next to you, and as long as I'm with you nothing can happen to you . . .'

'You don't know, you don't know anything,' Vincentas tells her, and again it feels as though he's not saying it but that someone is using his voice, his throat, his eyes and his hands, you don't know what happened to Baltramiejus today, it's strange, but I feel safe with you, but when I see armed men it's like I am naked. And I don't want to know, says Judita, I believe in you, that everything that you're doing is right, because it's unavoidable . . . or the reverse – it's unavoidable because it's right . . . Take me, take me, she says, and it's the one request that he can't refuse, that he can't shy away from, push away or make wait. You take me, too, eat me, he says to Judita, eat like you have fasted for forty days and nights, like I am but locusts and wild-heather honey, as though I am a wild mead that must be extracted from the depths, take me, suck me up, and she sucked as though she were a leech, like a snake, like a plaster on a wound, first touching just with the edges of her lips, then diving until she hits the end, until she collapses with her entire body, as though fighting with his desire, with her own desire, with her sensuality and abandon, with her holiness and innocence, I look at you and my heart rejoices, just don't look at other men, woman, because if you do you will betray me, you would do better to rip out your eye and throw it aside if it urges you to trespass, but don't cheat on me because that I won't be able to bear, thinks Vincentas, again feeling that he is rising upwards, rising and rising, and again sees the city, the streets, the continents and the oceans, as though they were all coloured maps or coloured stereoscope pictures that change at a crazy speed and then, clanging and whirring, vanish . . .

He must have fallen asleep, because the knocking frightened him. He jumped up in bed, confused as to where he was, who he was and what this awful darkness that pressed on his eyes could mean. He listened.

'What's happening?' he asked quietly.

At first he heard a low moan, and then Judita's quiet voice. 'Bloody hell.'

'Judita? Where are you? What are you doing? Why are you leaving?'

He turned on the lamp. Judita was kneeling naked on the ground; next to her lay Baltramiejus's coffin, which had fallen off its stand. She turned to Vincentas smiling guiltily, but her eyes were full of tears, and blood trickled slowly from her split upper lip.

'I was just getting up to go . . .' she said quietly and swore again, 'Bloody hell.'

'It's dark,' said Vincentas.

'Very dark,' agreed Judita. Then she added, 'I'll stay with you. Until things become clearer.'

After the final salvo in honour of Baltramiejus had died away, after the gravediggers had taken the ropes and, lifting the coffin, begun slowly to lower it into the grave decorated with young birch branches, in the bright July sunlight Vincentas saw that in one spot the lid of the coffin was not shiny, as though it had not been varnished. He wanted to get closer, to be sure, because he knew very well that he had varnished the coffin lid carefully, not once but twice, so he could not have left a blemish of that nature, especially on the lid. And only later, listening to the shovels rhythmically chomping on the sand, and the soft tapping of the earth being poured on to the coffin did he understand: it was Judita. She had gone to pee in the dark, bumped into and knocked over the coffin and split her lip. Then, kneeling next to it, had dripped some blood on to the lid, and Vincentas had not checked it before driving it to Baltramiejus's house. He had barely slept, was thinking about Judita, about how she would be living with him from now on, that he'd have to take care of many things, that he had wanted, had dreamed about this for two years, but when the possibility arose, when the possibility became an inevitability, he was not so sure that he wanted his life to go in this particular direction.

LESSONS IN ASCETICISM

Vincentas knew that he had not completed the job; he had not succeeded in photographing the people being shot. Jokūbas the Elder warned him that if he saw a camera lens aimed at him he would shoot without warning. And the people being driven into the pit and shot, that had been too unexpected for him. He had taken a few photographs of the bodies after they had become still, lying in the pit, chewed up by bullets, fallen one on top of the other. An unmoving body is a photographer's best partner. A child running through a meadow – bloody, tattered underclothes. A spotted angel in an awakening meadow. An angel soon to be caught by a bullet. There were also a few frames of the old sickly Jews in the back of the lorry. Those photographs had made a great impression on him. The faces of these old, sickly, hopeless people looked as if they were not of this time, not of this place. Strange, but these images were somehow more forceful than when he had seen them in the flesh. He knew why. Those people are no more; he knows where they are buried; he was the last person to photograph them alive. All of it made his head spin. What's more, looking at those photographs, he felt some kind of strange, shameful pleasure.

'These aren't at all the kinds of photographs that I was hoping for.' The SS officer threw them on to the table and walked over to the window.

Vincentas sat in silence. The German is unsatisfied. On the other hand, if he were satisfied Vincentas would also be sitting in silence.

'Maybe I expected too much,' added the German, turning towards Vincentas and smiling.

'I'm not used to working . . . in a slaughterhouse,' said Vincentas. 'It's . . . it's very unfamiliar. It was the first time for me. And the second time they wouldn't let me photograph.'

'I know. The slaughterer Haman. Best to stay away from him. The angel of death with the four horsemen of the apocalypse. You probably saw that he was followed by four sergeants. Next time everything will be fine. I'll arrange it.'

Vincentas said nothing.

'You must make an effort. Any one of our war correspondents can take photographs like these. But you are capable of more than that.'

'I don't quite understand. I probably just don't understand.'

'I want your perspective. I want your relationship. I want you to photograph not the fact but the whole – for you not simply to state but create. What is that pile of corpses there for? I want drama, I want a story; tell a story, use your imagination.'

Vincentas saw the absurdity of the situation: on one side stands a group of armed, drunken men – drunk from alcohol, from the smell of blood and death – and on the other the unarmed, half-naked victims. And he is there between them with his camera. An unwanted witness. A vulture, a hawk, a hyena.

'They could shoot me.'

'Who?'

'My own.'

The German laughed. 'Believe me, that's not the worst scenario.

I need faces. I need facial expressions. I need a face that is suddenly invaded by death. You must understand one basic thing: until now man was in charge of his own life.'

Vincentas thought that he had misheard. 'Was in charge of whom?'

'Of death. Of his own death. He gets sick, feels death approaching, talks about the signs that have appeared to him, calls for his servants one by one, his loved ones, takes leave, apologizes, blesses, because he has seen it before many times. But now we have the opportunity to see a person's death being taken away from him. He does not have the conditions for being in charge of it because *we* are in charge of his death. Is that not a moving thought?'

'I don't know. I am most moved by the thought of photographing the faces of those who are in the pit, who are often made to lie face down.'

'Yes,' said the German, waving his hands. 'I agree that it is not easy. But that is what distinguishes art from a document – it finds an unexpected solution. It is capable of looking at the same thing, at the same fragment of reality, in a completely unexpected way, differently, from another angle.'

Vincentas had a few photographs that he had not shown. He stuck his hand under his coat, pulled out a small pile and placed it on the table. 'Here.'

'What are these?' asked the German, curious.

'I thought that maybe . . .'

The German approached the table and took the photographs.

There were a few shots of the Jews siting in the back of the lorry. Old, infirm people.

'Expressive faces. Not bad. There you go . . . Why did you not give me these before?'

'I don't know. It's just a few shots that I took before all of it . . . before . . . I didn't think that . . .'

The Artist looked at Vincentas again, once again smiled briefly. 'Here is what I will say. Now that you are a soldier you must understand that it is only possible to tolerate the necessity of killing, the risk of dying and the constant presence of death by adopting a stoic attitude. You must learn to observe and tolerate everything with indifference. A strong immune system protects us from fear and compassion, and to some degree from ethical and moral questions, questions of conscience. What is conscience? It is not innate but rather a matter of collective agreement. A tiger does not have a conscience, he only has the instinct for self-defence, the need to satisfy hunger, the need to continue his line. There is no conscience instinct. There is no point in questioning what is happening around you and what you are participating in. It is essential to learn, through extensive practice, to drive away horrific images, to maintain a distance from loved ones, so that you do not become exhausted and can continue to be capable of acting rationally.'

'I'm not a soldier . . .' Vincentas started to say, but he could not finish.

Without a word the German pulled out a revolver, walked up to him and placed the muzzle against his head. Vincentas closed his eyes. It was not the first time during this war that someone had wanted to kill him, but the horror was still just as great. Paralysing, cold, it locked the muscles and flowed down his back first in breath-taking tremors, then horrible drips of sweat.

He came back to his senses only after multiple clicks. The weapon was not loaded; the SS officer had fired a whole cartridge of air into his head.

'This is how we, as soldiers in this war, must train ourselves,' he said. 'I want to see horror in their eyes, the horror of death.'

Any more and Vincentas would have soiled himself. What beasts these Germans were.

Then the SS officer picked up a photograph of the child running through a meadow in his bloody underclothes.

'Now there's something here,' he said. 'Very nice light.' He walked around the room. 'It's important to look at death more simply, as a part of life, as its extension. As sleep. In the fourteenth century, when Europe was stricken by the Black Death, people eventually decided not to be afraid of death because they became tired of fear. So they began to celebrate life, to make love, to enjoy themselves. It was a time of complete degradation, when the only thing of value was to experience as many pleasures as possible before leaving this world. War is much like the plague.' The German clicked his tongue. 'For that matter the Jews and the Muslims were often accused of causing the plague, so if we take the view that they are guilty of causing this war, not much has changed since the fourteenth century.'

'Are they guilty?' asked Vincentas.

'Now it doesn't matter at all,' replied the German. 'Sometimes retribution supersedes guilt.'

Vincentas was silent. He wanted to get out of there as quickly as possible, to get as far as he could from these strange reasonings, from the freshly shaved chin, the mouth that spoke so much of death.

'We spoke recently about the meaning of severed heads in art.'

'Yes,' he repeated automatically. It was always like this: the SS officer would speak and he would simply agree with a short 'yes' or nod of the head. As long as it did not annoy the German he could continue to behave this way.

'The shock effect,' said the officer, more to himself than to Vincentas. 'Beheading is one of the best ways to shock the viewer, to attract his attention – in other words to stimulate the passion of surprise in his spirit. When that happens the viewer explores the work further. To shock, to attract interest, attention . . . that is exactly what the Führer wants to do. To chop the head off Jewish communism in order to attract the world's attention, to shock, to force people to reflect deeply, to see the light.'

He remained silent. He remembered how, before the war, Judita had told him about a conversation she had heard somewhere – when there was also talk of the Soviet giant with clay feet, about the giant whose head had been chopped off. How many heads does that giant have that they have to keep being chopped off?

'The subject of beheading has been explored by those artists who liked to shock in all of their art. For example, the seventeenth-century Italian painter Caravaggio – he liked to shock in all sorts of ways – probably painted the greatest number of beheading scenes. That would be a corroboration of my thesis: if an artist who likes to shock often chooses beheadings as a subject, it means that it is a good way of effecting shock.'

'Yes, it is a good method,' he said in order not to remain silent. The Artist was not paying any attention to him. He was developing a theory. Maybe he was writing an article or a book. Vincentas was useful to him because he listened to him. He never asked his opinion. Perhaps that was part of his scheme. But what scheme?

'One of the most elementary ideologies – because it is a biblical subject – is the ideology of martyrdom, the theme of martyrdom. Another theme is male–female relations. The theme of the powers that lie within woman. In some paintings they look aroused. They hold a man's severed head and look intoxicated by this sight. The motifs of Eros and Death are intertwined in these narratives. Freud's theory also supports this – Eros and Death are very close. The French even call an orgasm *la petite mort*, the little death. The blending of Eros and Death can absolutely be discerned in these subjects. The nineteenth-century British graphic artist Beardsley, in his illustration for Oscar Wilde's *Salomé*, shows a young woman almost kissing John the Baptist's severed head.'

He imagined Judita holding a man's severed head. She appeared before him like a photograph, like a frozen thought. Realistic, more real than in life. A photograph waiting for him, which he just needs to take.

'Works like that can operate through the subconscious. They sow the seed of the connection between Death and Eros, Eros and torture.'

Judita stood with her back to him, but he knew clearly that she held a man's severed head in her hands.

'I have spoken quite extensively with soldiers – they say that the experience of pleasure, erotic arousal, at the moment of killing, is not foreign to them.'

The more that Judita turned towards him, the greater the anxiety that flowed into his chest.

'As for artistic devices – artists, especially in the Baroque period, employed a great deal of contrast: between old and young, between old and young faces, the contrast between withered and fulsome bodies. In this case – a man's head and a woman's head. The woman's head is beautiful, pure, radiant, and John's – old, bloody, horrible. A living head – a dead head. Breasts and a dead head. Woman – the embodiment of fertility, conception, the elements, nature, unconscious instinct, and in her hands a man's head, the symbol of reason, intellect, a symbol of power, a dead symbol, a symbol of defeat.'

Judita finally turned to face him, and she held a man's severed head in her hands, and when he could finally discern the bloody face with its half-open eyes a chill went through him – it was his.

The German led Vincentas to the door.

'I have a different kind of task for you. You will receive a package. You will have to bring it to me.'

'When?'

'You'll find out.'

THE GOOD SAMARITAN

They drove off in the morning, but everything was different from the times before. There were no Germans, there were no officers, and Jokūbas the Elder was in charge of the five-man party. Vincentas took his camera but soon began to wonder if he would need it.

They sat in the back of the truck. The weather was awful, the sky caked in heavy, murky, rag-coloured clouds.

Vincentas asked Matas, 'Where are we going?'

Matas shrugged. 'We got a report about some traitors.'

At first there had been a lot of denunciations. Sometimes a man would inform on his neighbour, claiming that he was hiding Jews. Sometimes the report was confirmed, sometimes it was just revenge out of envy or the settling of old scores.

They drove for less than half an hour. The truck turned into the empty yard of a farm. A sleepy old dog emerged from its kennel, barked lazily a few times, then went back in. The family was sitting at their table, apparently after a late breakfast.

The farmer, a tall man in boots and a dark shirt, invited them to sit down, put a bottle on the table.

'The harvest is ready to go, but the sky is stopping us,' he said and waved his hand. 'Help yourselves.'

They all had a drink. Vincentas thanked them but declined. Jokūbas the Elder, sitting on a bench by the window, leaned against the wall. 'It's been a long time since I've sat like this. With a family, at a table. My back and shoulders still ache from yesterday's work in the fields, and now again we have to go and root around in the bloody earth.'

'Yes,' nodded the farmer. 'That's for sure. Farming is hard.'

'We're looking for Jews. We heard that it's swarming with Jews around here.'

The homesteader laughed loudly, perhaps more loudly than was appropriate. 'I have neither seen nor heard anything. We see our neighbours rarely. I don't know, no one has said anything about Jews hiding around here. Our forest isn't big, there's nowhere to hide there. Sounds like rumours. You know how many rumours there are these days.'

'Yes, there are a lot of rumours floating around.' Jokūbas the Elder poured himself some bootleg vodka, threw it back, smacked his lips in satisfaction, reached for some bread and slowly took a bite.

'They say that there's shooting. That they are driven into pits and then pelted with machine-gun fire . . .' the farmer added. He scratched his head, shrugged his shoulders. 'Wouldn't it be better to put them to work? Or just shoot the communists? Let them work, let them be useful, now . . . They say that Lithuanians are shooting and the Germans are filming.'

Jokūbas the Elder smiled. 'Who knows what the truth is? Even Jesus Christ, when asked by Pontius Pilate what the truth was, didn't have anything to say. And we have our own photographers, too, don't we, Mr Photographer?' Jokūbas the Elder fell silent, gave the farmer a harsh look. 'So you're saying there are now Jews around here? Either above or below ground?'

The farmer said nothing and dropped his head. Then he stood

up suddenly. Jokūbas the Elder automatically raised the barrel of his weapon slightly. The farmer dropped his trousers and laughed, saying, 'Look – am I a Jew?'

There was a dead silence. For a few seconds nobody even stirred.

'I'll be damned,' whispered Matas finally.

'Mr Photographer, do you have your camera? This really is something.'

Vincentas raised his camera and then lowered it.

Pilypas stared stupidly. 'I'd like to have a record of it!'

The man's organ was impressive. The men stared at it, stunned, while the woman lowered her eyes modestly.

Feeling his worth, the farmer pulled his trousers back up slowly then buckled his belt.

'I'll be damned. It should be measured. Have you ever seen anything like it? That's a gift from God; that kind of gift shouldn't be hidden. The newspapers and magazines should be writing about it, I'm telling you,' said Jokūbas the Elder, although he was looking around the kitchen. His eyes finally stopped at the wood stove. 'That's a big stove,' he said.

'It's like a serpent!' said Matas, still stunned.

'Did our God not speak about that kind of reptile? Was it not that same serpent that was more cunning than all the other wild animals that the Lord had created? Was it not thanks to that reptile that our forefathers Eve and Adam realized that they were naked?'

Jokūbas the Elder stood up and walked to the stove.

'Do you remember, sir, the story about the viper warmed under a coat?'

The disheartened farmer said nothing, just looked straight ahead of him with unseeing eyes. He placed his hands on the table as though he were afraid that the table would suddenly begin to lift up and start flying around, together with the irritating flies that sting so painfully before the rain. His fingers shook almost imperceptibly.

Matas and Pilypas approached the stove. Tomas stood up and moved to the door. Vincentas stayed seated at the far end of the table, glancing now at the armed men, now at the family.

Jokūbas the Elder, Matas and Pilypas began to tap on the stove slowly with their rifle butts.

There were four of them: a man, a woman and two children, a boy and a girl. Jokūbas the Elder led the men, the farmer and the Jew, outside; the women remained inside the farm cottage. Having led them to a cesspit that had been dug some distance away from the outbuilding, Jokūbas the Elder stood the Jew by the edge of the pit and ordered him to perform some squats, and while doing them to shout, 'I am a Jew, a betrayer of Christ!'

The man did a number of squats, ran out of breath, fell silent, then Matas approached the pit and grabbed him by the hair.

'Repeat, you parasite, "I am a Jew, a betrayer of Christ!"'

The man just barely moved his parched lips and said nothing. When he squatted again Matas kicked him in the shoulder and the man fell into the cesspit. He lay unmoving in the wet waste, waiting for the shot. There was no shot. Jokūbas the Elder ordered him to climb out. The man crawled out of the pit with difficulty and sighed with relief: not just yet, he'll live a bit longer. Then a shot echoed, a hole appeared in the man's forehead and he fell back into the pit.

'Take some pictures, maestro!' shouted Jokūbas the Elder. 'You think that we just brought you here for the entertainment?'

Vincentas stood staring at the dead man lying in the pit. He stared and realized that he felt nothing at all, not even disgust.

Nothing at all. He raised his camera and clicked. Without aiming, without focusing. Shooting blanks is what that's called.

'Well then. Now it's the turn of the Good Samaritan. Just as it is said, "Do not go among the pagans or enter any town of the Samaritans" and "There is nothing covered up that will not be revealed, nothing hidden that will not become known".'

There was a space about a metre wide between the wall and the woodstove. That was where the hiding place had been built. Boards had been nailed from the top of the stove to the wall. A small trapdoor had been installed in the boards, through which the Jewish family could get in and out of the hiding place. The boards had been plastered with clay so that they would not stand out from the wall of the stove. A bag of onions hung above the little door to make it all look normal. If an informer had not revealed the location of the hiding place it would have been difficult to find.

'Do you know how it is said?' spoke Jokūbas the Elder to the ashen-faced, dumbstruck man standing by the cesspit. 'For this people's heart has become hardened; they heard poorly with their ears and they closed their eyes, so that they might not always see with their eyes, hear with their ears, nor understand with their heart and so they could not turn to me and I could not heal them.'

'I didn't realize that you were a doctor,' the farmer finally said.

Matas laughed, but Jokūbas the Elder said nothing, only looked angrily at Matas.

'They are like those corn-cockles, those weeds that the Evil One sowed in our soil, in our Lithuania.'

'I grew up with them.'

'Yes, I know, attachment is a complicated matter, complicated and painful when it is necessary to give up bad habits.'

'They are human beings, not habits.'

'I'll say it again: they are not people but weeds. Did human beings deport our brothers and sisters to Siberia? Could a human being horrifically torture innocent women and cut off their breasts, or cut off men's sex organs and stuff them into their mouths? Can Jewish communism appeal to human beings? I'll be damned – but no! Harvest time has come, and now it's time to separate those corn-cockles from the wheat, to root out and burn them. Well then, let's take another look at that gorgeous thing. Hold him, pull down his trousers.'

Matas and Pilypas grabbed the farmer by his arms, Tomas pulled down his trousers.

'If you love Jews so much you should look like them,' said Jokūbas the Elder. 'Take him to the chopping block.'

By the wood shed stood a chopping block with an axe stuck in it. Jokūbas the Elder pulled out the axe, checked the blade with his thumb, nodded.

'It's a good tool; you're a conscientious person. It's just that you're conscientious about the wrong things.'

The farmer shook as though he had gone mad. Matas and Pilypas could barely control him.

'All men want theirs to be longer, but the Jews shorten theirs,' said Jokūbas the Elder almost to himself, and Matas giggled again. 'Put him on the block.'

The farmer was now howling like an animal about to be slaughtered. Jokūbas the Elder swung, and then Vincentas closed his eyes. He waited for the blow, for the whack, for the cry – but nothing happened. He opened his eyes slowly. Jokūbas the Elder held the axe in front of him and looked at him mockingly.

'What, Mr Photographer, are your legs too weak for these kinds of pictures? Photograph, you son of a bitch. Do your job just like we're doing ours, otherwise . . . you'll up in his place.'

Again Vincentas pressed the button. Click, went the camera's mechanism. Whack, echoed the blow of the axe on the block. The farmer collapsed. Matas and Pilypas were wiping the blood off their hands and faces, their clothes also splattered with red.

Then the Jewish woman and her two children also fell into the pit. Jokūbas the Elder ordered that they be buried, then warned the farmer's ashen-faced wife and wailing children, 'That's what happens to Good Samaritans. Now you know, and you will tell others about it.'

A bottle of spirits went around as they drove back. Vincentas drank with the rest of them.

NEWS OF ALEKSANDRAS

Judita sometimes went into the city. She had carefully bleached her already fair hair with peroxide, and now – a perfect blonde – would go out walking. Vincentas did not like it, but he couldn't stop her. She found some contacts who, through other contacts, got her a fake passport and food card, important documents that proved her right to exist. Then she found work in a private translation bureau where a friend of hers from before the war was employed.

'But what if someone recognizes you?' Just the thought of it made the tips of Vincentas's fingers go numb. He and his mother would be shot, or at least thrown in jail.

'I can't lie around in a basement day after day,' she would say.

'Go and see my mother,' Vincentas would reply, knowing that it was a half-hearted suggestion.

Judita would shake her head quietly. She avoided his mother as far as was possible, but she would sometimes go to visit her but would then agree that the woman could only be taken in small doses. When she'd been drinking she would grab whoever was to hand and would not let them go until her reluctant companion finally managed to escape, sick of her endless stories about better days and the time when she sang and danced and was a desirable woman on Laisvės alėja.

Judita would bring work home. Each time it would be a meaningful journey for her – from 'the underworld to the kingdom of light', as she would say – but would return sullen and withdrawn.

'They have made slaves of us,' she said. 'I keep seeing brigades, all wearing Stars of David, creeping along side-streets – they do everything, all of the unbearably hard jobs. Prisoners of war and Jews have been turned into cheap labour that can be worked to death without adhering to any codes of humanity. The other day I saw some men hauling a wagon filled with logs, the kind of wagon that should be pulled by two strong horses, and just a few of them were dragging that wagon up a hill – and to make it worse, a guard was hitting them with his rifle butt. And today I saw my gynaecologist, a professor. He didn't recognize me. The poor man was walking in the gutter while his guard walked along the pavement.' She looked at Vincentas with eyes full of hurt. 'The guard wasn't a German, he was a Lithuanian partisan.'

Vincentas had nothing to say. He had seen that kind of thing more than once.

Their relationship deteriorated. Perhaps not deteriorated, it just became lukewarm. After the last operation, even though Vincentas had washed and scrubbed his skin with soap until it hurt, he still felt like he smelled of lime. And they made love less and less frequently. He had more and more difficulty struggling over the dead, the shot, the desecrated bodies, to reach his lover's, his only beloved's body. More and more often he made love drunk or having sniffed some powder. And he was still sometimes overcome by the fear that he would once more hear that cracking sound that had so frightened him at the beginning of the war and which he had subsequently heard more than once by the huge open pits filled with dead bodies.

After the Jews had been driven into the ghetto, Maksas Handkė's photographic studio, where Vincentas worked, had passed into the hands of someone who served the nationalists. He did not fire Vincentas, but he was clearly not thrilled to have him there. There was not a great deal of work, but Vincentas was spending more and more time at the studio.

When he returned home one evening Judita was more distressed than usual. She sat the table with her eyes fixed on a book. When he approached to kiss her she evaded his caresses, and he noticed that she smelled of alcohol.

'Your mother treated me,' she said, by way of explanation, then lit a cigarette with trembling fingers.

'Did something happen?' he asked.

'Yes. Something. A very big something,' said Judita, nodding.

His chest tightened. Suddenly he realized that he might lose her love. He did not know how or why, but it was a possibility. Anything was possible in this war. Before the war they had met secretly for almost two years. Their meetings were rare, but he always savoured each one for a long time afterwards. They were celebrations of emotion and passion that made living worthwhile, for which he would have given his life. Now, when he could see her every day, he was permanently worried that the whole thing could suddenly vanish, end, dissolve.

'Could it be . . . ?' he began but didn't finish. He did not know in which direction he should guess. Could she have found out that he was serving the Nazis? The whole time he had made excuses to himself that he was serving his homeland, but how long can such self-deception last? There is no homeland. And the Nazis consider themselves superior. Any number of shops, restaurants and cafés were now reserved only for Germans. The lowest German nobody considers himself above every Lithuanian. The soldiers in his brigade aren't issued with uniforms; they walk around in their own clothes. The warehouses are packed with Lithuanian army uniforms, but the Germans won't distribute them. They don't want the Lithuanians to look like real soldiers.

'Aleksandras has turned up,' she said finally.

'How? You've seen him? Where?'

'I sometimes go to a school where some of the Jewish women from the ghetto work. I take them some food.'

'We don't have enough food for ourselves.'

'No, we aren't short of food at all. You should hear what they tell me. They are half starved.'

'Fine, do as you see fit.' Vincentas's voice sounded unpleasant, almost hostile. He didn't care about the food. He was jealous. Judita was bringing not only food to those Jewish women she was also taking them a part of herself. Handing herself out to strangers instead of giving her whole being to him, Vincentas. He realized it was egotistical and maybe even absurdly childish, but he couldn't help himself.

Judita said nothing, just gave Vincentas a piercing look. It had to happen sooner or later. All those walks she was taking could not end well.

'In an inner courtyard next to the school a brigade of people with stars pinned on them was cutting firewood and washing soldiers' uniforms. I gave them a packet of cigarettes, and they were as excited as children. And one of them recognized me. I did not recognize him. It was Izaokas Lipceris. He had shrunk to half the size he used to be . . . He used to play with Aleksandras. He said that my husband was alive, in the ghetto. And he asked why I was not with him. I didn't know how to answer him. Why am I not with him? Why? I don't know. Maybe I should be with those who are already under the ground. In the pit, in the Seventh Fort!'

'It isn't your fault.'

'I should go back . . . I should go back to Aleksandras. I'm his wife. We were never divorced.'

'No, you can't, not under any circumstances. You have documents, you can get divorced and live here. With me. And become *my* wife!'

Judita shook her head. 'I have to go back. I feel like a whore.'

Vincentas did not know what to say. How to stop her.

TOTENKOPF

They arrived at the site of the operation a few hours early, so the men were allowed to go for a walk. Vincentas, too, went into the village. He took a few photographs of the church, then walked through the market square, and a few blocks further on he came upon the synagogue. He once again raised his camera and pressed the shutter-button. The Germans had given him a Leica II with a built-in rangefinder, an excellent camera. He didn't like photographing buildings, but lately he had ceased to be interested in capturing people. Their faces, their bodies – he was beginning to be afraid of looking people in the eye; he wanted to avoid their mockery, their contempt, their disgust. Walking around town, he would see the passers-by on the street and imagine them all dead – lying half naked in rows on top of one another in the pits. Anyone could find themselves there one day. All it would take would be one insane order and everything would change.

Looking around the market square once more he decided to photograph it from above, and so walked unhurriedly over to the church. The churchyard was empty; a few bouquets of wilted flowers lay by a recently filled grave. A natural death and an individual grave seemed like a curious luxury.

He looked around, hoping to see the priest or at least the sacristan, but he found no one, not a living soul. Perhaps that was the priest's grave, and the church had now been left without a shepherd. When he had gone to church with Juozapas as a child, Juozapas would call the priest 'Captain'. 'Why Captain?' Vincentas would ask. Juozapas would reply that the church was a great ship and that the priest was that ship's captain.

'Then who is Christ?' he once asked.

'Christ is life, the sea in which we – stupid fish – swim around, and only the nets of the holy apostles can catch our souls and drag them up to the true light.'

'Fish die on the shore,' said Vincentas. He had understood this once he'd started fishing with his home-made rod.

Juozapas laughed, ruffled his hair with a hand all calloused from working with his tools, and repeated, 'Fish die on the shore.'

The doors of the church were closed but not locked. Immediately to the right, inside the entrance, were stairs leading up to the bell tower. He took a few steps towards the inner doors, beyond which the nave was visible. Although the church was not big, in addition to the nave leading to the altar it also had two small transepts. A few bent-over scarves sat in the pews. There was no sign of the priest by the altar. It was not time for mass so there was nothing for him to do there. Or maybe he really was dead, buried right there in the churchyard. The women in the church simply hadn't noticed that the priest had died and had kept on praying out of habit. The captain dies and the ship just sails on regardless. Maybe they had failed to notice, in much the same way that they had failed to notice that half the town's houses were now empty, that half of the town's population had suddenly disappeared as if they had dissolved in water. In the sea that is life – just not for everyone.

Vincentas went back to the bell-tower stairs. He climbed the crooked wooden steps. Among the bell-ropes a rustling, a flapping of wings. A bird. A crow or a pigeon – a pigeon. A white feather floated and then, caught by a current, flew out and over the tops of the trees in the churchyard. He once again thought about his stepfather Juozapas. When he had found out that he was not his real father he wouldn't speak to him. He pretended not to hear what he was saying. He no longer wanted to sit in his workshop and enjoy the smells of the glue, the sap, the freshly planed wood. It seemed like the greatest deception that he had called him his father. His mother explained that it was she who had asked Juozapas not to tell him. I wanted to wait until you were older, wanted to find the right moment, she said, defending herself.

Any time is right for lying, but the truth requires a special moment.

The square was empty, strangely empty. A little further off, beyond a row of houses squatting along the street, he could see the sun reflected off the surface of a lake. He raised his camera several times but did not press the button. He could not see the image, could not see the photograph. When he took a shot he was always able to picture how it would turn out. Even before pressing the button he could see the photograph he wanted, waiting for him to capture it – he just came to fetch it, to confirm its existence.

The lens of the lake looked, blinking, up at the sky; it, too, was waiting. But for what images?

Vincentas looked down at the empty village square and could not see a photograph. There was nothing waiting for him here.

He wanted to go back down, but he picked up a sound. He could hear some kind of commotion coming from the direction of the synagogue. Leaning through one of the bell-tower windows he looked in that direction – the doors of the synagogue opened, and a crowd of people poured out of the building. There were men, many men, a couple of hundred at least, but no women or children. Bedraggled, wearing shabby clothes and with hair dishevelled, their cheeks sunken from hunger and lack of sleep. In truth, it was too away far for him to be able to make things out in much detail, but now he could see a photograph. Although he knew he would not be able to take it from the bell tower he could see their faces clearly. Not their real faces but the ones that would appear in the photograph, the one he would take if he were there, down there with them. But he did not want to be down there.

He remained in the bell tower.

He took a few panoramic shots as the crowd, being herded by local policemen, gathered in the square. He could hear commands in German. A foreigner was in charge of the police. The crowd stopped in the square, waiting for something.

A car drove up. An SS officer got out. Vincentas recognized him. It was the Artist. He had never before seen him at work. They always met at the German's apartment, where Vincentas entered through the back entrance and not the front door. As is fitting for servants.

To be safe he shifted to the side so as not to be visible. And he stopped photographing. He didn't want to be mistaken for an enemy sniper and be shot.

A German who had filmed and photographed an operation the previous week had told Vincentas how several of his war-correspondent colleagues had been shot by snipers who had mistaken them for enemy combatants. You're hoping for a photograph and you get death, said the German, wiping blood off his boot with a handkerchief.

Vincentas observed what was happening from the corner of his eye.

The officers ordered the corralled men to pick up all the horse dung. It looked like the market had been held there that morning. The men wandered around the square slowly, picking up the manure and putting it in bags. Some simply held a piece of manure in their hands and walked backwards and forwards staring at the ground. They did not want to get their clothes dirty. The policemen goaded them on, striking them with their rifle butts. The manure-gatherers could barely stay on their feet. They had probably not eaten for several days.

The Artist called over an officer and said something to him. The officer nodded, turned to the prisoners and shouted an order at them. The disorderly crowd slowly formed two rows facing each other.

Vincentas once more raised his camera but, after a moment's hesitation, lowered it again. The action was too far away.

The Artist would say, I need the poetry of death not the agony of dying animals. The poetry of leaking brains, the poetry of popped-out eyeballs, the poetry of swollen, rotting, reeking innards. That is the true poetry of death.

The officer ordered 'Fire!' The Jews stood there motionless. The command 'Fire!' echoed once more. No reaction. The officer said something to the policemen, who again started to strike the backs of the standing men with their rifles. The Jews finally began to throw the horse dung at each other.

Then he heard a loud command to lie down. Then to crawl. Then to stand. And, again, lie down, crawl, stand. When the Jews' clothes were completely soiled he heard the command 'Line up!' and a column of fours began to move slowly towards the lake.

He looked in the direction of the lake and he saw an image of naked, worn-out bodies in the water. Many naked men with bristly, sunken cheeks; they stand in the water, plunge in, surface, water running through their long, messy hair and matted beards. Their sex organs are limp, shrunken; everything says despair, hopelessness. Were it not for the presence of the Artist he might have gone down and taken the photograph that was waiting for him there.

He remained in the bell tower.

They did not allow the Jews to undress. They drove them into the water until they were up to their middles and ordered them to wash. But still he could still see them, up to their waists in the water, raising their thin, dirty arms up to the sky.

A huge, bearded old man wearing a camel-hair coat holds a water hose in two hands and shouts, 'You scum. Who said you could run from what's coming to you?'

Which image was real and which was only in his head? The one in the photograph or the one there in front of him? Which?

Then in a column of fours they returned. As the prisoners climbed the hill from the lake a woman came up to the first man she reached and handed him something. A policeman spotted this and tore the object from the man's hands. The policeman approached the officer and handed over the loot – a loaf of bread.

The crowd of men once more lined up in the market square. The officer said something, the policeman took the loaf of bread and, breaking it into small pieces, threw them into the crowd. The men attacked and fought over the scraps of bread, the unlucky ones pulling the victors' hair, hitting them in the face.

The bread was finished, and he heard the harsh command, 'Line up!' Their clothes dripping, their shoes full of water, the men moved out of the market square towards the synagogue. They were driven into the building, but one bearded old man was stopped and questioned by the guards, then led back towards the SS officer's car. The doors of the temple were closed; two policemen locked them and remained standing guard.

The Artist also asked the bearded old man something, nodded, laughed, patted him on the shoulder, then he got into his car and was driven off. The guards took the old man and disappeared behind the synagogue. A few people appeared in the square. They walked quickly, keeping close to the houses around the square, looking around suspiciously.

Vincentas left the church and returned to the building where the men of the brigade were being housed. Sometimes they stayed in barracks, but if the town was too small they would have to stay with a local in town or a farmer who had room. The house they were staying at this time was on the edge of the town.

He didn't know why, but he tried to walk through the market square as quickly as he could.

Vincentas was not at all surprised to see the Artist's car parked by the house.

The officer waved to him to come over to the vehicle.

'Leave us,' he told the driver, who obediently got out of the black Opel. The officer gestured with his head, inviting Vincentas to join him inside the vehicle.

'I have a task for you.'

It crossed his mind that the SS officer might have seen him in the bell tower, that this would somehow come back to haunt him.

The officer nodded at his camera. 'You've been taking photographs?'

'A few pictures of a church.'

'Good, but let's get down to business.'

'Yes.'

'At the edge of the town, going west, there is a large building – a dairy, I believe.'

'I'll find it,' nodded Vincentas.

'Go there after the operation. You will receive a package. You must bring it to me. This evening.'

'Fine.'

'And just one other thing,' said the German quietly, as though wishing to share an intimate secret. 'A photographer aiming a camera at armed men could easily be mistaken for an enemy sniper.'

JOKŪBAS THE ELDER SPEAKS IN PARABLES

The shooting is deafening. After the echoes of the last shot die away the sudden silence penetrates the ears with a stabbing sonorous sting – his head feels empty, like a football, but he cannot tell whether it is like a ball being inflated or one leaking air.

Vincentas's muscles ached, his back hurt. It had been a long time since he had done any physical labour; he did no exercise, did not even ride his bicycle any more. The Meister Fahrradwerke he had bought before the war had been stolen in the commotion of the end of June. The Jews, any one of his neighbours would have said. They were escaping from the city any way they could – on bicycles, trains, foot. But it could have been anyone. The war had fundamentally altered the understanding of personal property.

Although he had done nothing all day apart from trying to take photographs, he was exhausted. The images he had seen weighed heavier than any barbells. It was becoming harder and harder to withstand it all. Consciously or not he was always on the lookout for Andriejus. A dose of powder would be salvation.

He doubted whether any of the photographs would work. Again he had been scared of being shot by his own, again he could not concentrate and think about photography with hundreds of people dying in front of his eyes. He could not even remember how many times he had pressed the button. He would not be surprised if the film turned out to be ruined. He was not sure how he would explain this to the Artist, but it was increasingly clear that he was not suited to this work. He wants to quit, even if the consequences could be terrible.

The operation was over, but still it was not the end. Jokūbas the Elder was walking along the edge of the pit full of shot victims, shouting, 'If there's anyone alive, raise your hand. We'll let you go!'

He was joined by Andriejus and by Simonas, whom the soldiers of the brigade called Petras.

'If you're alive, raise your hand to the sky, and we'll take pity!'

'Only an idiot would believe that,' said Simonas Petras.

A few hands rose from the pit.

'Even an idiot wants to live,' said Jokūbas the Elder and aimed a few shots at the injured. Andriejus and Simonas Petras, not trusting their aim, stumbled, teetering over the dead bodies, and finished off the remaining ones point blank.

Having finished burying the corpses, a small group of Russian prisoners stood off to the side, sharing a cigarette the soldiers had given them. The prisoners worked on farms. Before an action the policemen would collect them to dig the pits, and later they would have to cover the remains.

'Can we go and rest now?' asked one of the Russians.

Jokūbas the Elder silently nodded his head. The Russians headed off slowly towards the town. A drunken policeman swerved behind them.

They were sitting by the ditch, drinking vodka. The Germans had already left; only the Lithuanians remained. Someone, perhaps Jonas, tried to sing a song, but suddenly Simonas, whom they all called Petras, started to search frantically under his shirt.

'Jesus, Mary, Holy Joseph – I've lost it!'

'What did you lose? Your brain?' asked Pilypas. 'You never had one!'

A few of the men laughed. Simonas, whom they called Petras, did not find it funny. He had lost a ring that he kept on a chain around his neck with a medallion his mother had bought him at the church festival in Šiluva.

'It was blessed by the bishop, it was blessed by the bishop,' Simonas, whom they all called Petras, whispered as if in prayer.

'The ring?' asked Andriejus.

'No, the medallion. On a silver chain. And the ring . . . my name and my wife's are engraved on it. I'm damned, I'm completely damned.'

'Calm it,' said Andriejus. He stood up and whistled loudly. The small group of Russian prisoners that was disappearing down the road slowed their pace, a few turned around. The policeman did, too. Andriejus waved at them to come back.

'Let them find it,' said Andriejus.

For a while they were all silent.

'It's not good to dig around in graves,' said Jonas.

'That's right, let them find it. Let them do it, the Red weasels,' added Matas.

'You've gone mad,' said Jokūbas the Elder angrily. 'A pit thirty metres long and three metres wide.'

'Twenty-eight,' said Matas quietly.

'What? What's up with you? What are you mithering about?' Jokūbas the Elder cried out.

'It's *twenty-eight* metres long,' Matas said more loudly. 'Two metres – that's quite a lot less.'

'Stick them up your arse!'

'And a metre and a half deep,' added Matas. 'I measured it. I climbed in.'

Jokūbas the Elder jumped up, pulled out his pistol and aimed it straight at Matas's face.

'You whore, how about if I measure your brains! How about if you measure the length of the stream of blood that'll gush out of your skull when I send a bullet into it! Three metres? Thirty-three?'

'Lower your weapon, Jokūbas, lower it!' said Tomas sternly, then he cocked his own gun and aimed it at Jokūbas the Elder's head.

Most of the others also grabbed their weapons. Vincentas still did not have one. The temptation to photograph all of them aiming weapons at each other was great, their faces distorted by rage and despair, as though they were at the same time both furious and terrified. And once again he thought regretfully how good it would be to have some of Andriejus's powder. He slowly took several steps away from the raging men. Something made a noise under his feet. A bottle of spirits. He picked it up and took a few swigs.

Suddenly Jonas started singing a folk song:

'Oh, my steed, my steed,
My dear bay steed . . .'

The song sounded completely ill-timed and out of place, and Jonas realized this and shut up.

The men looked at each other and some started shifting their feet uncomfortably.

Jokūbas the Elder lowered his pistol. 'Damn all of you. Damn you!'

Andriejus's thinking went like this: they should look where Simonas Petras had stood while shooting. The shooting had taken place in three stages: first at the men, then at the women and finally at the elderly and the children, who were brought on carts. The Russian prisoners who had been herded from the village hadn't made a particularly good job of covering the grave, so the layer of earth was thin. The bodies lay in the pit in four layers. Even Simonas Petras could not remember precisely whether, while shooting, he had stood in one place or had moved around.

'Even if you moved, it wouldn't have been more than a few metres,' decided Andriejus. 'Just from the pit to the vodka.'

It was decided that they would search for the medallion in a three-metre area.

'But I seem to remember he ran around along the edge like a madman,' said Matas.

'I've never witnessed a more idiotic business,' said Jokūbas the Elder, sitting by the edge of the pit. 'That's exactly how Lithuanians are different from the Jews. The Jews would never bother with this kind of nonsense.'

One Russian prisoner, probably the one in charge, came up to him and suggested cautiously, 'This is a desecration of remains. It isn't good to move the dead.'

There was a hush. Jokūbas the Elder turned his pistol in his hand. The Russian, understanding that he had behaved unwisely, retreated slowly to the pit.

'I'm sorry,' he said quietly. 'I'm sorry.'

Jokūbas the Elder aimed the pistol at him. The Russian closed his eyes.

'Bang!' shouted Jokūbas the Elder and started laughing. The other men laughed, too. Only the Russian didn't laugh.

The Russians began to dig up the dead, first by the edge of the pit, where the gunmen had stood.

Taking the occasional swig from a bottle, Jokūbas the Elder spoke. 'Do you know the story of the man who set out on a journey? Let me tell it to you. He called together his servants and gave them some money. He gave one servant five talents; another, two; the third, one. Each according to his abilities. And then he left. Time passed, then the master returned and asked for his money. The first servant said, "Here, master, you gave me five talents, and I used them to make five more." The servant who was given two talents had also doubled his money, but the one who had received a single talent said, "Master, I know that you're a very clever man – you reap where you did not scatter, you gather where you did not sow. Worried, I hid my talent in the ground. Here, take what is yours." The master praised the first two servants and rewarded them, letting them keep all of the money, then scolded the third, "You layabout, you should have invested my money, then I would have got it back with interest on my return. Take away his single talent and give it to the one who has ten."'

'So we're like that third servant?' Jonas asked, raising his head.

'What do you think?' replied Jokūbas the Elder.

'Instead of investing money we bury it,' said Jonas, gesturing with his foot towards the corpses just unearthed by the Russian prisoners.

The prisoners dug reluctantly. It looked like they did not believe that it made sense to look for some trinket or ring. They simply thought that they, too, could be shot.

'I'm not finished yet,' said Jokūbas the Elder. 'The story ends like this. The master said, "For to the one who has, more will be given, and he will have an abundance, but from the one who has not, even what he has will be taken away.'"

'My brother,' responded Pilypas, sitting at the edge of the pit, 'a few years ago he took out a bank loan. Then everything was taken away from him and given to the bank because he couldn't make the interest payments.'

'Such are Jesus's words,' said Jokūbas the Elder.

'Jesus was not a banker, for God's sake,' said Andriejus.

'No, no,' said Matas. 'When he was talking about the one who has not . . . He was talking about love. The one who does not love is the poor man, from whom everything will be taken away. That's what I think.'

Jokūbas the Elder nodded his head. 'That's written in black and white in the Jews' business manual. The more I think about it the more it becomes clear – that's all a lot more practical than what the priests tell us.'

The prisoners stopped digging. They had dragged several corpses to the side, and a dip appeared at the side of the pit. They were standing in it.

'What is it?' asked Andriejus.

One of the Russians gestured at a freshly dug-up body. The man, soiled with earth and dusted with lime, moved several times and tried to get up. Andriejus raised his rifle, let out a shot but missed. He shot again. The frightened prisoners squatted down in the pit. The body was still.

'Do you want to stay here with the Jews?' Jokūbas the Elder shouted angrily, raising his weapon. 'Faster, faster, you parasites.'

The prisoners resumed digging.

'That's blasphemy,' said Jonas to Jokūbas the Elder. 'It's not right to talk like that about the Scriptures.'

'Why?' asked Jokūbas the Elder.

'Well, you know . . . it's holy.'

'With all due respect, holiness is not the point here,' Jokūbas the Elder snapped back.

'Look, the master leaves you some money, and what do you do? You keep it safe, of course, so that it won't get lost. The Jew, on the other hand, invests it right away – he lends it out and receives interest.'

'And what's wrong with that?' asked Andriejus.

'Come on, it'll get dark. We won't be able to find our way back,' whined Simonas, who was called Petras. He was picking up the empty vodka bottles as though his valuables might have ended up at the bottom of one of them.

'There's nothing wrong with it. Nothing. But you can't disagree that interest is a Jewish invention. Making money by lending it out. You help someone but not for free.'

'Well –' Andriejus started, but Jokūbas the Elder cut him off.

'Let's take the famous parable with the multiplication of the fish and the bread . . . Only a blind man would fail to see that that's the same principle of interest. If you have two coins, lend them out so that you get two more in interest. Then lend out four and get eight back. This way you can multiply the fish you have so you can feed a crowd. Not for free, of course. Nothing in this world is for free.'

'So, what did Jesus get for feeding the crowd?' Pilypas, drunk, interjected. 'What did he get?'

'Nobody fed anyone. It's just a description of a very old Jewish business rule: the bigger the crowd, the better the interest.'

Simonas, whom everyone called Petras, hiccupped, waved his hands in front of him and said, 'I don't give a damn, do you hear!

You can be a disbeliever, you can mock and defame Our Redeemer, Our Lord, but I believe in God the Almighty Father, creator of Heaven and earth, in His only son Jesus Christ, who died on the cross, descended to hell and . . . all that . . . that He died for me and for you, as sad and wrong as that is! So that he could pay for our sins, damn all of you – our terrible, terrible sins! What? You want to shoot me? Then shoot me. I don't give a damn.'

'You'll shoot yourself,' replied Jokūbas the Elder indifferently. 'The time will come.' Then, with a bottle in his hand, he gestured at the prisoners toiling in the pit. 'By the way, they're still looking for your relic, in case you've forgotten.'

Simonas Petras looked them all over with drunken eyes, then croaked, 'I hate you. I hate all of you! You're animals, slaughterers, animals!'

The prisoners laboured, sweated, but found nothing. It was getting dark and they had to drive back home.

Jokūbas the Elder ordered the policeman to lead the prisoners back to the town. Then, after thinking for a moment, he waved to the one in charge, the one who had spoken about desecrating graves, to come over to him.

'Come here, come and get your reward,' and handed him a bottle.

The Russian, although exhausted, tried to look alert and approached, reached out his hand to take the bottle, and just at that very moment a shot rang out. The prisoner collapsed at Jokūbas the Elder's feet and lay there motionless.

'Throw him in the ditch,' waved Jokūbas the Elder, and the prisoners silently followed the order. They grabbed the dead man by the hands and feet and threw him in, then covered him with a few buckets of earth.

'Who else thinks he deserves a reward?' asked Jokūbas the Elder. The prisoners were silent. One of the men of the brigade sniggered.

The prisoners disappeared down the road, becoming shadows; it became hard to distinguish their dark figures from the blackening bushes lining the road.

Simonas, whom they all called Petras, walked swaying to the pit and stood by the edge; the sound of pissing was heard, then, after a pause, he lost his balance and his body fell into the pit, his loud curses echoing from within.

Andriejus and Jonas helped him climb out, but Simonas Petras fell back in on to his back. Then the men grabbed him by the feet. As they pulled, one of his boots came off and the long-searched-for medallion fell out. The ring was in the boot as well. When they shoved it in front of Simonas Petras he was too speechless to thank them or rejoice. He kissed it and wept.

The rumble of a motorcycle could be heard from the direction of the town. The motorcycle and sidecar approached quickly and stopped not far from the truck that was to take the brigade back to Kaunas. The motorcyclist approached and asked for Vincentas, then said that according to the Sturmbannführer's orders he was to pick up a package.

The men climbed into the truck. Simonas Petras could not crawl in on his own, so they threw him in like a sack and left him lying there. The truck rolled along the uneven road behind the motorcycle, its light disappearing into the darkness so that it seemed like a little boat was leading a big ship into the enormous darkness of the sea.

*

The SS personnel had settled at the edge of the city. When Vincentas approached the house, a shirtless soldier emerged. On the right side of his hairless chest he had a tattoo of a spread-winged eagle, and on his wrist, as was typical of an SS man, his blood type was etched into his skin.

'What do you want?' he asked.

'I'm supposed to pick up a package to take to the city.'

'Ah yes.' He smiled, then turned towards the house and shouted, 'Reinhardt, bring the package.'

Another man, also out of uniform but wearing a shirt, emerged. Large sweat stains darkened his armpits. He silently handed over a bag. The bag was not heavy and was tied with string using a fancy knot that Vincentas did not recognize.

'What is it?' asked Vincentas.

'A container for thoughts,' said the soldier with the eagle tattoo. The two Germans glanced at each other, laughed and went back into the house. Through the window he could hear a gramophone playing; he could smell meat cooking and alcohol. Vincentas remained standing there for a while with the bag in his hands – the soldiers inside were listening to a recording of *Carmen*.

Walking back to the vehicle where the brigade waited for him, Vincentas thought about Aleksandras.

'What's in that damned bag?' asked Jokūbas the Elder when the truck began to roll again.

'A package. For the SS Sturmbannführer.'

'Show me.'

Vincentas indicated the rope, tied in an unfamiliar double knot.

'Do you know how to retie a knot like this?' he asked Jokūbas the Elder.

'I don't give a damn,' he said and spat over the side. 'Untie it.'

'Untie it yourself,' said Vincentas and immediately saw the muzzle of a pistol appear under his nose.

'I've been wanting to shove a bullet into your vermin-like face for a long time,' said Jokūbas the Elder, now furious. 'You're not just a Bolshevik whore but a Nazi whore, too. What – do you like being fucked in all your holes?'

But Vincentas did not untie the bag. He sat there staring into the darkness swirling around the lorry; he even imagined he could see shadows running after them. They scurried from one side of the road to the other, rolling and tumbling, and if you listened carefully you could hear their moans blending with the sound of the lorry's engine. Now I'm imagining things, he thought, and even smiled. Why it was good he wasn't sure. The alcohol he had drunk was taking effect.

Jokūbas the Elder shoved him hard, grabbed the bag and with two hands quickly untied it. He pulled a lighter from his pocket, lit it and shone it into the bag. He stared, unmoving, then an expression of disgust distorted his dimly lit, unshaven face.

'Sooner or later I'll finish you off, you pervert.'

He threw the bag at Vincentas's feet. Tadas, who was sitting next to him, also wanted to take a look, but Vincentas quickly took the bag and retied the string. 'You shouldn't look,' he told him. 'Better if you don't.'

ODYSSEUS AND CHRIST

Aleksandras's ghost already hovered between them, but since Judita had discovered that he was still alive matters deteriorated. According to Judita, his ghost would haunt them and not give them any peace.

'I thought ghosts come here from the next world. If you know that Aleksandras is alive, how can he be a ghost?' Vincentas said with irony. Judita ignored him.

'I'm talking about a different kind of ghost. Hamlet saw his father's ghost. I used to think that was just a writer's fancy, but now I understand – the ghost is guilt. When you feel guilty you're visited by a ghost, the ghost of your guilt. Hamlet felt guilty for his father's death, that's why he was haunted by a ghost.'

'That's nonsense,' said Vincentas. But it was not such a stupid idea, at least not in the way he would have liked it to be. On three occasions now he had seen pits full of dead people. How many ghosts should be visiting him every night? Thousands. Does he feel guilty for their deaths? He can't answer that question. Simply can't – or doesn't want to. He's not yet sure how to word the charge he would bring against himself. That he does not feel pity for people who died like animals before his eyes? Strange, but the truth is, he does not feel pity. He doesn't understand if he feels anything at all. He knows one thing, though: ever since Aleksandras reappeared his relationship with Judita has gone downhill. Increasingly she turns her back to him or spends time with his mother instead.

Previously, she would sit in the workshop and watch him plane boards for coffins or crosses, smoking and telling stories about her trips to Paris or when she worked as a translator. He enjoyed listening to her low, gentle voice; just hearing her made him desire her, and the work went faster, and everything was smooth and effortless.

Now he sat for a long time at the workbench, doing nothing, staring at the rough surface of an unplaned board and seeing that it was full of knots; he sat there not wanting to move because movement would be painful.

Once again Judita was going to see his mother. He returned home exhausted, oppressed, still feeling deeply unsettled by the strange package he had delivered to the SS officer. The package was not heavy; he had known that it contained something unpleasant, something . . . wrong. He had not been able to stand it any longer and, once alone, had taken a look. And then immediately regretted it. Why had the German wanted Vincentas alone to deliver the package to him? Why?

He kissed Judita on the cheek, but she was getting ready to leave.

'You're going out?' asked Vincentas. 'At this time?'

'Your mother and I are going to make some lingonberry jam,' she said and left, as though Vincentas were a ghost. A dark shadow on a distant road.

He sat in the dark for a while, then put on a record. At first he listened to some guitar music, after which he began to hunt through a pile of records until he found the one he needed. A moment later the sounds of the overture to *Carmen* began to flow from the throat of the gramophone. He pulled out a cigarette.

'Cigarettes replace everything in the end, even sex,' he said to himself. Then he had a thought. He started walking up and down, put out the half-smoked cigarette, pulled out his box of photographs from under the bed, quickly selected a few, grabbed half a loaf of bread and left the house. Once on the street he looked around – no one was around, not even a patrol. Walking swiftly, Vincentas headed towards Vilijampolė, towards the ghetto.

He looked terrible, emaciated, much older; one of the lenses of his glasses was cracked, his face broken out in strange spots or pimples.

'Do you have anything to eat?' he asked Vincentas. Aleksandras did not seem at all surprised to see him. He did not ask what Vincentas wanted, why the soldier who had led him in stayed outside; the first thing he asked was whether Vincentas had anything to eat. When he saw the bread he was disappointed.

'White rolls are reserved for the Germans,' Vincentas said in justification.

Aleksandras nodded and sniffed the half-loaf.

'The whole time I have felt that Judita has a shadow,' he said, breaking the bread.

'I don't know what shadow you're talking about.'

'Really?' he looked at Vincentas. 'But Judita is living with another man, no? I think she had been seeing him for a long time, even before the war. Of course, we disagreed about certain things . . .'

'I thought that you had gone east,' said Vincentas, hoping to divert the conversation away from Judita, if only briefly.

'Without my wife? Surely you don't think that I would have run by myself and left her here?'

'Well, whatever happened, you disappeared . . .'

'We'd had a very bad fight that day. I suggested that we run, and she stubbornly refused to go to Russia. I went into the city. I wandered the streets for a long time, then I was caught by those shits, the partisans, the white armbands . . . They almost beat me to death. They threw me in the river, but by some miracle I survived . . .' Aleksandras bit off a larger chunk of bread and chuckled. 'Alive! I lay unconscious for a few days in someone's house, and when I came to they told me that Judita had gone, that she was no longer in our apartment, that new people were living there. And I didn't even have to move anywhere. I was already in the ghetto zone. The shoemaker Šlimanas and his family had pulled me from the river, from the otherworld. Maybe without good reason? Who knows. That is the whole story. And you? Have you seen Judita? How is she? A work crew recently saw her in the city. She was asking about me.'

'Yes, I've seen her . . . The situation is this, that –'

'I miss her. I don't have a single photograph. I once managed to sneak out into the city, but the new residents would not let me in; the woman said that there were no personal effects left, that they had thrown everything out.'

Vincentas was on tenterhooks. He regretted having come. He didn't know what he had expected from this meeting. It felt like self-inflicted torture.

'Do you remember how, before the war, I told you about Kafka's *Metamorphosis*?' asked Aleksandras, breaking the silence.

'No, I don't,' said Vincentas, shaking his head.

'We had gone on an excursion, we were drinking wine, sitting on the grass, outside the city, and I was telling you about a man who turned into an insect.'

'Ah, yes,' nodded Vincentas. Warm memories of those days flooded his chest – Judita's bare arms, warm, caring, protective, loving.

'It was a story about a man who woke up one morning and realized that he had turned into an insect. That is exactly what happened to me. I woke up one morning and realized that I had turned into an insect.'

'When they pulled you out of the river?'

'The river . . .' smiled Aleksandras. 'It is the river of death. It separates the living from the dead. Did you give the guard something?'

'A cigarette,' said Vincentas.

'You see? Now you have entered the land of the dead. Look around – this is what the world looks like after death. You have been given an opportunity; you are like Odysseus visiting the kingdom of the dead. But I'm not talking about the river, I'm talking about the ghetto, about the prison that the executioners forced us to construct around us with our own hands. Do you know how many people used to live here? Maybe about seven thousand. But thanks to the Nazis about thirty thousand are crammed in here now. There are thousands of us here – thousands of pathetic insects. Each one is allocated six square metres. Not much bigger than a grave. But does an insect need any more than that? Professors, scientists, lawyers, doctors, artists, grandparents and children – we have all become insects here. Do you know what the hardest thing is?'

Vincentas looked around uncomfortably, as though thousands of insects were swarming around him. 'I'd rather not guess.'

Aleksandras said nothing.

He died on the cross, descended into hell, appeared for a moment in Vincentas's head. Not Odysseus but Christ. Odysseus was concerned with personal matters, he wanted to return home to his wife. Christ went to the sinners in order to redeem them, to give them hope. Odysseus or Christ – is that the only choice there is in this life?

'You still think like a human, even though you turned into an insect a long time ago,' Aleksandras was saying. 'And people see you as an insect, they treat you like an insect, and there you are still thinking like a human. They give you insect food, and you grumble because you want human food; they tell you to live under the sofa, to crawl into a cave, a crack, to skulk in the damp and the dark, but you want light, you want warmth, you want space. This incongruity is the most awful part of it all.'

'It will all have to end someday,' said Vincentas, hardly believing the words himself.

'Yes, there are fewer and fewer of us. I think it will definitely end. And what is even stranger – more horrible – is that the mind slowly begins to adapt, and you slowly start to think like an insect, you are no longer tormented by emotions, sentiments, cultural needs, the only thing that remains important is to survive. Just like an insect you try to nick a little piece of mouldy cheese, a bite of rotten apple, and you are no longer ashamed of your insect body, your insect state; you are happy that even in the situation you're in you are still able to find some pleasures – memories of Judita, for example. Now that I know she is alive, and she knows that I'm alive, we will meet, and everything will be fine . . . I believe that, and that faith warms me. Faith – the most patient warmth there is, and the one that burns most painfully.'

Vincentas watched as Aleksandras stuffed the bread in his mouth, how he gathered the crumbs, and it looked to him that the man sitting opposite him did indeed resemble an insect. A repellent, disgusting insect. And such an insect, such an unpleasant creature will crawl all over Judita's body, over Judita's incredible body, that body which now and for ever had to belong to him, to Vincentas.

Vincentas did not know if it was the best idea, but he decided to show Aleksandras some photographs of Judita. The kind that he would not have shown anyone else. At first Aleksandras looked them over distractedly, almost as if he did not recognize her. Then again, and again.

'She looks well,' he said finally. 'So it is you, then. Are you working for them? You're a policeman, a white armband? She's living with a Nazi henchman? Tell me!'

'I . . . It doesn't matter, it just happened that way.'

'I thought we were friends. And behind my back you were plotting an affair with my wife.'

Vincentas wanted to get away from there as fast as he could. He had had only one thing in mind in coming to the ghetto – to show Aleksandras photographs of his naked wife. He had not thought about what would come next. He imagined that the photographs would automatically resolve everything, without words even. And now he was at a total loss for words. Before the war they had met only a few times, then the Soviets came and Aleksandras had thrown himself into his artistic activities – no, they were not close friends. They were just acquaintances.

'For a long time?' asked Aleksandras.

'You were busy building socialism,' Vincentas muttered. When the Reds came the concert halls had opened up to Aleksandras, and he had received numerous commissions, put together an orchestra, played on the radio, made recordings, planned to write – maybe even wrote – an opera. Judita had felt lonely.

'She felt lonely,' said Vincentas. 'It's not her fault. It's not only her fault.'

Aleksandras suddenly grabbed the remaining piece of bread and threw it in Vincentas's face. An insect, a real insect.

Vincentas understood that it was time to go.

'It's you – you insect!' Aleksandras spat out through clenched teeth. 'You and all those like you. You have taken away our homes, our women, our children, but it's you, you insects, you look like humans, but inside each one of you lives an insect with no conscience or honour, which cares only about satisfying the most primitive instincts – to feed and reproduce and kill all those who are not like you!'

Vincentas retreated slowly towards the door; Aleksandras remained seated at the table, facing away from him. His shoulders shook, and it looked like he was either crying or his entire body was seething with fury.

'I will still find her!' Aleksandras shouted in a pained, high voice without turning around. 'She's my wife, mine!'

Vincentas left in silence. He could feel his cheeks burning in distress and shame. The soldier escorting him asked, 'Do you want me to take care of that problem?'

'Which problem?'

'You're screwing his wife, right? What is she – a Lithuanian, a German? She's not a Jew, right?'

'No,' mumbled Vincentas. 'And how would you take care of it?'

'No person, no problem.'

'No person?'

'Well, we're talking about a Jew.'

'No, no, that won't be necessary. Everything's fine.'

'Up to you. I wouldn't charge much.'

Vincentas hesitated. When he realized that the pause had gone on too long he asked quietly, 'How much?'

MORTA AND MARIJA

He was already walking towards the gates when he met Jokūbas the Younger, who was carrying some boxing gloves.

'Mr Photographer, what are you doing here?'

'I was visiting a friend.'

'Is it true that you're a Jew, like Jokūbas the Elder says? Or maybe you have a girlfriend here? Do you like Jewish girls? They say that all the communist big shots marry Jewish girls – is that true?' Jokūbas the Younger asked mockingly. 'Let's go. Our boys are organizing a boxing match.'

Vincentas did not want to go but could not quickly come up with an excuse not to. 'OK, just for a bit.'

'Well, we'll see how it goes. Some are shorter, some are longer,' laughed Jokūbas the Younger.

For a while they walked in silence.

'The guard at the gate said something about peeling potatoes,' said Vincentas. 'He asked for a cigarette and then . . . about peeling potatoes.'

'You still don't know what that means?' asked Jokūbas the Younger in surprise.

Vincentas shook his head. Jokūbas the Younger stopped and made an obscene gesture with his hands, thrusting his pelvis back and forth.

'Here's what it means,' nodded Jokūbas the Younger. 'You know, now it's not at all the same . . . At the beginning of the war, at the Seventh Fort, that's where we stripped them good – that's where we had some fun. You could pick up as many gold watches, chains, earrings, brooches, medallions, wedding rings as you wanted. They hid everything, of course, but when you stick a hose down a woman's throat . . . You get it.'

Jokūbas the Younger was short and thin, with pronounced cheekbones, eyes close together and a long pointed nose – in the twilight he looked like an animal, perhaps a ferret or a stoat.

'There were about a thousand Jewish women there . . . We went around and picked out the best ones . . . it was dark, you shine your flashlight, you check that the face doesn't look like a rag, we were drinking before that, but a pretty woman is a pretty woman, then you take her to the next room . . . Boy, did we have some fun. Sure, some of them kicked a lot, had to kill them, but that was some night . . . a perfect night.'

'The St Bartholomew's Day massacre . . .'

'What?' asked Jokūbas the Younger, surprised. 'Why?'

Fairy tales on the bookshelf, toy soldiers, a rag reeking of lime covering the face.

'No, nothing. Baltramiejus, was he there, too?'

'Baltramiejus?' Jokūbas the Younger was surprised. 'I can't remember. He probably was. Most of us were.'

They approached a building that looked like a warehouse. A dim lamp hung from the ceiling. Several dozen men, most of whom Vincentas recognized, were sitting on benches, boxes, rickety chairs and stools. A space had been left clear in the middle of the room.

'Finally. What took you so long?' They heard Jokūbas the Elder's irritated voice.

'Here,' said Jokūbas the Younger, holding up the boxing gloves. 'The parasite didn't want to give them to me. He got some knuckles in the face.'

A man he had never seen before led two young Jewish women in from the recesses of the room. They were quite sturdy, wearing only shorts and undershirts, like they were about to play basketball. Their sporty appearance clashed with their bright make-up. Two whores who had decided to get some exercise. The girls moved lethargically, as if they were dizzy from medication, alcohol or drugs. Since Vincentas had spotted Andriejus among the spectators that wouldn't be a surprise. If required he could supply Stalin's entire army with his special powder.

The man pulled the boxing gloves on to the girls' hands and shoved them into the makeshift ring.

'Come on, you whores, box!' shouted Jokūbas the Younger, and the girls reluctantly started to punch each other. 'Listen up,' he continued, 'place your bets. In the red shorts we have Stalin; in the brown, Hitler!'

He sent a hat around, the shouting and laughing men placed their bets on the boxing girls and two more girls, naked to the waist, walked between the seated men offering snacks. As well as the hat, alcohol and cocaine were circulating, too.

The girls slowly got into it and hit each other more and more violently with their gloved fists. The intoxicated spectators urging them on, Jokūbas the Younger shouting loudest of all.

'The winner gets everything; the loser, nothing!'

Jokūbas the Elder was sitting with all the rest, but he neither shouted nor laughed. He watched the boxing girls glumly, taking pulls from a bottle that he kept between his feet.

Andriejus leaned towards Vincentas. 'Our spiritual leader had an unpleasant adventure,' he said gesturing with his head in Jokūbas the Elder's direction.

Vincentas shook his head. 'I don't understand. What adventure?'

'He was walking home from a restaurant, at night, with a girl, and he met a couple of Germans. He saluted, appropriately, but they still socked him in the face. You know how Jokūbas the Elder isn't a pushover – he gave it back to them. A patrol officer appeared immediately and dragged him to the station. The Germans made fun of his documents, called him a Jew-killer and, according to witnesses, he said, now you're butchering the Jews, next you'll be butchering us. That kind of thing. Then they let him go. The Gestapo returned his confiscated things – from what I hear the Germans want to smooth it over – but Jokūbas the Elder won't let it lie; he'll make a complaint.'

Vincentas said nothing, but he found the fact that a German soldier had punched Jokūbas the Elder in the face somehow gratifying.

The topless girls walked around offering food. He looked at their breasts and could not avoid thinking about Judita, about the afternoon he saw her like that for the first time – naked, holding a juicy plum in her hand, unbelievably attractive, simply radiating eroticism, then the image before him began to blend, to flow, and again he had the strange feeling that he was seeing everything from the side, as though he were not there himself but that his double, a shadow in the kingdom of shadows, was watching the girls beating each other up, Stalin was doing better than Hitler, her breasts were bigger, her punches more fierce, and he saw the girls sitting in the next room, and the men with those girls, and he was not at all surprised that he was one of those very men, and he asked one of the girls, is your name Morta, do you have a sister named Marija, there she is sitting by Our Lord's feet, by Jokūbas the Elder's feet, and is listening to His words, and you, Morta, you're running around and fussing, and you ask why the Lord doesn't care, why he leaves you to do all the work, why he doesn't tell Marija to help you, and the Lord replies, Morta, Morta, you worry and suffer over many things, but they are all worthless because only one thing is needed from you, while Marija chose the better fate, one that will not be taken away from her, Vincentas saw Marija, she was caressing Jokūbas the Elder's prick with her mouth, why are you killing us, asks Marija, why do you hate us, and she looks at Jokūbas the Elder with big, pure eyes, I was pulled from under a pile of corpses, says Jokūbas the Elder, I was supposed to die right at the beginning of the war, I was shot by Jewish commissars, said Jokūbas the Elder, and he struck Marija across the face, and she cried and still continued to pleasure him and then more men appeared in the room, they all wanted Morta to do the same to them, and Morta tried to please them all, but Marija was just Jokūbas the Elder's, then someone brought in the boxers, their breasts as big and firm as boxing gloves, and some bearded old man from the ghetto security force was talking about how when he shoots Jewish women he aims for the left nipple, when he shoots a man he aims for the belly button, but with women at the nipple, said the old man, that's bullshit, someone interrupted, no, it isn't bullshit, argued the old man, I want to preserve their healthy skin, why should the skin be damaged, skin is a good thing, the Germans make all sorts of nice little things out of it, laughed the old man, a hideous, drunken oaf, the kind that shoots people in the back, shoots them lying down, shoots invalids, children, they don't need breasts, they don't need . . .

And again that day, the day he saw her for the first time, the plum juice on her dark nipple, a target for a bullet, and she is standing by the pit, shivering from the cold, from the lewd, hungry expressions of the drunken men, and she, Judita, is trying to cover her breasts, her nipples, with her hands so that the hideous bearded old man wearing a sheepskin coat girded with a wide leather belt could not see where to shoot, and then it was as though he had awoken from a trance, had come to and seen where he really was, although he would have difficulty saying what that 'really' means, and Jokūbas the Younger was ramming a pistol against Morta's head and shouting, 'Move, and I'll blow your brains out! The train races forward, only forward!' and she wasn't planning to turn to the side, she was moving rhythmically, it did, in fact, look like an engine racing, Matas was smoking a cigarette, his mind had long since sunk into a dark bog, he took one last puff and stuck the cigarette's glowing eye into the door of the engine's firebox, you Jewish girls, you're so hairy, even your arseholes are covered in fur, shouted Matas, and then Jokūbas the Younger let out a terrifying cry.

From the unexpected pain she had bitten down on him hard, and Jokūbas was behaving irresponsibly, he had released the safety catch, pain had come before clear thinking, the dead Morta had clenched her teeth hard, and it was all they could do to prise her off, smashing the dead Morta's face, and they had to try to avoid ripping Jokūbas the Younger's member off, and Andriejus joked, Jews bite even after they're dead, Jokūbas the Younger was not laughing, he was in serious pain, the fucking whore, he screamed, then calmed down, he got some powder and calmed down, and they dragged the dead girl into a corner, wrapped her in an old sheet, we'll cart her away when we leave so there won't be any fuss, said Jokūbas the Elder, now I want to eat, give me some bloody food, eat and drink, you sons of bitches, because you never know when it'll be your last supper, they found places to recline in various corners, wherever they found a spot, as there was no table, and Vincentas asked Andriejus where Tadas was, he didn't know, he was around and now he wasn't, he's always like that, there are rumours that he's been recruited by the NKVD, but now he's milling around the Gestapo, why do you have such strange names, asked Vincentas, why do you call each other such strange names? Andriejus smiled, it was Jokūbas the Elder, the former seminarian who was thrown out of the seminary, served in the army and did six months' time before the war for a fight he had with a lieutenant, he thought it up, and it wasn't a bad idea, we're Christ's soldiers, we're the damned apostles, we cut off bunches of grapes and pour them into the winepress of God's wrath, and from that press pours blood, and the blood rises as high as the horses' bits, or whatever, what the hell do I know, ask Jokūbas the Elder, he's the talker, he's the great talker, but Vincentas did not ask, he had had enough, he was a glass boxer with glass fists, he wanted no one, no one ever to touch him, he wanted only to sleep, to cover himself up, to cover his head, block his ears, close his eyes and sleep, as far as he could from here, as far as possible from the twilight, from this bloody, boggy, all-consuming twilight.

SALOME

She had gone. Judita had disappeared. And that was that. By the time Vincentas returned from the ghetto the sun had risen. He desperately wanted to sleep, his head ached, he was hungry. After sleeping for a few hours he woke up with a bad feeling. Judita still had not returned. He went upstairs to his mother's. She was sitting, wearing her glasses and knitting.

'I knew it wouldn't end well,' she said, putting her knitting aside. She reeked of alcohol. Where did she get it? Maybe she had stocked up. 'Just yesterday we were making lingonberry jam. She's sweet, we were chatting like two close girlfriends. She said she wanted to tell you something important. Maybe that was the important news – that she's leaving you.' His mother's brow furrowed. 'Listen, have you checked if any valuables are missing? Go and check if my jewellery box is there. Bring it to me.'

He reluctantly brought her the jewels. They both knew it was an absurd procedure, but Vincentas did not have the energy to argue. His mother opened the box and carefully looked through it.

'My ring isn't here. Do you remember? The one with the little stone, a tsarist general gave it to me . . . What was his name . . . ? Aleksandras, I think. He waltzed beautifully. And my brooch is gone.'

'Mother,' said Vincentas angrily.

He did not believe that Judita could have robbed her. And he did not want his mother even to joke about it.

'Fine then, fine. I found a good buyer. Do you think I can survive on your salary? I liked her, your Judita. She'll be back, don't worry. Women can get like that.' And his mother smiled mischievously. She knew something that Vincentas didn't. That irritated him even more.

'Like what? What do you know?'

'Sometimes we just like to go out to be alone, without you – without you men.'

'Are you talking about a convent?'

'Calm down. Everything will be fine,' his mother waved and once more buried herself in her knitting.

He went out into the city. He walked around aimlessly, skulking along the streets in the hope of spotting her. Her desirable, incredible figure. The Gestapo? No, it couldn't be. They would have taken Vincentas and his mother away, too. They would have turned everything upside down.

He stopped by the translation bureau where Judita had often found work translating from Lithuanian to German. No, she hadn't been there today; nobody knows anything.

Jokūbas the Elder? He hates Vincentas. Maybe he doesn't think he's a Bolshevik spy any more (Vincentas was almost sure he never had), but he doesn't like him and wishes him harm.

It was no good. He even went to the ghetto and gave the guard a cigarette – no, he did not think that a young, fair-haired woman carrying a suitcase or a bundle had come to the ghetto today. If she had decided to go to the ghetto to find Aleksandras, wouldn't she have needed to bring some of her things?

Maybe he had been stupid to refuse the offer of the guard's services – for just thirty packets of cigarettes Aleksandras would have disappeared for all time. Or maybe it was the unconscious but rationally practical sense that sooner or later he would be eliminated. For free. No, he didn't want to think about any of it. Even though he saw Aleksandras as his rival he did not wish him dead; he did not want and nor did he have any reason to seek revenge. If he had not by pure chance met Aleksandras by the river that evening and been invited to the opera, Vincentas would never have found Judita, he would never have experienced such joy – a joy that was now turning into heartache. Where is she? Where?

Vincentas returned home. No, Judita's meagre possessions were where they should be – several items of clothing, some underwear, her shoes were all there, even a folder of translations lay on the table. She was thorough enough that she would not have left a piece of unfinished work. Vincentas was beginning to find it all very suspicious. She would have written something. She would have at least taken several essential items. Now she had disappeared without a trace. She had taken nothing, had left nothing.

In the evening he began to feel a pressure on his chest. A great hole formed by his heart. It felt as though that hole was expanding and sucking him in. He loved Judita. He didn't want to lose her. He tried to console himself that it might be better this way. But what was better, and for whom? The Germans were approaching Moscow; soon they would take Leningrad. Somewhere, at the edge of his consciousness, he had a bad feeling that they had no future together. Especially if it continued to go so well for the Germans. Did he have to think about things like the distant future? Nonsense. But it was also shocking that only now, as he felt her loss, did he realize how precious Judita was to him, how much he needed her – how much he missed her smell, her look, her embrace.

Where could she have gone? To her friend Greta's, a German woman who had married a Jew? Her husband had been arrested and shot at the beginning of the war. Judita had spoken about that option. When her landlords had thrown her out of the apartment she was renting she had stayed briefly with Greta. It was only later, after the majority of the Jews had been moved to the ghetto, that she had agreed to move in with Vincentas. He didn't have Greta's address, although he had some idea where she lived.

'If you should ever begin to feel that I'm a burden, I'll leave.'

'Where would you go?'

'To Greta's. She lives on the outskirts. She has often offered to let me hide there. She lives with her daughter. The Nazis killed her husband.'

'Do you think that would be safer?'

'I don't know.'

'I want you to be with me.'

'I know. But if you ever start to feel that you don't want that any more I'll disappear from your life.'

'No, I don't want you to disappear.'

'And I don't want to.'

They were lying naked and tired. Judita smelled of sweat and a mixture of other smells, a mixture that he could never analyse. They were sharing a cigarette, listening to a scratched Louis Armstrong record on the Odeon label. Judita had put her head on his chest; his heart was still beating faster than normal – for a second it seemed to him that his and Judita's hearts were beating to the same rhythm.

'I was washing your clothes yesterday, and your trousers smelled bad,' she said, lifting her head.

He did not know what to say. It was probably the lime, which, for reasons of sanitation, was sprinkled over the pits full of dead bodies.

'I have no idea. I must have rubbed against something.'

'You must have rubbed against it pretty hard. Or swum in whatever awful thing it was.'

'It's awful everywhere these days. Everywhere. It's hard to avoid it.'

'Really? It seems to me there's always an alternative.'

'It isn't that simple, Judita. It isn't that simple.'

'I'm not saying it's simple, I'm saying there's always an alternative.'

'Sometimes there isn't anything at all.'

'That isn't true.' She turned on to her back. 'A friend was recently telling me a story . . .'

'Greta again?' Vincentas asked.

'Yes. She was telling me about a family, about a mixed family, the man was, as it's now common to say, an Aryan, the woman was not, and because it was a mixed marriage their two daughters were also tainted. Because the husband did not want them to be separated, they were all ordered to move to the ghetto. And, guess what? They committed suicide. The whole family.'

'And you call that an alternative?'

'The husband shot the younger daughter and then himself. And the older daughter shot the mother and then fired a bullet into her own heart. Yes, I do think that is an alternative. One can take that way out, too.'

To depart for the afterlife. After making love it seemed absurd to Vincentas. There is no reason to go anywhere, everything that is good is right here. But, unfortunately, so is everything that isn't. And the fact that one is constantly facing evil in this life must be the firmest proof that we won't have to pay for pleasures experienced here somewhere over there in eternity. We pay for everything here. For everything. In spades.

Maybe she had departed, too, and not just from his life. To eternity. Would Judita have had the strength and courage to kill herself? I don't know her at all – a chill came over Vincentas. They had known each other for almost two years; at first they would meet only briefly, then they would suffer long weeks of separation, and now, when they had the chance to be together – for eternity, till death parted them – Judita had simply vanished.

After night fell someone knocked cautiously on his door.

He jumped to his feet. Judita had a key.

It was a man from the brigade. Tadas. It was Tadas.

'Are you alone?' he asked.

Vincentas looked around. He and Judita had been careful to avoid leaving any signs of a woman's presence around: clothes, footwear, jewellery, even too much order. Judita liked to tidy. She just didn't like to cook. Lately, more often than not, she had been sullen rather than happy.

'As you can see.'

'I can see.'

Tadas sat down on a pile of boards stacked next to the wall. He tapped it with his hand.

'Good material.'

'It's for coffins. They've been dried for coffins. I bring them in here so the heat from the stove isn't wasted.'

Tadas laughed.

'I always wanted to have my own apartment so that I wouldn't have to talk in the morning, wouldn't have to say good-night to anyone in the evening, so that I could sit in the dark and look out of the window and just watch people walking down the street, nothing else.'

'This is a closed yard. You can't see people walking by.'

'A coffin is something like an apartment,' said Tadas, ignoring Vincentas's comment. 'Small but secure. And just for one. It's good that it's just for one. I wouldn't want to end up in a pit with a crowd.'

'There's no window.'

He looked at Vincentas. 'What window?'

'A coffin doesn't have a window.'

Tadas shook his head. 'She's really pretty, that Jewish girl, and doesn't even look like a Jew.'

'What are you talking about?'

'You know.'

Vincentas knew. 'Where is she?'

'We were shooting in the Ninth Fort . . . In the ninth heaven, as Jokūbas the Elder likes to say . . . They were undressed, stamping around by the pit, suddenly I hear my name . . . I see Emma, a fiery brunette, naked, reaching her hands out to me and she's saying, save me, I don't want to die . . . We went to school together; she looked like Marija. We even kissed. She was probably in love with me. That was the first time I saw her naked. And the last,' Tadas chuckled strangely. He looked disconcerted, depressed, unhappy.

'There's always an alternative,' Vincentas said carefully, adding cautiously, 'Some kind of . . .'

Tadas nodded. 'I could have saved her, God knows, but it was too late. Too late.' He stood up and pulled a silver chain with a small precious stone from his pocket. 'This is what's left of her. She gave it to me so it wouldn't get lost. She said if it was too late, I should at least take it.'

Tadas put the piece of jewellery away, pulled his pistol from under his belt, cocked it and put it back under his belt.

'Come on. And bring your camera.'

They walked along the darkening city streets. It was unnerving knowing that an armed man was walking behind him, one who had abducted Judita. What had he done to her? What was he planning to do to Vincentas? Tadas tried to avoid the main streets, choosing alleyways and smaller streets.

In one of those streets they approached an abandoned house. The building was crumbling, there had been a fire on the second floor, but part of the building was intact. It looked like the fire had been recent and that the residents had moved out. Or it had been a Jewish home. That was more likely.

'What a dump,' Vincentas said, coming to a stop.

'Forward,' Tadas muttered. Could he be hiding Judita in this house? What does he plan to do with her? He'll kill her. First he'll rape her, and then he'll finish her off. He'll force him to watch. To photograph it. His blood began to freeze. Maybe he'll shoot him, too. Should he run to the nearest German soldier and ask for help? To help him save a Jewish woman he has been hiding in his apartment, with whom he has lived as man and wife, deceiving the Reich and mocking the sacrament of marriage? How would he explain it all?

They continued.

The master of the house opened the door. It was the Artist. He was wearing a long velvet dressing-gown. He was in an excellent mood.

'Come in,' he said.

Vincentas entered.

He could hear music coming from the main living-room and light from candles, not electricity, was shining through an open door.

Vincentas turned around. The Artist gave something to Tadas, who nodded, looked at Vincentas, winked slyly and disappeared. He received his thirty pieces of silver. He had done his dirty work. He would wait in the vestibule like a dog on a doormat. When had he met the Artist? Had he informed on Judita? How had he found out? Had he seen the photos in his darkroom? Damn it – he had shown the Artist the photographs of Judita himself the first time he had been called to the SS officer's apartment. He had wanted to show off and had betrayed her.

'Oh, how lovely a confused, frightened, shocked human face looks,' said the satisfied German. 'You must be wondering what on earth is going on here? Let me admire the shock and awe in your twisted face!' He sunk into an armchair, picked up a glass of cognac from a side-table, took a sip and continued to study Vincentas. 'Do you know that living with a Jewish woman these days is at the very least foolish? How old are you? Not even thirty?'

Vincentas nodded. What difference does it make how old you are if you're good for nothing – which was exactly how he felt at that moment.

'These days it's foolish to live at all,' he muttered from his parched throat.

The German laughed. There was no sign of Judita. Maybe she isn't here? Maybe Tadas has already killed her?

The German went to the gramophone and raised the volume, waved to some invisible person and then turned to Vincentas.

'This seat is the most important object. Set up your camera so that you can take some *good* photographs.' And he sank into the large sofa that had been draped with red fabric. 'I like good photographs, I like images – images containing contrast. The old and the young, old and young faces, the contrast between withered and plump bodies. That is what we will be trying to achieve this evening – contrasts. Will you have enough light?'

Vincentas nodded uncertainly.

'A woman's head is beautiful, pure and glowing while John the Baptist's is old, bloody, ghastly. A live head and a dead head. Breasts and a dead head. A woman – the embodiment of fertility, the beginning of life, the elemental, nature and unconscious instinct; and a man's head – the symbol of rationality, the mind, power, a dead symbol, a symbol of defeat – in her hands. And your woman is so perfectly suited to our subject. Her body is full but not fat, a very attractive moderation. I can't fault you. Excellent taste.'

He spoke in a strange, excited way, as though in some kind of ecstasy. Then Judita appeared.

It was the first time Vincentas had seen her this way. She was dancing. Vincentas did not know that she was a talented dancer. In fact, it seemed he did not know much about her at all. He was increasingly convinced of that – that we know the people who are closest to us least. The people we live with sink into us like a smell, and with time we stop noticing that smell, we begin to confuse it with our own. Then, when something happens, an accident, an unexpected event or some other unpleasant thing, we suddenly realize that we don't really know anything about those with whom we share a bed.

Judita was wrapped in a multitude of scarves, she was fluttering around the room throwing them off one by one. The Artist sat

down in the armchair smiling, then opened his dressing-gown –
he was only half aroused. He turned to Vincentas.

'Do you even have enough intelligence to appreciate this? It's
the Dance of the Seven Veils! Strauss's *Salome*! Who better to play
the part of Salome than a Jewess? Such a wonderful concept – I
am a genius!' The German pulled out a small bag containing white
powder from his dressing-gown pocket, poured a little on to the
surface of the side-table, inhaled first into one nostril then the
other; with a look of satisfaction he rolled his head back and settled
into the armchair.

Judita was still dancing. She spun around the room as though
she were chasing somebody, as though she were being chased
herself, she turned and turned, and Vincentas started as if he were
under a spell, unable to tear his eyes away, and fear and anxiety
flowed into his loins, horror and despair, this can't be it, he thought,
this can't be the hour of our deaths, if not the hour then the day,
the evening, the night, the German won't let them leave here alive,
the German will destroy them. For what? Regret pierced Vincentas's
chest. For what? He had done nothing wrong.

Finally Judita was almost completely naked, a single transparent
silk screen remained. She stopped dancing and stood frozen in
the middle of the room. In the candlelight she looked so beautiful,
so lonely. And sad. Perhaps that was her role. Vincentas was utterly
confused. What's happening here? He understood only that she
and the SS Sturmbannführer had rehearsed and that this show
was clearly not for him. The Artist waved his hand. Judita followed
his orders as though drugged. She approached him, kneeled down
and stretched her hand towards the Artist's penis, but he shook
his head. Judita was kneeling before him, looking into his eyes.
The German grew more aroused. Then Judita shifted over to the

table and snorted some of the cocaine. The German turned slightly towards Vincentas and gestured. He understood that he should now take a shot. He raised the camera and then lowered it again. Despair constrained his movements. Judita stood up and walked over to a small table in the corner of the room, gave it a little pull, and the table began to roll across the floor. It was on castors. On the table was some kind of object covered with a shroud.

She pushed the table towards the Artist, then, with a graceful movement, she pulled away the shroud and screamed – a muffled, hoarse, terrified scream. She had not known what was under the shroud. Or perhaps she knew and this was part of the performance, the game. The Artist sighed with satisfaction. Or perhaps he laughed. He was having fun. It was the head of a rabbi. Of the same rabbi that the SS officer had picked out by the synagogue in that provincial town. The same head that Vincentas had brought him yesterday in a bag.

'Kiss it,' ordered the SS officer.

Judita stood there looking at the bearded head, its dishevelled hair stuck to the forehead. The thick beard was matted with blood, the dead eyes half open, condemning.

'Well then . . .'

Judita leaned towards the head. The SS officer stood up, opened his dressing-gown, approached her from behind and raised the silk scarf.

'Spread your legs, you Jewish bitch!'

She followed his command obediently.

'Now, photograph!' the German shouted.

And he fucked Judita right there in front of him. Vincentas struggled to concentrate, to see the photograph. He simply didn't want that photograph – something prevented him from seeing it.

Fear, jealousy and despair paralysed his hands and his mind, and he was sure nothing would come out of it.

The Artist shoved Judita to the side, grabbed the rabbi's head, threw it on to the armchair, then bent Judita's head towards it and entered her again from behind, moaning in blissful satisfaction.

'Yes, yes, yes!' he shouted, then, without looking at Vincentas, shouted again, 'Shoot! Shoot, you son of a bitch! And you kiss the head, you Jewish whore. Kiss it, kiss it, kiss it!'

Judita let out a moan, and it flashed through Vincentas's head that he wasn't sure if she was moaning from pleasure or shame. Perhaps there is no difference in the end. Maybe those moans coming from lovers' beds are the cries of both bliss and shame. He felt a strange fog flood his brain.

'Now I would like to remind you of the most important thing. There is only one principle that unconditionally applies to a member of the SS – we must be honest, polite and faithful with people who share our blood but with no one else. We have come to lands inhabited by different nations, but we must never forget that whether these other nations live well or reek of famine should not matter to us in the slightest. It can only concern us to the extent that they can be of use to us as slaves, nothing more. Our concerns, our duty, shall be for our nation and our blood alone – our nation and our blood, our nation and our blood!'

When he began to climax, when he was grunting like a pig, Vincentas could not stand it any longer. He fell on him him, drew the leather strap of his camera around his neck and began to strangle him from behind. The German was stunned by such impudence, and for a few seconds did not even resist. He was still inside Judita; Vincentas thought that she was still moving with the Artist rhythmically, automatically, and he pulled the strap even tighter. The German moved backwards, and they both fell to the floor. Although the German fell on to Vincentas, he did not release his grip on the strap around the man's neck. It was even easier that way – he was waving his arms but could not reach Vincentas. He was not heavy or well-built, but he was very energetic, and he kicked and squirmed. Then Judita joined in. She lay on top of him and pressed the weakening German's hands to the ground.

They sat on the floor next to the corpse, listening to the opera.

'I can't stand Strauss. I never liked him,' Judita finally said. 'Now I *despise* him.'

'We're finished,' said Vincentas. 'Now we're truly finished.'

'No one knows we're here.' Then she suddenly remembered. 'Except . . .'

'Tadas.'

'His name is Tadas? He drove me here.'

'He's a member of the security brigade. He brought me here, too. I thought Tadas had abducted you.'

Judita sat down on the floor.

'It would be good to have a smoke.'

He began to search in his pockets. He had left his cigarettes at home.

Judita was pondering something intensely. She went into the other room and quickly returned, now dressed. She stopped by the side-table, where there was still some cocaine left. Then she rummaged in the German's dressing-gown pocket and pulled out a little bag.

'Come here, now we really need some.'

The cocaine began to work, and his head cleared. Vincentas was sure of only one thing – they had to get away. Anywhere they could and immediately. They needed to get his mother, some food and run.

'You know what, we should find some rope,' said Judita.

'Rope?'

'Yes, and a good length of it. Even some twine would do, but thin rope would be best.'

Vincentas wanted to turn off the gramophone but decided against it – he let it play, just lowered the volume. The rabbi's head lay bloody on the armchair, the beard sticking upwards. Next to it, on the floor, sprawled the dead German. His abdomen shone in the candlelight, Vincentas bent down – the sweat of a death-agony orgasm. There's your little death, there's your poetry of severed heads, there's your Bible for the illiterate, Vincentas wanted to scream, and maybe even screamed, just somewhere very far from here, from very deep down.

Judita came back from wherever she had been. She held a length of clothes-line in her hands.

'Don't stand there like a statue. Help me.'

Judita swiftly tied a complicated knot, he raised the Artist's head and she slipped the noose over it. Then, just as swiftly, she tied two smaller loops and slid them over the Artist's feet.

'Now we just need to tighten the ropes – help me.'

'What does it all mean?' asked Vincentas. He didn't understand what she was doing, but it was obvious that she was not doing it for the first time.

'I'll explain later.'

'To hell with later! Have you done that with him before? Did you know each other? That dance and everything – what's going on here, Judita? Tell me.'

'Later.'

'You liked it – I could see it!'

'What did you see? What? An animal demeaning a woman, debasing her nation? What did you see?'

'I saw you writhing and moaning with pleasure, that's what I saw! And now all of this – what is this? Did the two of you meet and do this before? Answer me! Answer!'

'No, no, no!' Her face changed, went grey, looked at once tired and enraged. 'It's Aleksandras!'

'What about Aleksandras?'

'He no longer desired me, he was always telling me how he no longer wanted me . . . that he was old, unhappy, that I didn't love him. Oh! Then, on one occasion, after he came back from Berlin, he showed me something . . .'

'Jesus Christ, what else don't I know about the two of you? Aleksandras?'

'Hurry up, someone could find us here. Let's lift him on to the sofa.'

They managed to roll the corpse on to the sofa. Judita decided that it would be best if they laid him face down. Then, thinking further, she put the rabbi's head on the side-table, where it had earlier sat under the shroud. There was no longer any need for a shroud.

'We might get away with it,' said Judita. 'Might . . .'

The scene in the room began to swim before Vincentas's eyes: in the fading candlelight, on a red-draped sofa, lay the dead Artist, almost prone and strangely twisted, with the rope around his neck and his feet. It looked as though by pushing against the rope with slightly bent legs, he was trying to raise his lifeless head from the sofa's armrest. Before the sofa stood the small table on wheels, and on its silver tray the severed, bearded, bloody rabbi's head with its half-open eyes. A little further away, next to the camera, a tired, half-naked Judita.

'Now we need to pull him by the feet,' said Judita.

'I don't understand.'

'You pull him by the ankles, I'll hold his head.'

'Is it necessary?'

'When the heart stops pumping blood and he no longer gets oxygen, the blood collects under the skin and it turns a pinkish purple. It's called post-mortem bruising.'

'OK, OK, I'll pull him by the feet.'

It seemed to Vincentas that his own hands had become pinkish purple and were starting to bruise. That's what he'll look like when the Gestapo find him and hang him.

'We might be lucky, and the point at which the rope is tight will look like strangulation marks.'

He pulled the Artist by the feet a few times as Judita held his arched-back head. They were in the German's apartment, once more strangling their dead host; around them the candlelight slowly faded, the severed head loomed on the silver platter. He wanted to get out of there as fast as possible.

'Now let's pray that that awful guy isn't outside the door.'

Judita looked around. 'Take his weapon.'

'If his weapon disappears it really will look suspicious.'

'All right, don't take it then.' Judita carefully examined the dead man. 'But we'll need some come.'

'Come?'

'Semen. If they find him strangled like this, by his own hand, and there's no semen, it will look suspicious.'

Confused, Vincentas looked at Judita. She was unrecognizable.

'All of his come ran down my thighs,' she explained. It pained

Vincentas to hear her say that. He felt a distinct pang of jealousy in his breast. He suddenly understood what Judita wanted of him.

'No, I can't do that . . . I won't be able to.'

'You have to, my darling, my beloved. I'll help you.'

Vincentas understood the seriousness of the situation perfectly well, but that didn't help him. He could not become aroused. It had come full circle, it was just like at the start of the war, his masculine instincts had abandoned him, a cracking sound kept echoing in his head, there was the dead rabbi's head on the platter, the strangled officer on the sofa, Judita is trying to help him, should I undress, she asks, at first Vincentas doesn't understand what she's saying, he stares at her full round breasts, but all he can think about is that bastard from the ghetto security forces bragging about aiming for women's nipples so as to damage the breast as little as possible, so that the skin remained intact so that it could be used, pretty handbags made from it, and then Judita began stroking him with her hands, he sees all of it, and it seems to him that this is just an extension of the performance, that Judita will suddenly break out in laughter and will say that it's all a big joke, and the Artist will get up and will begin theorizing about little deaths and great orgasms.

When it was all over he went to the Artist's study and found what he was looking for – a stack of photographs – his own photographs. Some of them had been pinned to the wall, but most just lay on the table. Just in case, he looked through the drawers – masses of documents. He thought there might be some mention of him, but if any documents disappeared it would be even worse. There was also a weapon in one of the drawers. He could only take it under one set of circumstances – if he and Judita decided to shoot themselves.

'Why do you need all of that?' asked Judita when she saw the papers and the photographs.

'It's evidence.'

'What evidence?'

'It proves that I had business with him.'

Vincentas passed her the photographs of the elderly people sitting in the back of the truck.

'These are your photographs?'

'I'm a photographer. There are photographs and film here, so I could be a suspect.'

'There won't be any investigation. Plenty of intellectuals have choked themselves that way.'

'But what if there is?'

'Then we're really done for.' Then she grinned. 'If you were Jewish we could hide you in the ghetto.'

Vincentas looked Judita in the eyes with hesitation. 'Yes, they are my photographs.'

THE LETTER

It is cold and damp in the room. Yesterday a long, emaciated rat crawled out from under the floorboards. Do you remember how I kept asking you to close up that hole in the floor, but you never had time? She looked at me so pitifully that I soon began to wonder which of us was more human – the haggard rat or me.

Do you remember how I once said that photo negatives are like unborn children? You asked if I wanted children. What did I reply? Well, something about how it's a horrible time for having children, that only the mad could do that.

I don't know where to start . . . It was a warm day yesterday. I opened the window. A light wind was blowing and the frame creaked. I only had one cigarette left – maybe that was a good thing since I don't want to smoke any more. When I found out . . . I suddenly felt very lonely. Even when we're together I still feel lonely.

I try to go out into the street as little as possible – people are being hunted in restaurants, movie theatres, cafés, work permits are being checked, those without them are rounded up on to trucks, they're taken to collection points and the next day are transported to Germany to work in factories. I can't take such risks any longer. Now that it's no longer just me I don't want to.

Your mother once said – she was very drunk as usual – suddenly, out of the blue she said, 'I like fish. I like fish. They're the only ones with any decency. They don't gossip for no reason. All the other animals make a noise – they growl, bark, roar, squeak and come out with all sorts of nonsense, but fish are quiet.'

The funniest thing is that she herself never shuts up.

It's looking at me again, the rat. Maybe it can smell the remnants of food on my mouth. The smell. The smell of life. Or maybe something else.

I remember the last time I was by the sea. The summer that we met. Aleksandras did not go, he never had time, he was always listening to music in his head, I would say to him that one day I would find a little knob on his head, would turn it and music would start blaring out of his ears.

I was there with Nataša – we worked together at the translation bureau. I'm not a very good swimmer, and the waves were so big. Nataša shouted, 'They're as tall as horses,' and they really were like great steeds with arched necks coming towards us, then they would rear up, their heads pouring cold water over us. The Baltic is cold even on a hot summer day. At first it was frightening, but then a strange elation came over me, and I felt like I was a huge, two-legged fish, but one that screams and shouts.

Do you remember when you came to see us for the first time? I was sitting in the kitchen . . . That was the first time we saw each other. No, it wasn't by chance. I had bared myself on purpose. I wanted to enjoy your confusion. And it really was fun. You blushed so deeply, you were so confused, you couldn't get a single word out. I almost exploded with laughter, barely controlled myself. Your timidity was so childlike, like a little boy's, so innocent . . . You said that you had been with a woman before, but I'm not sure . . . I'm not talking about sex, but about a woman, about love. You had never loved until you met me. And I had never loved until I lost you.

I can hear her again. She's playing the piano and singing. I'm sure she has already drunk half a bottle. Her voice is sober enough, but her fingers sometimes miss the keys. If circumstances were different I think we'd get on pretty well. Now, whenever I speak to her I feel indebted. I do not like to feel indebted. After all, it's you I love, you I share everything with. I don't want to share it with anyone else, I cannot, there would simply not be enough of me.

I do not know what else to say. I had intended to say something important, but it seems as though everything that is important is unsayable. Because when you say it, it feels that maybe it's not that important after all, that there are more important things. I'm not good at writing farewell letters. Does such a profession exist? Farewell-letter writer?

I wanted to go back to Aleksandras. I'm his wife. To go back to certain death. But when I realized I was pregnant it changed everything. Aleksandras could not have children. An empty score, as he himself used to say. At first we thought that I was barren. We saw several doctors, but in the end a French professor, Julien Robbe-Grillet, confirmed that it was Aleksandras who was infertile.

I wanted to curse you, to curse this greedy, bloodthirsty little nation that worships God and suffering, but I changed my mind. I don't believe in curses; I believe in punishment and memory. You will never see your child. And if you survive you will always remember that. Always.

You once said that there are similarities between Christ and photographers – you only observe people, but you cannot change them, you cannot help them. Rats also observe. They wait for a crumb to fall so they can grab it. But we are not rats, we are not idols decorating temple walls, we are people. We have to make choices; we have to answer for our actions. No one else, just us.

How are you any better than a monster who rapes a woman while looking at a severed head? You watched as thousands of people died – not only watched, you recorded it; you did it to give someone pleasure. And you would return to rape a woman, still savouring the images of the dying in your head. Yes, it was rape, because a deceitful love is a greater violence than an open crime. It's as though I had been making love with a rat that had temporarily taken the shape of a man. War tears off all masks.

Don't look for me. I never want to see you again, even if it breaks my heart. I can't, not any more.'

That's all. Nothing more. Just a letter.

CHRISTMAS

Christmas was approaching. The first Christmas of the war, the feast of the baby Jesus. Only a madman like Christ could have chosen to be born at such an awful time.

Vincentas was sitting in the studio. Beyond the window it was dark; he could see the occasional shadows of passers-by. Again that same feeling, that state he had sometimes been in last summer when walking along a country road by a pit full of the executed – as though he were stuck in a cave, as though he could see only shadows, as though he had become a shadow himself. Everything had changed so quickly after Judita left; life stopped. He read her letter a thousand times but found nothing, not the slightest hint that she might return. He tried unsuccessfully to find her. She was not in the ghetto. And Aleksandras was no longer in the ghetto either.

Vincentas felt pain – the pain of loss, separation, even of betrayal. But at the same time this pain provided some relief. Scenes from that night would appear before him, and the feeling of hopelessness would leave him gasping for breath. But more and more he felt pain combined with relief: maybe it's better that Judita is not here with him, maybe it's better that he doesn't have to look at her, doesn't have to caress her, kiss her, maybe it's better . . .

He stood up, went to the gramophone and looked through the records. He felt like listening to some French music.

Again someone appeared outside the window, but this time lingered. They stopped and looked inside. A 'stone guest', he thought, and a moment later he heard knocking at the door.

'It's open!' Vincentas shouted and continued to sit facing the gramophone, his back to the door. Whoever it was, he was not expecting anyone except Judita. But she'll never come back. He no longer entertained the slightest hope that she would.

'So, you're still taking pictures,' he heard a familiar voice say. Vincentas turned around. It was Simonas, the same one that the men of the brigade had called Petras.

'Yes,' replied Vincentas, 'I still am.'

The time before they had sent Tadas; this time they sent Simonas Petras, thought Vincentas. I wonder if he'll shoot me on the spot or perhaps take me behind the house first.

Simonas, whom they called Petras, stuck his hand under his coat and searched for a long time. He was looking for a pistol, it couldn't be a very big weapon. Finally he pulled out a sheet of paper. It looked like the sheet had been crumpled, then smoothed out and carefully folded.

'You know German – translate it for me.'

Vincentas took the sheet and quickly scanned it. 'Do you want me to translate it and write it down?'

'No, read it out right now. If you have time, of course,' said Simonas, who was called Petras, glancing around the empty workshop.

'Sure,' said Vincentas and began reading aloud. '"To the General Commissar in Minsk. Regarding the Jewish operation. On 27 October, at approximately 8 a.m., a senior police battalion lieutenant arrived from Kaunas (Lithuania) and presented himself as the aide of the security police battalion commander. The first lieutenant stated that the police battalion had been issued the order to liquidate all the Jews here in the town of Slutsk within two days. He further explained that the battalion commander would be arriving with a battalion of four companies, two of them consisting of Lithuanian partisans, and that the operation must begin without delay. I replied to the first lieutenant that I ought first to discuss the operation with the commander. Approximately thirty minutes later the police battalion appeared in Slutsk. Further to my request, as soon as the commander arrived we exchanged opinions. First of all I explained to the battalion commander that it would not be possible to implement the operation without preparation, as our troops had all been sent out on work duty and it would cause serious disruption. It was his responsibility to give me one day's notice. Therefore I requested that the operation be delayed for one day –"'

'Christ, those Germans are so picky!' said Simonas Petras, frowning.

'Maybe that's enough?' asked Vincentas.

'No, no, read.'

Vincentas continued. '"Therefore I requested that the operation be delayed for one day. He rejected this, noting that he had to execute operations everywhere, in all towns, and that only two days had been designated for Slutsk. Over those two days the town of Slutsk had to be completely cleansed of Jews. I immediately protested, pointing out that the liquidation of Jews should not be executed in a random manner. A large number of the Jews remaining in the city consisted of craftsmen or craftsmen's families. It would be impossible to manage without these Jewish craftsmen as they were essential to production. I went on to say that there were practically no Belarusian craftsmen, and that the liquidation of all Jews would force all essential factories to halt operations immediately. At the end of our conversation I also mentioned that all essential craftsmen and specialists have documents and cannot be removed from factories. And that, further, we had agreed that all the Jews in the city, and in particular craftsmen's families, must first be moved to a ghetto for reallocation. This distribution was to have been carried out by two members of my staff. The commander did not in any way counter my opinion, therefore I was firmly convinced that the operation would be executed in this manner. But within hours of beginning the operation considerable difficulties arose. I was forced to conclude that the commander was not acting in accordance with our agreement. Despite our agreement, all the Jews were removed from the factories and workshops and were rounded up and driven away. In truth, some of the Jews were transported through the ghetto, where I was able to locate and distribute a considerable number of them, but the vast majority of them were put straight on to lorries and, without any delay, liquidated on the outskirts of the town. Immediately after midday complaints began to pour in because the removal of all the Jewish craftsmen meant the factories could no longer operate. Because the commander was not there but in Baranovich, after a lengthy search I contacted the captain under him and demanded that the operation be halted immediately because it was being executed without following my instructions, and the economic damage done up to that point was already irreversible. The captain was quite surprised to hear me express this opinion and said that he had received an order from the commander to cleanse the entire town of Jews without exception, as they had done in other towns. This cleansing had to be carried out for political reasons, and to date economic factors had not played any role anywhere else. Nevertheless, because of my insistent demands the operation was halted by evening.

'"As for the way this operation was executed, I am sorry to say that it approached sadism. During the operation the town was a scene of horror. German police officers and, notably, the Lithuanian partisans, were extremely cruel in the ways they drove Jews as well as Belarusians from their homes and crowded them into one location. Shots rang out all over the town, and some streets were simply filled with piles of Jewish corpses –"'

'Remember how I almost shot you at the beginning of the war?' Simonas Petras asked, once again interrupting Vincentas.

'Do I keep reading?'

'I could have shot you, and that would have been that . . . And now you're taking pictures of me . . .' He smiled. 'No, that's enough. Jokūbas the Elder got so upset when he read that text. I don't understand.'

'Where did you get it?'

'What's it to you?'

'It's stamped "Secret".'

'Well then, if it says that keep your trap shut,' Simonas Petras replied sternly. 'I don't get the Germans – we do a good job for them, and they complain. The two-faced idiots.'

Simonas Petras fell silent for a moment. 'You wouldn't believe what it was like, what some of our boys who escorted a group of Russian POWs described. A guard shoots a horse, and they all fall on it and eat it raw, innards and all. Some die and others survive, but later they all still die from the cold. You know, it was fifteen or seventeen below, they lead them along a road while waiting for the lorries to come. As they wait for the transportation to arrive many of the prisoners freeze to death, and the ones who are still alive strip the dead ones naked, but some are still dying, and they crawl towards the bonfires, fall into the flames and burn. Our boys then shoot all the ones who are dying or trying to escape, apparently about a hundred Russians in all.'

Simonas, whom they called Petras, was in a good mood. He was treating Vincentas like a good friend even though they had only seen each other a few times, and not always under the most pleasant circumstances.

'Remember Tadas?'

'Yes.' Vincentas nodded, and he felt an unpleasant chill in his breast.

'There you go.' Simonas Petras cleared his throat. 'We were on our way to an operation to catch some partisans. There were German and Latvian squads with us. We surrounded two neighbouring villages; the officers ordered us to shoot anyone who showed the slightest resistance – they were all partisans, paratroopers from Moscow, and if not, they would be locals harbouring Soviet partisans.

'The shooting started in the north. There was a really loud hammering from the Latvians' MG 34s. Our guys were mostly armed with MP 40s. That's a good thing. Better than a Mauser carbine. The partisans retreated in all directions, and we met them with a wall of fire. Because they were caught by surprise the resistance died down pretty fast and the armed partisans pretty much disappeared, all that was left were innocent, peaceful residents. Peaceful and innocent,' repeated Simonas Petras and fell silent. 'Are you going to photograph me or what?' he asked after a pause.

'I'm ready. Don't move,' said Vincentas, and he stuck his head under the cover, pressed. Click. A guillotine that chops a person in half, leaving one half in the light and the other in the darkness.

'Once we'd taken the villages there wasn't a moment's rest – we got the order to round up all the men, though it became clear later that women and children were rounded up, too,' Simonas, who was called Petras, continued. 'We drove most of them into a bakery storehouse, the rest into a wooden barn. A Latvian officer ordered that the women and children be herded into the storehouse, and then that the soldiers pack all the windows with as thick a layer of dry straw as possible. A regular soldier, not one of us, was already holding a bundle of burning straw, but at the last second there was an order to let all the women and children go. The soldiers were cursing because they had done all that work for nothing. "Never mind, we'll bake some bread out of even better dough," Tadas joked. But no one had given the order to set fire to the bakery storehouse. A German staff sergeant ordered that a machine-gunner on a motorcycle be stationed a bit further off in case any of the prisoners tried to get away. They he ordered that the Bolsheviks be brought up from the basement four at a time, and the staff sergeant shot them himself by the bakery wall. We threw the dead bodies back into the basement. About fifty men. Which of them were partisans, which were villagers, nobody asked. "They'll be classified up there," said Jokūbas the Elder, pointing up to Heaven. You know how he likes to use heavy phrases.'

Oh yes, thought Vincentas, his words were heavy, his work even heavier.

'We were already thinking about taking a break, but then, suddenly, all the vehicles were started up and a non-stop honking started. "Let's go and see what's happening," said Jokūbas the Elder. We took our weapons and went over to the barn. When we got there it was already in flames. You could hear the screams even through the honking. All the Germans standing around the barn lifted their weapons and started shooting in every direction. I didn't know if I should stay and shoot or go to try to find a drink. And then, listen to what happened next.' Simonas Petras became more serious, fell silent for a moment and cleared his throat. 'What a viper! A real viper. This woman came out of the closest cottage, a bit of a looker, big chest – you know those Russian women – and she was carrying a basket of eggs. She walked up to a small group of soldiers and a couple of German officers, and our Tadas was standing the closest to her. And then suddenly – that bloody woman's eggs exploded!'

Simonas, who was called Petras, fell silent. 'The sergeant was just injured, but Tadas was killed. He got some shrapnel through the eye.'

Simonas Petras pulled a silver chain with a small jewel from his pocket.

'So this is what's left of Tadas. He had this little chain around his neck. Not a cross, but this little piece of crap.' Simonas Petras held up the chain, let it swing in the air and then put it back in his pocket.

Vincentas remembered Juozapas. 'At the end someone hammers down the points of the nails,' he said.

'What nails?' asked Simonas Petras.

'Even the ones that no one can see.'

Simonas Petras did not like Vincentas's words. He made a face, took a step towards Vincentas and, barely taking a swing, whacked him around the ear. Vincentas's mouth dropped in surprise. Simonas Petras stood there with clenched fists and looked at him angrily.

'And what are you going to do to me?' Vincentas finally asked. 'What?' He pressed his hand against his hurt ear – it was bleeding.

'Nothing,' he replied. 'Nothing.'

ESCAPE

He wanted to die. Sitting there injured by the lake he felt weak, helpless and useless, he wanted to end it all because he saw no point in going on. But then, from somewhere very deep, from the darkest corner of his unconscious, came the realization that the only reason for which it was worth living and suffering was his son. He didn't care any more what future generations might think of him; he didn't know those generations and never will. The most painful thing was that he would probably never know his son either.

Although Judita had written in her farewell letter that he must not look for her, he had tried. The more so because one day he had found a small piece of paper wedged between the door and the door jamb of Juozapas's workshop. There were only two words on it: 'A son'. Why had she done that? To torment Vincentas, to hurt him? Or maybe she still loved him and wanted Vincentas to know that their short, unlucky love had borne a wonderful fruit – a son.

And a strange desire awoke and grew and spread inside him – the desire to explain to his son who his father was, who *he* was. To justify himself. To apologize. This simple, even banal thought, this desire saved his life. He began to resist death, and death withdrew a little. Sometimes he felt its presence, sometimes he even imagined it standing in a corner, but in its hand it held not a traditional scythe but a seven-tined harpoon. When he felt better he thought about his life; he couldn't blame the way he had behaved on the times he had lived through. To him it was as colourless as developing fluid.

His mother did not want to flee. Who in Germany would want an old whore? she asked Vincentas ironically when he suggested that they leave the country together. On the last night they sat together in silence, drank some alcohol mixed with cranberry juice, and he asked his mother to take care of Judita if she should ever turn up – when the Reds come, when the Reds come back.

He had managed to get a permit from the now-defunct general commissariat and had bought a ticket as far as Vienna with no trouble. At the border his permit did not raise any suspicions with the border guard either, then Tilžė, Königsberg, where he had a long wait for the train to Berlin – the military were allowed through first – then Elbing, Berlin . . . He decided to get off in Berlin. He had seen it only in photographs, had read things in books and newspapers, and the city enchanted him immediately – *Friedrichstrasse, Hallesches Tor, Museuminseln, Alexanderplatz*, he muttered the names under his breath, and it all seemed like a childhood dream or memory, although he knew that he had never been here, and he spent a whole day riding the metro in every direction, enjoying the rhythm of metropolis, which is best felt underground. Sometimes he felt as though he were a photograph, as though he were an image captured and fixed on film, a negative that rises from the catacombs up to the light, revealing the light contained in him. No matter how many times he came up to the surface, there was still no more light in his eyes, but here were Berliners taking the metro, people who looked as though the war had never happened – all well turned out, shoes polished to a shine, and then for a while he did small carpentry jobs, and worked as a mechanic at a factory in Spandau, and when the Russians got closer to the city he and other refugees retreated further south.

Wandering among the ruins that Germany was gradually becoming, he felt his personal circumstances mirrored what he saw around him – his life, too, was in ruins, and when he tried to imagine what he might say to his grown son all sorts of complications arose.

He imagined a measured conversation between two grown men ... Love is real madness, he would tell him, a disease, an obsession, like being poisoned. And when you recover you can't understand how you could have behaved that way, thought – or rather not thought – that way. Love is like war. In both love and war you can act as though you've lost your mind. You have to be mad to be able to kill your fellow creature. Of course, war causes death, love brings life.

And yet, when I think about Judita, about your mother, he says to the son he imagines, a feeling of bliss comes over me. Of intoxication. I think about her; I think about her, and I don't want to stop, I don't want the bliss to end. It's a strange feeling – as if when I lived with her, back then, when we were together, it's as though I wasn't living but just waiting. And now, when she's no longer here, when I may never see her again, I have started to live. With her. I remember her much better, feel her more deeply, know her in the finest detail, very differently from when we were together. I still love her, I still lose my mind when I look at photographs of her.

Thankfully he had managed to save some photographs of Judita. Not all of them, but a few. He pored over them constantly, every day; it was like praying, a ritual for him. And every time he looked at those photographs it was as if he understood just how beautiful she was for the first time, how amazing her body was and now that a few years had passed he couldn't quite remember if he had always understood that, if he had always told her that she was beautiful, that she was the most wonderful woman on earth. There she is, leaning her full head of blonde hair on her arm, her other arm resting on her curved hip, she isn't looking into the camera but just above – there was a small window there, light fell through it, just like here. Only Judita is not here.

Among the photographs of her he found a scrap of newspaper. The negatives, which he had not looked at since the war, were wrapped in it. It was old.

Lithuanian brothers and sisters!
The fateful hour of the final reckoning with the Jews has arrived.
Lithuania must be liberated not only from Asiatic Bolshevik oppression but from Jewry's long-standing yoke.

Where are you now, my liberated brothers and sisters, you miserable refugees, now that you have been freed from your homeland?

He keeps losing his train of thought. It breaks like a strip of film. Some frames are exposed, in others there are white spots, he doesn't even know if they were good shots or if he had just been shooting randomly. Sometimes the image yields only after several tries. It is as if he were not looking through his own eyes but through someone else's, or – even more strangely – through a rangefinder, through a lens. He looks at that image through the lens and senses that it is there but just can't find its contours, can't grasp its essence. Then suddenly it reveals itself, all by itself. Then other times it happens on the first attempt. Exactly as it should be. Like the image was waiting to be found, to be extracted from reality. Then he walks through that same place, in his thoughts, and there is nothing left; it has disappeared, melted away. Everything seems to be the same, but all the objects and shapes are nailed down where they belong, like they are decorations. But when the revelation occurs everything looks as though it has just been created – it hovers in the air, rises barely a few millimetres above the ground, like a soul trying to liberate itself from the confines of its corporeal prison.

More and more the world seemed like a giant darkroom to him, with people's lives pegged to a string to dry – or, more accurately, reflections of their lives, shed skins, copies that no longer had anything to do with the original.

I would like to talk to you, he would say to his imaginary son, nothing more, just exchange a few idle words. Do some of those silly little things that fathers do with sons. Go fishing, take some photographs, talk about girls, first kisses and the final colours of a sunset. Ride bicycles towards the horizon. Ride and never stop.

But still he was tormented by another unpleasant thought – what if it was all a big joke? A note about a son? Judita's big joke? But a joke would be too light a punishment. Another thought crept along after that, a much darker, crueller one: what if the son did exist, but the father was not Vincentas but the Artist, that poet of severed heads? This was unbearable, but it was with this thought that the conversations with his imaginary son usually ended.

PAINTINGS

Vincentas's doctor – although in his thoughts he called him 'the butcher' – was not in any way a dilettante. He talked about having treated wounded German soldiers during the war, he claimed to have seen everything. He had been ready to give his life defending his country, but in 1944, as the front approached, he realized he was not made for heroism. He described to Vincentas a scene he had witnessed that definitively convinced him that he was not cut out to be a soldier. A young Lithuanian captain put a couple of sandwiches in his pocket, a loaded pistol and two turnips, kissed his wife goodbye and calmly walked off down the road – as if he were not going to war but was simply on his way to work. I understood then, said the doctor, that I wouldn't be able to show the same courage, and I decided to flee.

One way or another, whether it was the doctor's qualifications and experience or Vincentas's survival instinct that saved him, he slowly began to recover. He regained a ravenous appetite and the desire to know what was happening outside the walls, what was happening in the camp. Strange things were going on in the refugees' world: they were all dancing, singing, publishing newspapers and books, staging plays and talking about how they had escaped from their homeland and how they would return to it. Some were enraptured with the idea of the exile's fate, others by visions of return. Almost no one lived in the here and now – except for the dead and the sick. When Vincentas's doctor offered to take him to the French zone he was surprised but elated. The doctor said he had some friends there, a family; the wife has an administrative job and the husband is a teacher. There's a lot of culture in the French zone; they're always putting on plays and having films brought in.

'In southern Germany, where the French are in charge, they make sure that the soldiers are exposed to culture; they screen French art films in the soldiers' cinemas, they bring in concerts and plays from Paris,' the doctor told Vincentas. 'Your body has recovered sufficiently – now your soul needs to be healed.'

Vincentas smiled, for the first time in a long time. If he still had a soul it probably looked like an insect. Like an insect that's been crushed by a soldier's boot.

'There,' said the doctor, pleased. 'That's the first sign that things are improving.'

Vincentas did not try to argue any longer, but he was quite sure that after this war his shares in a soul, faith and God had fallen drastically. The Son of God may have risen, but mankind had not.

They took the train. Permits were required to cross between the American and French zones, but the two men did not have any. They travelled to the last possible station, then got off and started walking through the fields.

'You know, of all the stories you have told me there are a few that require more detailed explanation.'

'In other words – they sound like fabrications?'

'Well, I wouldn't be quite so specific, but still . . .'

'For example?'

'Well, the woman sitting in the kitchen, naked to the waist.'

'Why is that odd?'

'Well, I don't know. It doesn't seem to me like something that normally happens – you enter a kitchen and a half-naked woman is sitting there. It's not usual.'

'Doctor, I can't prove anything, anything. The only thing that's certain is that Judita was not an ordinary woman. She was an *extra*-ordinary and unusual woman.'

Vincentas was lying, he could have proved it. He had Judita's letter, but he didn't want to show it to the doctor.

'That's your emotions talking, not reason.'

'To hell with reason.'

'All right. Let's say she was an unusual woman. But the story about the SS officer . . . it, too, raises some questions.'

'Yes, that's an unbelievable story. And I am certainly not happy that it happened to me.'

'I have the impression that he in some way fascinated you, that officer. Would that be true?'

'Really? I would say more that he frightened me. But I don't know. He, too, was an orphan of sorts – he also grew up without a father.'

'And it's also hard to believe that there was no retribution after an SS officer died in such a mysterious way.'

'What do you mean?'

'They would have burned half the town for something like that.'

'Didn't they burn enough towns?' mumbled Vincentas.

Yes, the doctor was right, but how could Vincentas have calmly described that he had watched that animal rape his beloved – that he had just stood there and done nothing? Who would gain anything from that? Both the executioner and his victim know the real truth, but the witness, the viewer, he only receives an impression of the truth. It doesn't matter whether that impression is strong or weak.

One way or another it will fade, will become a dim and distant memory, but the victim and the executioner will never forget the truth. And that is what is most important.

So it may as well just go on like this.

After that awful night he was no longer required to attend any more operations, maybe because all the Jews in the countryside had already been killed, or maybe for other reasons that were unknown to him. He waited, for many days and nights he waited, for someone to knock on his door – for that fateful knocking. Simonas Petras had split open his ear, but that was unrelated. Vincentas no longer had to be killed. He was already dead.

'War is like a scalpel – it exposes man's rotten innards pitilessly, with a single cut. And, unfortunately, there is no way to fix him,' said the doctor.

Is it possible to heal a dead man? Vincentas wanted to ask. Even our God hangs dead on the cross. Judita, seeing how cruelly and disrespectfully Lithuanians were treating Jews, had once said to him, 'What can be expected from a nation that worships suffering and death?' But he remained silent. It would change nothing. Nothing in this world had changed for a long time, apart from the man guarding the cemetery.

It suddenly became cooler; it began to rain. Vincentas and the doctor continued, all the while trying to find some shelter, from bush to bush, from one grove to another, but sometimes, when there was no shelter, they walked with their heads lowered and hunched over so as to be as inconspicuous as possible.

'We look like criminals,' said the doctor. 'But what is our crime?'

'Some things have to be done in the dark, doctor, some things cannot tolerate light,' Vincentas replied.

'What are you talking about?'

'About photography.'

The doctor laughed. 'I'll bear that in mind.'

They came across a huge puddle in the road and skirted it, then suddenly heard a commotion beyond the bushes.

They froze.

'Well, here we are,' whispered the doctor. 'A patrol.'

'Shhh,' Vincentas silenced him.

The voices beyond the bushes became louder. It seemed an entire squad was approaching them.

At first Vincentas thought they should run. He looked around. The soldiers were quite short, wearing winter uniforms much too early in the season, and when they saw the two crouching men beyond the bushes they began to bleat.

'Bloody hell – sheep,' the doctor laughed, relieved. 'It's just some bloody sheep!'

'If there are sheep, there will be shepherds near by,' Vincentas warned him.

The doctor looked at him curiously, seemingly surprised by this new ironic tone in Vincentas's voice.

The two men slowly moved ahead, now surrounded by a flock of sheep.

'We're like wolves in sheep's clothing,' said the doctor.

They approached a cluster of buildings that stood at some distance from the road. The doctor went up to one of them and whistled gently then began to wave at Vincentas to move away. The letters were big and the sign could be made out from some way away: 'Gendarmerie Française'.

Without looking around the doctor quickly ran back to Vincentas. 'If they look out of the window our journey will end right here,' he said.

Then they heard the sharp creak of a door. There was nothing left for them to do but pretend to be shepherds and go to tend to one of the sheep that had strayed from the rest of the flock. The gendarme said nothing, the door creaked again and thudded softly as he closed it.

'So that's what that saying means – one lost sheep can be more important than the whole flock,' said the doctor, sighing with relief when the danger had passed.

Now on the French side, they had to wait quite some time for a train. By evening, chilled to the bone but still good-humoured, they finally reached Reutlingen.

The doctor's friends were very nice people. The husband was a teacher and the wife a translator working for the local administration, so they received regular salaries and lived in an apartment furnished with real furniture – a sofa, armchairs, sideboard and dining-table – not the kind found in the camps. Everything was real, and it almost felt like life before the war. Almost like life.

The woman, Sofija, was tall and thin, her uniform suited her very well, and she clearly knew it: as she passed the tall, almost-ceiling-height mirror she always stopped and critically, but not without satisfaction, looked herself over from head to toe, then, after the guests had eaten their macaroni with stewed preserved meat and were enjoying American cigarettes, she again stood before the mirror, trying on a hat.

When their hosts went into the kitchen, the doctor leaned towards Vincentas and whispered, 'If she glues herself to that damned mirror one more time I'll stand right there next to her and try on that hat, too.'

Vincentas merely smiled. He was not at all bothered by a woman wanting to be a woman, by a human being wanting to be a human being no matter what was happening around them.

The next day she walked with them as far as her workplace, showing them the town along the way. Then she suggested they go to a concert – one of the Bach concertos was going to be performed in a nearby Lutheran church. She and her husband would join them in the evening.

As soon as he saw the musicians Vincentas felt sick. He was overcome by a heavy mood, or maybe the disturbing feeling that he might know one of the musicians. Aleksandras – every man with a musical instrument reminded him of Aleksandras. He mumbled an apology to the doctor and went outside. At first he thought of waiting until the concert had ended but then decided to go for a walk around the town.

In his meanderings he noticed an enormous building that from the outside looked like a warehouse, which it may have been before the war, or maybe it had been a factory. Now all he could see was an empty space, but a great many paintings had been hung on the walls. Part of the roof had been glassed, so there was plenty of natural light in the space. He asked a man in uniform what it all meant.

'It's a collection of paintings that was discovered recently, sir. The National Socialists wanted to send them all to South America, but they didn't manage it in time. While it's being decided what to do with the paintings the soldiers can enjoy them . . . as well as other people,' he added after a pause. Other people – that is, people without a place, refugees.

There weren't many people viewing the exhibition, so Vincentas could look at the paintings without interruption. French, Italian, Dutch painters, then he caught himself looking around for something, something frightening and familiar. The Artist's shadow. Here was a young woman with a severed head on a platter. Girolamo Romanino's *Salome with the Head of John the Baptist*, Bernardo Strozzi of Genoa's *Salome with John the Baptist's Severed Head*, her plump arms are so soft, her cheeks blushing, her young breasts are compressed but trying to escape, with her plump, gentle hands she gingerly holds a strand of hair from the hideous, severed head as if to make sure that the head is really dead and will no longer cry out or open its eyes when its hair is pulled. He stood there looking for a few minutes, as though waiting, as though knowing that something had to happen here. And the girl's hand moved ever so slightly, her cheeks became redder, and with a barely visible movement she pulled at the hair and the head opened its eyes and looked straight at Vincentas. He closed his eyes. When he opened them again the head was no longer looking at him. He was just tired. It was too stimulating, for the past month he had been battling death. It was just exhaustion. Then he started to imagine that he saw Judita, yes, the longer he looked at that unfamiliar Italian artist's painting the more clearly he saw that this was some kind of trick; the painting could not have been executed in the seventeenth century, as it said on the card; he went up to the uniformed man and asked when had this painting been painted, three hundred years ago, the man replied, but it seemed to him that he detected something like a smile on the man's face, Vincentas looked around, all the visitors walking along the walls were also smiling, they were not looking at the paintings, they were looking at him, and he finally understood that it was a trap, that Judita was hiding somewhere, she was laughing with the rest of them, she wanted to hurt him, make fun of him, he was overcome by the fear that he would be wrapped in a canvas and set on fire and would explode, lighting a path for the millions of souls that were circling above Europe, and, scared almost to death, he ran from the building and kept going for a long time until, exhausted, he reached the railway station.

THE EMPTY GRAVE

Vincentas could not remember how he ended up on a train returning to the camp. Why had the doctor left him? No, it was he who had left the church, leaving the doctor there. He did not want to listen to music. Aleksandras, a ghost. Then he had walked the city streets, stumbled into an industrial area, a warehouse, some paintings, yes, he had looked at paintings. The last thing – he could still see it before his eyes – a woman holding a large silver platter with a man's severed head on it. The exhibition. He had walked around the exhibition, then came to on the train. Had he and the doctor agreed to meet on the train? Either way, in front of him sat not the doctor but an unfamiliar middle-aged man with a hat pulled down over his eyes. He ignored the other passengers – the soldiers, the refugees – but he could not stop looking at this man.

'Now, that little church that we passed is the Church of St Denis. St Denis', the stranger told him, 'was the first bishop of Paris. He was beheaded on the Hill of Martyrs, where Montmartre is now, which, in fact, means "Hill of Martyrs". After he died his body stood up, picked up his head and walked away. That's right, carrying his head, his body walked for several kilometres, to a village outside Paris, and there it lay down and rested – indicating that here was where he wanted to be buried. The paradox is that the Roman

Dionysius was not at all holy. If they had wanted to disgrace and punish him, it's certainly not his head that should have been cut off.'

The man lifted his hat slightly, and Vincentas had a chance to get a better look at his face. There was only person it could be, the only person Vincentas never wanted to see again, but it was him, Jokūbas the Elder. He was considerably changed: he was dressed like a farmer, a prominent scar on his cheek ran into his dark, thick beard; his hair was also quite long, almost to his shoulders and covering his ears.

'Why are you telling me this?' asked Vincentas. 'What are you doing here? Are you following me?'

'People like stories, people are happy to listen to stories, it's just that history never listens to man. But you're attracted to severed heads, no?' And Jokūbas the Elder winked at him. 'I saw you by the paintings. That's what I thought – the Photographer, only he could stand there for an hour staring at a severed head. Let's go and have a smoke.'

The two men went out into the corridor of the carriage.

'The Russian has come back to Lithuania,' said Jokūbas the Elder, lighting a cigarette for himself and giving one to Vincentas. 'It wasn't supposed to happen that way. They betrayed us. They tempted us and then betrayed us, dumped us like a pregnant girl, the bastards – and everything was going so well, so neatly; we had almost wiped that garbage off the face of the earth. Our goal was noble. We wanted to free the world of Jewish communism, and now look where we are – now I have to hide like a cornered wolf, run from my homeland. I can't even be myself.'

Jokūbas the Elder opened the carriage doors. He stuck his head outside. The train was slowing down – evidently they were approaching a station. It almost stopped, hesitated, then slowly picked up speed again.

'This war revealed an interesting thing about the Lithuanian, a nasty aspect of his character: if you're doing well a Lithuanian will be your friend, but as soon as you're in any kind of trouble he'll turn away from you just like that. Better a communist or a fascist – you always know that you're looking at an enemy, and that enemy tells you straight that he wants to kill you. The Lithuanian wants to stab you in the back. Don't be lukewarm, or, as it is said, "I will spit you out". It's those lukewarm ones – they're the worst.'

Vincentas struggled to swallow. Jokūbas the Elder was probably referring to him, too. After all, he was neither hot nor cold. He was lukewarm; he was an observer.

'It's cold,' said Vincentas to Jokūbas the Elder. 'Let's go inside.'

Jokūbas the Elder said nothing but grabbed him by the shoulder and tried to throw him out through the open carriage door. Vincentas barely had time to grab the handle. They struggled for a few moments, Jokūbas the Elder started smashing his hand, the thought flashed through his mind that if he let go now it would all be over very quickly – he'd break his neck, and that would be that. The train once again slowed down, and, with the last of his strength, Vincentas pulled the hand that was holding him towards him, grabbed Jokūbas the Elder by the hair and then let go of the handle.

They rolled down the embankment together. For a while Vincentas lay there, stunned from the impact of hitting the ground, then he tried to move his arms and legs – he didn't feel any pain. He lifted his head – Jokūbas the Elder was nowhere in sight. He couldn't have sunk into the earth. He was somewhere here, somewhere there – in the dusk, in the shadows, in the dark.

Vincentas stood up and started walking in the direction the

train was going. Soon he heard steps behind him – he was chasing Vincentas. He stopped and turned – Jokūbas the Elder was holding a knife. Vincentas tried to run, but he didn't have any strength. He turned around again – in the twilight it looked as though it was not Jokūbas the Elder following him but an unfamiliar man dressed like a bishop and holding a severed head in his hands. The head looked familiar – yes, it was the same head that he had taken to the Artist. He quickened his step, but the man following did not fall back at all – on the contrary, he was getting closer and closer. Vincentas ran through a wide, open meadow, someone flashed white before him and waved a small hand at him, a little boy in bloodied underclothes, a little boy in a meadow lit by the rising sun, lost between three pine trees, a little boy whose name Vincentas did not know and would never know, but when he got closer, the child began to recede, and, finally, when Vincentas was just a few steps away, he saw a small flock of sheep run off to one side, leaving a solitary lamb standing there, letting out its mournful cry.

Where the meadow ended Vincentas noticed a lone, crumbling building – it could have been a house or a stable, in the dusk he couldn't tell, but he ran towards it. The building had no roof, only bare walls. There was hardly any furniture apart from a few broken chairs; the owners or someone else must have removed everything. Vincentas quickly ran through the rooms – there was nothing there that he could use as a weapon. He realized that he had set his own trap and there was no way back. He heard someone coming up the front steps. Heavy, thumping steps, it was Pushkin's Commander rising from the grave, it was the rabbi carrying his severed head, coming to get him, no, it was Jokūbas the Elder, and he would not leave him there alive, he heard the steps on the other side of the wall, he would soon enter the room he was hiding in, and there was nowhere to hide within the room. With all his strength he pushed against the crumbling brick wall, and it shifted, then he pushed again and again, and the wall fell down, and a cry was heard on the other side. A cloud of dust rose, and when it had cleared he could see a man's leg sticking out from under the rubble and one arm thrown wide.

'Help, help me,' came a voice from under the pile of bricks, but Vincentas no longer had the strength to do anything, he sat down next to the pile and heavily, painfully drew some air into his lungs, like he had been holding his breath under water and had now suddenly come up to the surface and, for the first time in a long time, could breathe in real fresh air, air that was like light.

Jokūbas the Elder continued wheezing for a while, then slowly quietened, fell silent, and Vincentas took a closer look: no, there was no way he could get out from under the bricks.

Having caught his breath, Vincentas quickly placed a few more bricks on what was already a significant pile pressing down on Jokūbas the Elder, and then he withdrew.

The following day he went out for a walk. He was not at all surprised that his legs took him back to the building where he had buried Jokūbas the Elder. He circled the building several times, looking for any signs that might mean he should be cautious. Nothing suspicious. A building at the edge of a meadow by a narrow road.

He stepped inside and approached the pile of bricks carefully, as if worried that he might awaken the man lying beneath it, and then what confusion, what amazement overcame him when he saw that in the middle of the pile where Jokūbas the Elder had been buried there was now a gaping pit. The grave was empty. He began frantically moving bricks to the side but found nothing apart from a long cigarette butt. He left the building and sat down at the edge of the ruins – it looked like he'd gone. He'd disappeared, he'd left, he isn't here, and that's all there is to it.

He wasn't sure how long he sat like that among the ruins before two men in shining garments appeared. They kept coming closer. Vincentas knew he should do something, maybe simply get up and walk, but he did nothing. His body wouldn't obey. His thoughts, feelings, memories, everything that made up his personality suddenly disappeared, and all that remained was emptiness, an empty hole – dark, indiscernible, droning, pulling him deeper and deeper. And the men in shining garments were coming closer and closer.

That was how two British soldiers who had been passing by found him, sitting there. They asked him something, but he did not understand English.

'He was dead; he was buried here,' said Vincentas, pointing at the pile of bricks.

'He's saying that his friend died,' one of the soldiers explained to the other.

'Tell him the grave is empty, that he should not look for the living among the dead.'

AFTERWORD
by Tomas Vaiseta

The following fact is more important than the remainder of the text – and, in fact, more important than all the discussions that have taken place around this issue in Lithuania: between 1941 and 1944, under the occupying Nazi regime, roughly 196,000 of the Jews living in Lithuania – that is, 95 per cent of the Lithuanian Jewish population – were annihilated.

Although the Holocaust was conceived, initiated and organized by the Nazis, several thousand local inhabitants, mostly ethnic Lithuanians, were involved in implementing the mass killings. Lithuania was especially awash with blood in the summer and autumn of 1941, when, during a period of less than six months, 80 per cent of Lithuania's Jews were killed. In villages and small towns, homes became vacant in the blink of an eye – over a month, a week, a day. It would have been impossible not to see the tragedy that was taking place. They were led along main streets, held in temporary ghettos and then – in a manner different from how the Holocaust unfolded in Western Europe, where Jews were transported to concentration camps in Germany and Poland to be exterminated – they were executed close to their birthplaces, sometimes right in front of other local inhabitants. People living in larger cities such as Vilnius and Kaunas had a different experience; here the Jews were driven into long-term ghettos, and the massacres took place at some remove, so that urban non-Jews experienced the Holocaust not as the sudden, incomprehensible disappearance of specific faces but as a slow, strangely steady death-process that other residents could avoid witnessing directly.

It is impossible to know how these two experiences of the Holocaust are related, but it is significant that, in recent years, the question of memory and the Jewish Catastrophe in Lithuania has primarily been raised by authors originally from small towns. Born in the village of Obeliai, Sigitas Parulskis has described how, on a visit to the Imperial War Museum in London, he came across a diagram indicating the locations across Europe where Jews were exterminated during the Second World War and how he found the statistics for his own town – '1,160 Jews were killed there by the Nazis and local collaborators' – leading him to the realization that he had avoided and been afraid of acknowledging those facts his whole life.

What are the reasons for that forgetting, ignorance and avoidance on the part of the children and grandchildren raised by the inhabitants of those small towns – people who could not have been unaware that their neighbours had been driven from their homes and brutally murdered?

Throughout Europe, reflection on the Holocaust has been a complicated process; in each society it has taken place in a different way, uniquely, painfully and with unavoidable disputes and accusations. But, after the war, in the Soviet Union and the countries it occupied, including Lithuania, such reflection was generally impossible until the collapse of the Soviet regime in the late 1980s. With their strict control of public discourse and memory, the Soviets prohibited any differentiation and commemoration of the Jewish Catastrophe as the tragedy of a specific nation. The Jews, as a description and as a people, had to dissolve into the mass of Soviet citizens and the Holocaust itself become just one more of Hitler's crimes. As it worked on establishing an international Soviet people, the regime did not want to highlight the suffering of any individual group, perhaps in an effort to hide the fact that the tragedy of the Jews mattered to them only in terms of how it helped the USSR emphasize the 'evils of fascism' and its victory over it, no more than that. As a result, if the sites of executions of Jews that were scattered across occupied Lithuania were marked at all, it was only as places where 'Soviet citizens had fallen as a result of Hitler's crimes'.

During this era of enforced silence about the Holocaust, memories of the killings flickered in the minds of people who had witnessed them or were passed on in private conversations, often transformed into stereotypical and historically erroneous accounts along the lines of 'they say that Lithuanians participated in the killings as vengeance against the Jews for their role in the soviet-ization of Lithuania during the first Soviet occupation of 1939–40' or 'the Lithuanians have suffered so much themselves that they should not also have to think about the Jews' misfortunes'.

With the restoration of the country's independence in 1990, Lithuanian society had to begin unravelling the tightly wound skein of pain, guilt, shame, indifference, nightmares, stereotypes and lies around the memory of the Holocaust. But at first the newly restored Lithuanian state seemed to promote Holocaust remem-brance as if from a safe distance – in order to not disrupt fragile romantic national ideals nor to minimize the suffering of the hundreds of thousands of Lithuanians who were deported or killed by the Soviets. It is probably for that reason, as historian Hektoras Vitkus has noted, that the memory of the Holocaust was more often sanctified than critically examined in a way that would promote the analysis and debate of sensitive and uncomfortable questions. Whenever such questions arose, sparks would immediately begin to fly and the smell of burning would spread, along with the noxious fumes of conflict, blame, fear, complexes, conspiracies, anger and anti-Semitism. Keeping consideration of the Holocaust at a safe distance was a more convenient strategy, but the formality and cautiousness of this position prevented deeper discussions from reaching people and, more importantly, from helping Lithuanians understand the Holocaust as *their* tragedy – as the tragedy of Lithuania's Jews. Here again, distortions of memory were fuelled by forgetting, ignorance and witnesses' reluctance to tell their children and grandchildren what they had seen. If the topic arose, it could cause middle-aged men to blush like six-year-old boys.

For ten or fifteen years a small group of Lithuanian historians applied themselves to researching issues around the Holocaust, reconstructing events and examining awkward questions in order to attempt to explain how the killing of Jews was organized and implemented, how many Lithuanians were involved and why, thus countering the myths and stereotypes that were circulating in the country's collective memory. But society as a whole took little notice of the historians' efforts. Although their findings were incorporated into educational reforms and other initiatives contributing to the education of new generations, it would require a stronger, bolder and more effective impulse to disrupt Lithuanians' Holocaust memory. Although no single action, initiative or artefact would be able to do this single-handedly, if one had to identify a moment from which a distinctly new, deeper and more open – if not always consistently effective – rethinking of the Jewish Catastrophe began, it would have to be the publication of Sigitas Parulskis's *Tamsa ir partneriai* (*Darkness and Company*) in 2012.

Looking back, it now seems that only Parulskis could have done this, offered Lithuanian society a bold, even shocking novel about the events of the Holocaust in Lithuania, a novel that raises the key questions of why Lithuanians became involved in the killings and what their role was in that tragedy.

Parulskis arrived on the literary scene just as Lithuania regained independence, first as a poet and then very quickly also as a critic, social and political commentator, playwright and essayist. Solitary, overwhelmed by longing, communing with the dead and with death itself, rebellious, unpitying, presenting himself as an outsider, a stranger, and at the same time almost contradicting this image, he became a widely read, respected and influential author. The same themes kept recurring in his writing, and he developed a new, harsher, bleaker existentialism to suit the times: the solitude that lingers within all human relationships; a sometimes deeper, sometimes more vulgar psychological battle with a father; unquenchable, death-oriented desire; a complicated relationship with faith, with God; a very sceptical view of the Church as an institution but a sensitive aesthetic relationship with church architecture.

Parulskis's 2002 novel *Trys sekundės dangaus* (*Three Seconds of Heaven*), about the violence and harshness of everyday life in the Soviet army, is a distillation of all these motifs. At the time it seemed that, even though a new millennium had just begun, its best Lithuanian novel had already been written. Older generations were affected by the work's descriptions of the brutality, still vivid in their own memories, experienced by Soviet military conscripts. For his own generation, which Parulskis described as one that the great political changes left mistrustful, indifferent, lazy and lacking enthusiasm, the novel reflected them and their fate. But perhaps most important was an even younger generation, the youngest readers, who may not have known Parulskis the poet or critic. For them, the Soviet past was but a vague childhood memory and of little concern, but they discovered and identified with Parulskian existentialism. This connection enabled different generations of readers, regardless of age or experience, to recognize that Parulskis spoke for them all.

Darkness and Company appeared a decade later, and Parulskis is again addressing difficult themes. The central motifs of his writing are even sharper, but this time, during the Nazi occupation of 1940–4, Lithuanians are the executioners rather than the victims. Hoping to save his Jewish lover Judita, the protagonist Vincentas succumbs to the will of a Nazi officer and agrees to photograph the executions of Jews. Travelling with a brigade made up of Lithuanian Nazi henchmen, he remains a passive, lethargic observer who finds himself caught between the executioners and the victims, unable or unwilling to take a clearer position or any firm stand regarding responsibility or moral dilemmas. Taking photographs at once involves and detaches him – Vincentas only has a whiff of the death and horror, of the chill of the deepest darkness about him. As if the brutal executions of Jews and the dumping of their bodies into pits were not enough, as if doubting whether that would cause enough of a chill, the author pulls in all of his characteristic symbolism – biblical motifs, overwhelming desire, perverse scenes of sadism – so that the edge of the precipice of shock would be reached but not stepped over, so that the chill would numb.

Other Lithuanian writers had written about the Holocaust and

Lithuanian responsibility, but those works, in terms of time and atmosphere, in terms of their very language, were too distant from newly independent Lithuania's audiences and were therefore incapable of moving them. For the memory of the Holocaust, sanctified and as though preserved under a glass case, to reach readers, an author was needed who would dare to desanctify the Jewish Catastrophe and thus make it current and present to contemporary readers.

'I don't know how people can read this book. But I read it,' wrote one reviewer on a social-media site and gave *Darkness and Company* four stars. This accurately reflected most readers' feelings – the 'sex-and-God' formula (as one critic put it) against the background of the massacre of the Jews was hard for many to stomach, but from public reactions it is clear that this is partly what helped the novel achieve its goal of initiating a new examination of, as well as an individual and collective reckoning with, this great tragedy in our past. The provocative style, the theme of the Holocaust, the depiction of Lithuanians as passive observers or executioners also had to evoke the familiar smell of burning. The author's inbox was flooded with anti-Semitic emails, there were public and private laments that the novel would further diminish an already small and beleaguered nation, in anonymous comments and virtual discussions Parulskis was accused of betraying Lithuania and selling himself to the Jews, all of which suppressed the occasional more rational and well-founded discussions about the question of individual and collective responsibility, about the historical basis for the author's interpretation of the historical origins of the Holocaust, about identification of the Lithuanian nation with the murderers and the significance of murderers' national identities in general. But this only confirmed that in the early 2010s a new, deeper and more open reconsideration of the Jewish Catastrophe was just beginning in Lithuania. That 'just beginning' probably still applies today.

Darkness and Company caused passionate debates and discussions that can be seen as Lithuanian society learning to talk about the Holocaust, to shatter the glass case and discover how to speak when that protective cover is no longer there. The novel defiantly erased the safe distance Lithuania had maintained from the Holocaust and opened up an unfamiliar, and therefore risky, discourse. Parulskis understood this risk. In one meeting with readers he said that the path to memory, to the past, is like walking on thin ice, so we are scared to go there. Is that not why *Darkness and Company* has a feeling of numbing cold about it – so that this thin ice would grow thicker and that fear vanish?

Tomas Vaiseta
Department of History, Vilnius University
2018

KAI AARELEID
Burning Cities

Translated from the Estonian by Adam Cullen

978-0-7206-2029-0 / 320pp / £9.99

Kai Aareleid's lyrical novel *Burning Cities* is set in the southern Estonian city of Tartu. Destroyed during the war by the German and Soviet armies then slowly rebuilt, the city is home to many secrets, and little Tiina knows them all – even if she does not quite understand their import. The adult world is one of cryptic conversations and unspoken dread. From the death of Stalin to the inexorable collapse of her parents' marriage, Tiina experiences both domestic and great events from the periphery, ultimately finding herself powerless to prevent the defining tragedy in her own life.

The smells, colours and atmosphere of a given time and place always remain in a person's memory, and Aareleid, through Tiina's story, reminds us that revisiting old memories, while often painful, is essential. The past leaves an indelible imprint on the future, and Aareleid vividly shows how childhood recollections and the world of one's early life can follow a person for ever – and how every secret must be shared, if only once.

KRISTĪNE ULBERGA
The Green Crow

Translated from the Latvian by Žanete Vēvere Pasqualini

978-0-7206-2025-2 / 240pp / £9.99

The Green Crow follows two parallel narratives. The present-day strand describes the day-to-day life of the protagonist, a young woman in a psychiatric hospital, incarcerated because of her hallucinations – most significantly that of the Green Crow who has been her companion since childhood. The other strand comprises the stories the woman narrates to her carers – with a dark irony that has been compared with the writings of Michel Houellebecq; these tell her life story, and through them she slowly reveals how she has ended up in her present predicament.

The dreamy melancholy of the early part of the novel – the childhood memories, the hazy hospital surroundings – soon gives way to the difficulties and realities of the protagonist's coming of age and adulthood. After her parents separate, she drifts from one destructive relationship to another, seeking refuge in men and alcohol and slowly losing what is left of her already-tenuous connection with reality. Throughout all this the Green Crow becomes a part of her daily life, sometimes as a giant imaginary friend to soothe her pain and at others as a regular European roller, a bird known as a 'green crow' in Latvia, who appears at her window to offer solace.

PETER OWEN WORLD SERIES
SEASON 1: SLOVENIA

JELA KREČIČ
None Like Her
Translated by Olivia Hellewell
978-0-7206-1911-9 / 288pp / £9.99

Matjaž is fearful of losing his friends over his obsession with his ex-girlfriend. To prove that he has moved on from his relationship with her, he embarks on an odyssey of dates around Ljubljana, the capital of Slovenia. In this comic and romantic tale a chapter is devoted to each new encounter and adventure. The women he selects are wildly different from one another, and the interactions of the characters are perspicuously and memorably observed.

Their preoccupations – drawn with coruscating dialogue – will speak directly to Generation Y, and in Matjaž, the hero, Jela Krečič has created a well-observed crypto-misogynist of the twenty-first century whose behaviour she offers up for the reader's scrutiny.

EVALD FLISAR
Three Loves, One Death
Translated by David Limon
978-0-7206-1930-0 / 208pp / £9.99

A family move from the city to the Slovenian countryside. The plan is to restore and make habitable a large, dilapidated farmhouse. Then the relatives arrive. There's Cousin Vladimir, a former Partisan writing his memoirs, Uncle Vinko, an accountant who would like to raise the largest head of cabbage and appear in the *Guinness World Records*, Aunt Mara and her illegitimate daughter Elizabeta who's hell bent on making her first sexual encounter the 'event of the century'. And, finally, Uncle Švejk, the accidental hero of the war for independence, turns up out of the blue one Sunday afternoon . . .

Evald Flisar handles the absurd events that follow like no other writer, making the smallest incidents rich in meaning. The house, the family, their competing instincts and desires provide an unlikely vehicle for Flisar's commentary on the nature of social cohesion and freedom.

DUŠAN ŠAROTAR
Panorama
Translated by Rawley Grau
978-0-7206-1922-5 / 208pp / £9.99

Deftly blending fiction, history and journalism, Dušan Šarotar takes the reader on a deeply reflective yet kaleidoscopic journey from northern to southern Europe. In a manner reminiscent of W.G. Sebald, he supplements his engrossing narrative with photographs, which help to blur the lines between fiction and journalism. The writer's experience of landscape is bound up in a personal yet elusive search for self-discovery, as he and a diverse group of international fellow travellers relate in their distinctive and memorable voices their unique stories and common quest for somewhere they might call home.

PETER OWEN WORLD SERIES
SEASON 2: SPAIN

CRISTINA FERNÁNDEZ CUBAS
Nona's Room
Translated by Kathryn Phillips-Miles and Simon Deefholts
978-0-7206-1953-9 / 160pp / £9.99

A young girl envious of the attention given to her sister has a brutal awakening. A young woman facing eviction puts her trust in an old lady who invites her into her home. A mature woman checks into a hotel in Madrid and finds herself in a time warp . . . In this prize-winning new collection Cristina Fernández Cubas takes us through a glass darkly into a world where things are never quite what they seem, and lurking within each of these six suspenseful short stories is an unexpected surprise. *Nona's Room* is the latest offering from one of Spain's finest contemporary writers.

JULIO LLAMAZARES
Wolf Moon
Translated by Simon Deefholts and Kathryn Phillips-Miles
978-0-7206-1945-4 / 192pp / £9.99

Defeated by Franco's Nationalists, four Republican fugitives flee into the Cantabrian Mountains at the end of the Spanish Civil War. They are on the run, skirmishing with the Guardia Civil, knowing that surrender means death. Wounded and hungry, they are frequently drawn from the safety of the wilderness into the villages they once inhabited, not only risking their lives but those of sympathizers helping them. Faced with the lonely mountains, harsh winters and unforgiving summers, it is only a matter of time before they are hunted down. Llamazares's lyrical prose vividly animates the wilderness, making the Spanish landscape as much a witness to the brutal oppression of the period as the persecuted villagers and Republicans.

Published in 1985, *Wolf Moon* was the first novel that centred on the Spanish Maquis to be published in Spain after Franco's death in 1975.

JOSÉ OVEJERO
Inventing Love
Translated by Simon Deefholts and Kathryn Phillips-Miles
978-0-7206-1949-2 / 224pp / £9.99

Samuel leads a comfortable but uninspiring existence in Madrid, consoling himself among friends who have reached a similar point in life. One night he receives a call. Clara, his lover, has died in a car accident. The thing is, he doesn't know anyone called Clara.

A simple case of mistaken identity offers Samuel the chance to inhabit another, more tumultuous life, leading him to consider whether, if he invents a past of love and loss, he could even attend her funeral. Unable to resist the chance, Samuel finds himself drawn down a path of lies until he begins to have trouble distinguishing between truth and fantasy. But such is the allure of his invented life that he is willing to persist and in the process create a new version of the present – with little regard for the consequences to himself and to others.

José Ovejero's existential tale of stolen identity exposes the fictions people weave to sustain themselves in a dehumanizing modern world.

PETER OWEN WORLD SERIES
SEASON 3: SERBIA

FILIP DAVID
The House of Remembering and Forgetting
Translated by Christina Pribichevich Zorić
Introduction by Dejan Djokić
978-0-7206-1973-7 / 160pp / £9.99

To save the young Albert from the horrors of a Nazi concentration camp, his father makes a hole in the floor of the cattle truck taking his and other Jewish families to their deaths. He then pushes Albert's brother Elijah and then Albert through and down on to the tracks, hoping that someone will find and take pity on the two boys in the white winter night. In an attempt to understand the true nature of evil, David shows us that it is necessary to walk in two worlds: the material one in which evil occurs and the alternative world of dreams, premonitions and visions in which we try to come to terms with the dangers around us. With its intricate plot and interweaving of fact and fiction, *The House of Remembering and Forgetting* grapples with the paradoxical and painful dilemma of whether to choose to remember or to forget.

MIRJANA NOVAKOVIĆ
Fear and His Servant
Translated by Terence McEneny
978-0-7206-1977-5 / 256pp / £9.99

Belgrade seems to have changed in the years since Count Otto von Hausburg last visited the city, and not for the better. Serbia in the eighteenth century is a battleground of empires, with the Ottomans on one side and the Habsburgs on the other. In the besieged capital, Princess Maria Augusta waits for love to save her troubled soul. But who is the strange, charismatic count, and can we trust the story he is telling us? While some call him the Devil, he appears to have all the fears and pettiness of an ordinary man. In this daring and original novel, Novaković invites her readers to join the hunt for the undead, travelling through history, myth and literature into the dark corners of the land that spawned that most infamous word: vampire.

DANA TODOROVIĆ
The Tragic Fate of Moritz Tóth
Translated by the author
978-0-7206-1983-6 / 160pp / £9.99

Ex-punk Moritz Tóth is languishing in the suburbs when he receives a call from the Employment Office offering him a job as a prompter at the Opera. While trying to cope with the claustrophobia of long confinement in a rudimentary wooden box, struggling to follow Puccini's *Turandot* in a language he doesn't understand, Moritz gradually becomes convinced that he is being pursued by a malevolent force in the hideous person of his neighbour Ezekiel, a.k.a. 'the Birdman'. In two parallel narratives – one earthly strand detailing the growing paranoia of our reluctant hero and the other, more heavenly one of Tobias Keller, the Moral Issues Adviser with the Office of the Great Overseer – the plot develops in the atmospheric style of Kafka and Bulgakov as Tobias discusses the life path of Moritz with the Disciplinary Committee. As the pieces of the puzzle finally come together and the connection between the two storylines becomes clearer, Todorović, mixing philosophy with first-class story-telling, coaxes us towards a surprising finale.

SOME AUTHORS WE HAVE PUBLISHED

James Agee • Bella Akhmadulina • Tariq Ali • Kenneth Allsop • Alfred Andersch
Guillaume Apollinaire • Machado de Assis • Miguel Angel Asturias • Duke of Bedford
Oliver Bernard • Thomas Blackburn • Jane Bowles • Paul Bowles • Richard Bradford
Ilse, Countess von Bredow • Lenny Bruce • Finn Carling • Blaise Cendrars • Marc Chagall
Giorgio de Chirico • Uno Chiyo • Hugo Claus • Jean Cocteau • Albert Cohen
Colette • Ithell Colquhoun • Richard Corson • Benedetto Croce • Margaret Crosland
e.e. cummings • Stig Dalager • Salvador Dalí • Osamu Dazai • Anita Desai
Charles Dickens • Bernard Diederich • Fabián Dobles • William Donaldson
Autran Dourado • Yuri Druzhnikov • Lawrence Durrell • Isabelle Eberhardt
Sergei Eisenstein • Shusaku Endo • Erté • Knut Faldbakken • Ida Fink
Wolfgang George Fischer • Nicholas Freeling • Philip Freund • Carlo Emilio Gadda
Rhea Galanaki • Salvador Garmendia • Michel Gauquelin • André Gide
Natalia Ginzburg • Jean Giono • Geoffrey Gorer • William Goyen • Julien Gracq
Sue Grafton • Robert Graves • Angela Green • Julien Green • George Grosz
Barbara Hardy • H.D. • Rayner Heppenstall • David Herbert • Gustaw Herling
Hermann Hesse • Shere Hite • Stewart Home • Abdullah Hussein • King Hussein of Jordan
Ruth Inglis • Grace Ingoldby • Yasushi Inoue • Hans Henny Jahnn • Karl Jaspers
Takeshi Kaiko • Jaan Kaplinski • Anna Kavan • Yasunuri Kawabata • Nikos Kazantzakis
Orhan Kemal • Christer Kihlman • James Kirkup • Paul Klee • James Laughlin
Patricia Laurent • Violette Leduc • Lee Seung-U • Vernon Lee • József Lengyel
Robert Liddell • Francisco García Lorca • Moura Lympany • Thomas Mann
Dacia Maraini • Marcel Marceau • André Maurois • Henri Michaux • Henry Miller
Miranda Miller • Marga Minco • Yukio Mishima • Quim Monzó • Margaret Morris
Angus Wolfe Murray • Atle Næss • Gérard de Nerval • Anaïs Nin • Yoko Ono
Uri Orlev • Wendy Owen • Arto Paasilinna • Marco Pallis • Oscar Parland
Boris Pasternak • Cesare Pavese • Milorad Pavic • Octavio Paz • Mervyn Peake
Carlos Pedretti • Dame Margery Perham • Graciliano Ramos • Jeremy Reed
Rodrigo Rey Rosa • Joseph Roth • Ken Russell • Marquis de Sade • Cora Sandel
Iván Sándor • George Santayana • May Sarton • Jean-Paul Sartre
Ferdinand de Saussure • Gerald Scarfe • Albert Schweitzer
George Bernard Shaw • Isaac Bashevis Singer • Patwant Singh • Edith Sitwell
Suzanne St Albans • Stevie Smith • C.P. Snow • Bengt Söderbergh
Vladimir Soloukhin • Natsume Soseki • Muriel Spark • Gertrude Stein • Bram Stoker
August Strindberg • Rabindranath Tagore • Tambimuttu • Elisabeth Russell Taylor
Emma Tennant • Anne Tibble • Roland Topor • Miloš Urban • Anne Valery
Peter Vansittart • José J. Veiga • Tarjei Vesaas • Noel Virtue • Max Weber
Edith Wharton • William Carlos Williams • Phyllis Willmott
G. Peter Winnington • Monique Wittig • A.B. Yehoshua • Marguerite Young
Fakhar Zaman • Alexander Zinoviev • Emile Zola

Peter Owen Publishers, Conway Hall, 25 Red Lion Square, London WC1R 4RL, UK
T + 44 (0)20 7061 6756 / E info@peterowen.com
www.peterowen.com / @PeterOwenPubs
Independent publishers since 1951